"Impressive . . . Price's characters are an appealing collection of originals. Rosa shows once again the novelist's ability to create believable women. . . . Long may she endure!"

USA Today

"The stamp of [Reynolds Price] is unmistakable. . . . There is much pleasure to be taken in the characters' honesty, humor and stubborn integrity—qualities they share with their creator."

Newsday

"While the heart of the novel belongs to Rosa and Wesley, its secondary characters are so finely etched you can almost smell the Sunday suppers."

The Boston Globe

"The book is studded with revealing, cropped-to-the-bone conversations—as always, Price's ear for laconic dialogue is so right that whole chapters snap into place."

The Village Voice

Also by Reynolds Price:

A LONG AND HAPPY LIFE
THE NAMES AND FACES OF HEROES**
A GENEROUS MAN
LOVE AND WORK*
PERMANENT ERRORS
THINGS THEMSELVES
THE SURFACE OF EARTH*
EARLY DARK
A PALPABLE GOD
THE SOURCE OF LIGHT*
VITAL PROVISIONS
MUSTIAN*
PRIVATE CONTENTMENT
KATE VAIDEN*
THE LAWS OF ICE
A COMMON ROOM

*Published by Ballantine Books
**Forthcoming

GOOD HEARTS

REYNOLDS PRICE

BALLANTINE BOOKS • NEW YORK

Library of Congress Catalog Card Number: 87-33327

ISBN 0-345-35707-8

This edition published by arrangement with Atheneum Publishers, an im-
print of Macmillan, Inc.

Manufactured in the United States of America

First Ballantine Books Edition: April 1989

for

MARCIA DRAKE BENNETT

and

PAUL CLIFFORD BENNETT, JR.

ROSA WESLEY

ROSA REACHED OUT AND SWITCHED OFF THE LAST light. Then she said "I hope we both sleep safe." It was what she said many nights at this point. It meant what it said. But also, and often without her knowing, it also meant *Sleep please, nothing else*.

Wesley gave his usual answer, "Anything you say, lady. Good night."

They both always entered sleep on their backs, so they lay flat now and waited for their eyes to adjust to the dark —dim slats of street light on the ceiling and a glow on their skin like the shine of phosphorus on underwater life. Neither one of them was thinking. They'd each worked a normal full-day, had a light supper, watched two hours of dumb television, and expected the same tomorrow. Now they were each exhausted and empty, normally tired—no panic or sudden waves of despair.

1

You though, if you'd been transparent there, would have seen an apparently young married couple. Both of them looked young because they'd mostly avoided fat and because the dark conceals small furrows. They looked married because of the ease in one another's nearness, the benign neglect which permits two bodies so warm and fine to resist quick union.

In fact Rosa and Wesley Beavers had been married twenty-eight years that month, a wedding forced on them by pregnancy after years of old-time country courtship. Beyond a hurried wedding, the outcome of that accident was Horatio, their grown son who lived half the state away—an only child, kind to his parents but mostly helpless in emergency. And their visible ease with one another's bodies was also misleading, a dangerous illusion shared by Rosa.

She thought they were aging but content (she was forty-eight). So nothing now stood between her and sleep, and in fifteen seconds she'd said her short prayer and was walking through the first light dream of the evening.

IN THE DREAM SHE WAS STANDING IN A BIG ROOM OF PEOPLE. None of them wore her family's faces or even her friends'. But she knew them all and knew they wanted her. Somebody in the farthest back circle raised a hand, as if she was the teacher, and said "Please Rosa, recite us a poem." And she did. In real life when she was fourteen to twenty, she wrote lots of poems. They were long gone now, since she burned her diaries and scrapbooks the first time Wesley vanished from home. But in tonight's dream, one of the best poems suddenly swam up in her mind; and she said it straight through,

I ought to try to say what you gave me—
Didn't we know the darkest brightness that can be?

Even in the dream, she knew when the poem was written and for whom—Wesley when he'd finished high school. He had signed up for three years in the Navy, and gone straight off during the Korean War where actual local boys were dying. It had been Rosa's way to say what she hoped they'd accomplished (and by then they hadn't ever touched completely; she meant just the hope). So the dream was happy, and it led her on into deeper sleep and the chance of more stories as good as that.

Wesley though, at fifty, was in real pain. It had been part of him all his adult life, a way of walking into a day with a sense of happy blessing only to come up at four p.m. with his nose flat against a blank wall of defeat. Nowhere to go, no way back, no other human to turn to for help, nothing more awful than now except the risk of death. When those ambushes happened, he could never say why. So he blamed nobody but himself.

Tonight lying here at the end of a decent work-day toward the end of the year (it was the third week in December), Wesley had lain down thinking he might join his wife for the slow close fun that would lead to long sleep. But now he was faced with Rosa's polite refusal or at least her hope of separate rest. Well, he always respected her. He hadn't forced himself on her for maybe twenty years. He granted that she mostly joined when he needed her and with a nice cooperation that might not be enthusiasm but was surely not grudging.

So he said to himself over and over "This is just one night, not the end of the earth. Get calm and wait." And though he was not one for regular prayers, he also said a short sentence, "Thank you for everything good that happened, that we didn't do ourselves. Help us to do more." He was even surprised when he felt himself slide off the ledge into sleep. And it deepened pleasantly for almost an hour till the first dream started.

IN IT WESLEY WAS A BOY AGAIN, MAYBE SIXTEEN. HE WAS standing bare in a room full of strangers. He didn't feel naked, though there was a big mirror on the wall in which he could see his whole body. Young as he was, he was already proud of it. He'd seen enough other boys in the baseball-practice showers to know that, in Warren County anyhow, nobody had made a finer body than he. It seemed well fixed to manufacture strong good children any day. It sure God *meant* to, in every cell. But when he faced the strangers around him, their eyes were glassy. And they shook their heads as if to say "Anybody with nothing but this to offer should quit right now and not crowd the world." Yet he knew they didn't have the right to kill him. He'd have to hang around, crowding up space with himself—a failure he couldn't repair.

In the dream, Wesley understood he was dreaming. So he tried to wake up by rocking his whole body back and forth and yelling his name. He could see that clearly from overhead—his thrashing body, his loud mouth. But he didn't come to, and Rosa didn't hear him or feel his panic. He truly was balked and he sank on deeper into more and more dreams the whole night ahead.

IF YOU'D KEPT WATCHING THOUGH WHAT YOU'D HAVE SEEN through every hour was the same fine couple, enhanced by darkness. Whatever your rate of attraction to bodies, you might well have thought you'd seldom been given a chance to watch people any gentler than these on the eyes and ears (neither one of them snored or scratched, and even in dreams their breathing was calm). You might have chosen to stay on till daylight revealed their faces and their eyes opened finally, of course their best features. And once you'd seen eyes so clear and keen (so ready to know you like a trusted friend), you might have wished you could go on watching their moves and words—learning their luck, washed in a steady stream of deeds from hearts as good as any you've met unless you meet more saints than most.

When the clock rang though at half past six in winter dark, Rosa and Wesley were there alone. For all the strange night, the clashing dreams, they both looked calm as children who'd stroked through steady rest toward a welcome dawn and the day's first words.

Wesley silenced the clock and rubbed at his eyes.

Rosa switched on her lamp and looked his way. "Sleep good?"

He lied. "Good as ever."

With all the signs of their age plain to see, they'd come through again as what they'd been most days of their lives —people worth watching and hoping to know.

BY SUNDOWN WESLEY'S DREAM AND WHAT CAUSED IT HAD driven a man strong as him to leave for parts unknown, with no word to Rosa.

The second night Rosa sat down alone at a kitchen table to think on paper, hoping to crack or at least describe this big new mystery that had struck so hard.

ROSA'S DIARY

I**T'S ALMOST THE SHORTEST DAY OF THE YEAR, AND IT** ends in an hour. But I'm sure you aren't coming back tonight either, so I'm beginning to write this page. If there's a midnight tomorrow in Raleigh, N.C. and I live through the day to write a second page, then I may have made myself a place I can come to and run and yell in at night. It will be an account of what I did all the time you were gone, if you ever come back. If you decide to, and I decide to stand here and join you, then you're bound to grin and say "Of course you thought it was a good idea. All your ideas about me are good and have been for thirty-odd years. But no, I won't be needing it now."

We had the office Christmas party today. Everybody had got their final exams finished and the grades turned in. So for the four thousandth eon, Jean and I cooked the annual St. Nick Picnic and trucked in with it. I brought a ton of

fried-chicken knuckles, and Jean brought one of her foot-
ball-field size congealed salads—the dark colored ones
with mysterious ingredients that you've always been suspi-
cious of. But not those world-traveled PhDs. They shoveled it in by the square yard. Every inch of it went too,
while I had several baskets of chicken knuckles left to
bring home and freeze. In all the years of those celebra-
tions, we've never had such a turn-out.

Maybe everybody's poor and hungry. Or a Christian
again. Anyhow nobody had a foaming fit or struck anybody else, though the usual dozen aren't speaking to each
other and popped their necks out of joint trying to be sure
their enemies knew they weren't smiling *their* way. That
much went according to plan and was a reward.

I got the usual gifts of whorehouse bath-products and
paperclip holders with moron-smile faces. And I tried hard
to look grateful, even when I know they're bought by
wives who wish the old secretary would just go on and
retire if not die. The surprises this year were a pair of
tickets to a February concert from my chairman and a *pint*
of Chanel No. 5 from the youngest professor.

He must think I've got more influence than I do. But
he's shy enough to vaporize if you meet his face. I happen
to know his salary wouldn't keep a widow in black ink,
and I didn't know he'd noticed there were women on earth.
So when I saw that lifetime supply of French sweetener, I
gave him a hug that set him back years. He may not speak
again before spring. Bless his heart.

I've got it on right now, the perfume, and am laying
down a fog all round the dinner table where I'm writing. A
big nose-fiesta for me and Roger and that one mouse you
still haven't caught. He just negotiated the far corner at

ninety m.p.h., flashing me a grin before he managed his vanishing trick.

Roger was gentlemanly as usual. He crept farther and farther from me till he could tactfully retreat to the kitchen and his old basket with the new cedar pillow you bought. Otherwise he's put his usual emergency plan into effect. He eats twice the amount of his dry chow. I think when he doesn't see you for twenty-four hours, he decides to try to swell up till he fills however much of the world it takes to bring him back up against your dry knee and he knows he's back where he

—BELONGS. THE PHONE RANG JUST THEN AND JOGGED MY hand. I thought it was sure to be Horace, but there was just live silence. I first thought "Good, this is going to be my first obscene phonecall since I was forty." You remember the boy that called here eight years ago on my fortieth birthday by happy coincidence, saying he was taking a consumer poll and would I tell him what size cup I wore in brassieres, and I told him they didn't cup all that much anymore, and why wasn't he doing his homework on a weeknight?

But the silence lasted. I stopped asking questions and set in to wait it out. I think the person took at least one breath, and I guessed it was a man. In ninety more seconds he kept his peace. I thought I could hear his arm move to hang up. But then this voice—man, woman's, talking bat's—said "Never you doubt I watch you by the instant. Others may be fooled. I've got the damned *facts*."

Then I hung up. Now I'll try to go on to bed, trusting it wasn't you. Whatever else I've accused you of all these years, it was never cheap tricks or mental illness. If I plan to sleep, I'm also going to need to assume it wasn't anybody with a long clean knife and our address. Mine anyhow.

The honest balance at the end of this second day seems to be this. You left the shop two evenings ago and went on somewhere else. Nobody down there claims to have seen you since, and they've never lied to me before. I've looked in your usual places and don't find any note or cash advance. I've got plenty money, as you well know, so that's no concern. And I don't feel the pure terror I felt when you did this same thing for four days when Horace was born and shorter times since. I'm not running for police chief or anything else that bold, but for the first time in my life at about ten o'clock tonight, I said out loud to the room and Roger, "Rosa, you can stand alone."

You said fairly recently that you were not a real prop for me, and I called you wrong. Maybe you were right. Maybe you're giving me a chance to test it. I wouldn't have asked it of you, not now—least of all with Christmas at the door and me having to go to Mama's and explain your absence, if you're still absent Christmas. But there again, those were my plans not yours.

I trust you're alive, Wesley. Safe and indoors and that, whatever's wrong enough to drive you off, it will heal itself in the night. Or you'll call me tomorrow and say what it is and let me try to change it. I can't claim I've loved you longer than anybody else above ground, but I have loved you harder. Every doctor on television says love is supposed to change as any two people walk forward together through more than junior-high dates. I can look at you still, as recently as last Sunday when you were nodding in your chair by the football game, and know why

I've wanted to be in reach of you for all but the first thirteen years of my life.

Every picture of you in this house is standing in place, not turned face-down or hidden in drawers. I see you this instant and want you back, strong as ever. Say your prayers, be good to your body, sleep deep. I've got one consolation in knowing you're not a drunk. I can trust you not to be sleeping in gutters. But also I can't blame your absence on liquor. What you've done, you've done clear-headed.

I know, I've gone on more than a page. You always said the worst thing about me was how I loved words, how I talked my way to victory in every fight we had. I know that's true and I'm sorry. I know I've driven you further back into silence to the place where, to get my attention and make your point, you practically have to walk out one dawn and slash my tires. Or slide through those slim tall trapdoors in the outside world that you've always known how to find with your nails and that gladly close behind you. Please reappear.

CHRISTMAS EVE AND NO WORD. I JUST TALKED TO HORace. They're staying in Charlotte this year, you remember, with the Mama-in-Law. So he called all bent down with guilt and apology. I told him I was fine, which is not but three-fourths a lie. I told him Christmas was sad enough without him taking on further reasons for misery. I was hoping he wouldn't, but you know what he did next—ask after you. I planned to lie there too, but my mouth wouldn't do it. It just plunged on and told the whole truth. I said you'd been gone since right after eating a big normal breakfast on the eighteenth.

He asked had I checked your sock drawer for notes, remembering the times from his childhood. (Was it two or three times you left back then? I've honestly forgotten.)

I told him I'd about worn your socks out but no, not a word.

Horace said "In that case I'm leaving this minute. I'll see you in three hours."

I almost let him. The thought of seeing my son *alone*, without that wife, for one more time seemed sweet in the mind. But I told him I wouldn't sit still for him to run out on his promise. Just act like the well-brought-up child he is and not go strowing his sad family's mess around the outside world like hog shit down near another man's creek. Not that his mother-in-law's squatty house constitutes the world exactly, but the one sure thing that would wreck me now would be knowing half-strangers are pitying Horace. Or me and you. Or you.

Wesley, you were always so slow to speak up for yourself that it took me long years to realize how I mowed you down time after time with all my orations and grand epistles. Of course I *didn't* mow you down. I never really won. You'd just tuck your square chin, nod, walk on off, and do your will in your own sweet time. But I wish I'd had the fairness to see years sooner how I shut you out of my own calculations and thought I was Miss Country Genius and Judge.

I can plead that I got it from my mother. Our father was so good to watch but so weak, and Mama just got stronger and harder till she thought she knew more than Justice Holmes or John-the-damn-Baptist and the mixed choir of saints. So I naturally kept my eyes on her. I'd have rather watched Daddy, but he was mostly gone—drunk laid out under some cool low tree. And what I learned was "Men are meant to be loved and not trusted." Or "served not loved."

I know I loved you—God knows you heard me moan it enough—and women my age just learned from birth that service was what our hands were for. Hands, eyes, titties, bladders, all. I thought I was going to want to serve you till we'd both worn to dust and blown on away or at least been tucked underground by Horace with one granite stone saying both our names till an H-bomb dissolved it. With all my new education and self-respect, I still think so more often than not.

You think otherwise. So your absence seems to say. Unless you're kidnaped by Shiite Muslims and rushing toward Beirut right this minute with your wrists bound bloody and your eyes tight-blinded.

Forgive me please. Don't let my busy imagination jack this private trouble way past its true size. But isn't that part of what's so strange now? People not one bit grander than us, just broke-down retired old Jews on vacation or sailors on leave with pimples and toilet-paper patches on their chin can step round a corner or sit in the wrong chair and— woom!—be pitiful stars on the news, the urgent business of presidents, popes, and assorted kings.

Of course, all of us matter to God that much. Poor God. Poor us. How can things weak as us bear so much care? If I let myself really dwell on it, it's likely to burn me right to the sockets. You asked me two or three years ago why I'd just quietly given up on church. I wasn't that sure I had, till you noticed. But now I see why. I really don't want to matter as much as church says I do. Reminds me too much of me as a girl, me gazing at you like you were the Holy

Ghost in blue jeans with tongues aflame and angels behind you stretched east and west towards dawn and dark. Idolatry.

Am I punished now for that? Are you telling me finally, you and God, to lay off the worship? I quit though, Wesley, some years ago now. It was how we got back at ease together once Horace had packed up for college and gone. You noticed it; you said so. One night you dropped a raw egg on the stove, right down in the eye, and left me to scrounge out the awful glue. I said "Goddamn it! You're a permanent mess." In an instant I was ready to beg your pardon.

But you laughed hard and said. "Exactly. I was hoping you'd learn."

You *are* a mess. You were set down here to stir things around. I am a stuck-up missionary nurse sent to press and fold and hide mess in drawers. We had one child, sadder than we two combined. Together we made up my favorite team. Now we're strown round the map like Esso stations, and I hate it worse than anything yet. Christmas Eve and eleven o'clock!

This is meant to be the best hour on earth, long year after year. Stop, sit still, and wait—there, hear the Boy coming. Hold your arms out to greet Him.

I can't speak for you, your arms tonight. Mine are here in my lap. I am sick with shame for my big share, whatever it is, in this wreck we're in.

I BROKE OFF THERE AND CALLED YOUR MOTHER. I KNEW IF you'd kept to your old customs, you'd have called her by now. I also knew she'd keep her own counsel unless I pried. I chose not to pry, and she chose not to tell.

She wished me a very nice day of rest. She said she was warm and dry, thank Jesus. She thanked me for my "little thoughtful thing." I knew she'd already forgot what it was —five pounds of chocolate, already rushed down her throat. She said "I'm right here alone as a handsaw."

I didn't know quite how alone a saw was, but I said "I know it and I'm sorry as you."

She finally laughed. I hadn't heard her laugh in years. Then she said "I'm happy, Rosacoke. Get that straight."

I'll try, all night. I hope you've found the Salvation Army and have put your order in for turkey and dressing. Or I hope you are by some kind soul that means to give you Christmas without signing on for a whole life with you. I mean to get up at day with the sun and drive to Afton and face my mother. She let me know by mail late as yesterday that you and I are looked for, us and all other souls bearing one small drop of her strong blood through the fields of the world—*Come hither and feed!*

I slept last night, to my great surprise. That's bound to mean you did. I pray for the same on us both, now and always. Sleep, dark brown rest and no dreams of day.

CHRISTMAS NIGHT, 10:30. I GOT BACK FROM HOME SOONER than I expected, and tired as I am, I'll turn to this in hopes of burning myself all the way down to the gutters. Who but me wouldn't be cold white ashes after a day full as this? But you know my nerves *eat* trouble. They're standing on end down my whole body this minute, playing "Reveille" on those little Yankee Doodle flutes that etch glass.

And I got up before the sun, finished wrapping the presents for home, fried me a big breakfast, enjoyed every bite of it, watched the Bethlehem, Judea service on t.v., took Roger for a stroll round the block among all the children with their new realistic toy implements of destruction, then settled Roger in with a day's supplies. At the whiff of me leaving too, he started that puppydog trembling that comes nearer to breaking my heart than most human signals.

Horace called up just as I was heading out the door at 8:30, so I laid back five minutes to let him put in enough writhing to stoke his shame. He said he'd rather be with you and me than any thirty of the Lomaxes.

I said "Me too."

And that made him worse.

Finally I had to say "Son, I truly don't want you here. We've had enough Christmases together to last us till Heaven. I'm beginning to realize I love a little freedom. I'll call you collect the next time I'm blue. But don't hold your breath."

It shocked him badly. I thought he was about to hang up in my face. But then he said "Promise me you're lying."

I waited and said "Of course I am. Come down early in the New Year—by yourself if you can—when everybody's not blue as indigo. I'll cook you exactly what your heart desires."

He accepted and I ran.

All the way up home though, I knew I hadn't lied. I didn't want to see him and least of all Priscilla. Horace turned out as satisfactorily as we have any reason to expect, and I'd write him a good job reference tomorrow, but till I get a lot older than now, I won't be needing many days of his time.

You though. The nearer I got to Afton, the more I felt the shape of your body being cut out of me like a live

paperdoll—a shape that was leaving me with less than I
need to live on. Once I got on past Louisburg and people
gave out and God took over, I got worse by the mile. In
ways I'll never understand, you are so personally involved
in that one stretch of pines and oaks, the white sandy soil,
that blond broomstraw that looks like it's growing from
buried Viking giants (their beards, chests, and crotches),
the way the sky huddles down and cups the land like a pale
blue dome that seems to be promising to protect it forever.
The way you can come round a long curve of road through
woods and slowly build up the expectation that—yonder
just the instant you break out into view of that halfway hid
rock up yonder—a fourteen-year-old boy, a little old for
his age, is going to rise up from sitting on that rock, wave
you down, step up to your window, motion you to open it,
and then without saying anything but your name reach out
and hand you a folded slip of paper that, when you read it,
says either "You can stop now, Child. You've finished.
And you've won perfect rest" or "Stop. You have failed.
Step out of this car, leave your keys on the seat, head
straight for those trees, and brace your face. Your punishment begins"—both in God's handwriting, tall straight
black ink.

I've always known the boy's face will be yours, the face
you had the day I found you. The one I tried to earn for so
long till it vanished behind what the years did to you. You
and me and everybody else but my good mother.

I was into Mama's road drying my cheeks with the back
of my hand when I caught sight of her standing straight by
the door. You recall how she always knows when I'm due.
No air-traffic boss can foretell arrivals like my Emma
Mustian. I was a few minutes late, so she'd got a little

chilled. I could see her flinch once, and someway that scared me much worse than finding you gone the other night. The thought that my mother might ever go underground, agreeing to die, still won't run through me without hard snags and bloody cuts.

Nobody was there yet but her and Rato. When was the last time you saw Rato?—two or three years? My next-older brother has genuinely got younger. For a few years there around forty, his face looked like it might crackle all over the way a white cup will. But it didn't. Whatever clouds blow through that mind, they blew on away and left him calm as a good April evening.

He could be that boy on the road too—Rato, the boy that hands you news from God. In fact I remember thinking, just before I met you, that Rato might stand up at the supper table some night or when everybody was ready for bed and say "I know you thought I was human, your son and brother, but no. I'm an actual angel and I've noticed some things. Get ready to hear me." I don't think I'd have been the only one that halfway expected it.

Mama says he stays indoors with her from Thanksgiving through the middle of March and does every possible chore for her. But let the first leaf show on a tree, and Rato's off to roam the woods from dawn till dark like when all of us were young. "I might just as well not be here," she said. She doesn't know what he can be doing out there. I wondered if he might not have a big profitable liquor still, and Mama said "He does seem to have his own pocket change."

When I climbed the steps to Mama and kissed her cold cheek, Rato was suddenly there behind her in that scary way he has of condensing out of nowhere.

I said "Merry Christmas."

He looked me over closely and said "Let me see your passport." You know how he's always liked spy movies and used to claim he was a spy but wouldn't say who for.

I said my credentials were out in my car with the presents if he'd please go get it all, which he did.

After that it went very much like a normal Christmas visit. Milo and Sissie drove up from Henderson while Mama and I were putting dinner on the table. With how Milo's acted in recent years (leaving the farm for a truck dealership and neglecting Mama), I wondered if the eldest brother would appear. But they did, grinning like they still lived upstairs and helped the family through thick and thin.

It was Mama's usual light lunch—the turkey with cornbread dressing and cranberry sauce, country ham, corn pudding, snaps and little butterbeans she'd put up last July, spiced peaches, cold crisp watermelon-rind pickle, macaroni and cheese, creamed potatoes and gravy, then her own angelfood cake and ambrosia. Every mouthful made the only way, from the naked pot upward by hand. I hadn't eaten with her since the Fourth of July, and it was a real shock to my tongue—that many kind flavors, all happening at once like good deeds intended for me. Whenever I compliment her on it, she just says "It's the only way I know to cook. I know they've got a lot of fine speedy things now, but I haven't got the time to read all those instructions they put on the boxes, and anyhow my glasses are generally lost." Even when she and Rato are there right alone, she turns out three of those meals a day—every one of them simple and appropriate as the original patent-model Last Supper.

The only new strange thing was that nobody mentioned

you till after dinner. It was four o'clock and we were halfway through opening presents in the front room when Sissie as usual finally stepped in it. She picked up your
present, dangled it toward me, and said. "Am I going to be
the first one to ask if Wesley is alive?"

Milo laughed. "I *knew* you would."

Even Mama had somehow held back, so I'd made it a
game to help me through the day—who could keep quiet
the longest and not ask Rosa the oldest question, "Where's
Wesley?" At first it hadn't seemed that hard to do. But by
the time Sissie blundered ahead, I was ready and relieved.

I said "I very much hope he's alive and well. His body
at least has not been found. He left for work several days
ago and kept on going."

Sissie had to ask "Is he still up to that?"

"Still?" I said. "It's happened a time or two in twenty-
eight years. I don't call that an everyday event."

Sissie said "Thank God it's something Milo never
tried."

Milo stood up and said to my face "Too true, too right.
That's why Milo is no more living back of *these* two eyes
than Tyrone Power." He rubbed both eyes with his hard
thumbs like Milo was gone and his eyes didn't matter. In a
second—whoever he was—he was gone out the back door
toward the woods. That was my old trick, bolting dinner
when my feelings got bruised.

Sissie said "He'll be back before dark. He's scared of
dark." Then she begged my pardon. Sissie learned the secret of family diplomacy in early childhood—say everything you think, *then* apologize. You get the best of both
worlds.

As always I excused her. But my own nerve was up, so

I told Mama I'd get some air myself and would be back
directly.

She said "You haven't opened my present yet."

I told her I'd save the best for last.

And I went to Milo like a heat-seeking rocket. All I had
to do was walk double-time. I knew where he'd be, the
path he'd take.

He heard me coming in the thick dry leaves and slowed
down his pace, though he never turned to face me.

When I got up behind him, I didn't try to speak and he
didn't either. I think we'd have circled the globe like that if
I finally hadn't said "Can we sit down a minute?"

Milo said "I didn't know *we* were doing this."

I said "I need you."

He thought that over for what seemed a mile. Then finally we came in sight of the saddle tree, the one bent
down by a snowstorm years ago but kept on living. He
suddenly turned back, grabbed me round the waist, and sat
me up on the saddle easy as if I was still a lightweight
skeeter. He sat on the ground three paces beyond me,
found my eyes, and said "What do you need?"

I told him I'd never been worse than now, that you were
gone with no word of why.

He wanted to know what I had done wrong?

I was mad at once and said so. Why did he think, first
pop, I was wrong?

He said "Wesley's two years younger than me and gone.
No man in his fifties will push off from home if he's got a
home."

I said "Then you're way too far out of touch. Wesley
hasn't said one hard word to me in the last five years."

Milo said "Him leaving is a sermon, commencement

address, and the twenty-third damned psalm all together. Check his last words. What's the last thing he said?"

I tried to remember. The last real act of yours I could see is how you put your straw hat on once your father was buried and went to the car, not waiting for me. The last unusual words were maybe two years before when we'd made nice love and were resting. You said "For a Baptist missionary, Rosa, you can sure damn *dance*."

Milo shook his head. "No, the morning he left. Did he say he'd call you or see you or what?"

I said I'd gone back upstairs to dress.

"So you didn't speak at all? No wonder he's gone."

I asked him what we had left to say after so many mornings? "What can Sissie tell *you* that she hasn't said ten zillion times?"

"—Some mess she's just now heard on t.v. or a secret chuckle from our honeymoon."

I told him I bet that was one long laugh.

He said "Well, it wasn't Jackie Gleason, but then you and Wesley aren't the only food for laughter. Me and Sissie have had our pretty moments too."

I told him I was glad. I didn't say it was a bigger surprise than you leaving. If I knew the answer wasn't bound to be you, I'd have thought deep and told him the next-closest truth—that Milo Mustian my oldest brother was the most important person on earth to me. As it was I said Wesley was the name that came to me when anybody mentioned a boy's name and love or happiness.

Milo said he understood me.

I said I thought my family in general looked down on Wesley.

Milo stood up and came over toward me. Those eyes he

got from Mama were big bowls of water that looked like
tears. He was facing the ground, but he said "Rose, I don't
look down on anybody. A man'd have to be digging fast
toward Peking to be farther down than me."

I took both his wrists and pulled his eyes up to meet me
again.

The tears had drained on away, no sign of water. He
said "You and me ought not to have give up on each other."

I said "Maybe not." Then I kept on looking. He kept on
moving back faster and faster till soon he was too much
like the brother I'd known so well and trusted. Then I finally bent down enough to kiss him. He's of course my
brother, though I don't think I'd ever kissed him outright
before—just dry cheek brushes. It ended in no time.

But it got Milo's attention. He didn't try to force anything else on me, not from that direction. But he said "Oh
Rose, why in God's poor name did I let all these strangers
in on us?"

You know how, anytime things have gone bad between
you and me, Milo has blamed himself for introducing us.
The hundred times I've told him the way we really met—
me sighting you in the woods up a tree—are just waste
breath.

He wanted to know if you had abused me?

I told him absolutely not. I said there were times I could
imagine you murdering me frankly with a gun or a quick
knife but never with meanness or poison. And I said I'd
always figured I could stop you cold if you came at me
violent.

Then he wanted to know if we had "given up on the
bedroom"? He put it exactly that way. All those t.v. sex
seminars have got to him.

"Not given up," I said. "But it never did seem like the answer to anything between me and Wesley. It was always more like the question itself. How come we wanted that out of each other and went for it at such different rates and times?"

He told me more than I'd ever wanted to know about Sissie and him. How she'd pretty well cut him off at the spring years ago, which I figured. How he'd found a willing ample girl at that Farm Bureau motel-weekend he spent up here studying soy beans right after the Vietnam war (the time he came out and barbecued chicken for us). How he wanted to set her up in a house in Florida and find his way to pull out of here and eventually be an orange-grove worker near Orlando with her. Her name was Spain, I seem to remember—her first name, a redhead, Spain Russell. Milo thinks she's still down there, and he still thinks he knows her phone number but has never tried to call it again. He said it out to me like a lesson I'd someday need —area code so and so, dot dot dot dot dot dot dot.

I smiled and said "Thank you."

He turned to head home, back to Mama's (I keep calling it *home*). Before the trees gave out completely, he looked back at me, took both my elbows, kissed my forehead, and said "You ever get tired of being this lonesome—Christ knows, *I* do—you call me collect. We could both pick oranges another twenty, thirty years. Then we'd be right there in retirement heaven. We could drop in our tracks. They've got boys in white coats roaming the streets day and night, to shovel you up for the incinerators."

I thought it was the foolishest proposal I'd ever heard but also the kindest and, right then, welcomest. If you get to read this ever, don't be mad or jealous. And don't even

mention it to Milo or me. It means too much to either one
of us. Just remember *old* Milo—the one that was better
than you and me both for sweet open-heartedness and eyes
like the temple altar of God, incense coals fanned red by
troops of angel wings. That boy's still hid somewhere way
down in this scorched old man, fifty-two years old and
worn to the threads.

Back at the house Sissie and Rato were watching t.v.
from opposite sides of the kitchen, and Mama was ironing
the latest gift wrappings to save for next year. She's got a
little deafer in the last twelve months, so I had a short
second when I came through the door before she saw me.
She's seventy-three years old and seriously she doesn't
look in any important way a bit different from how she's
looked ever since I remember. And that goes back to 1939,
me two years old staring from the baby bed at that same
face beyond me, the hair a little darker, otherwise the
same—my perpetual moon, always at the full.

WHAT DOES THAT MAKE YOU? WOMEN AREN'T SUPPOSED
to say this anymore, but doesn't it make you the sun?
Aren't you the power I've moved around and because of?
In those eleven or twelve years when Horace needed more
or less all of me, I guess I was his sun or—again—his
moon. Maybe I was getting power from you and shining it
on to him. But surely Mama didn't get one amp of power
from my poor father. So was I wrong all that time? Was all
my strength mine? Did I just imagine you?

How much of whatever you and I made through these
past thirty years was sex?—just the big force of God working through us to make a new relay of people? Is it what
went wrong between us, the reason you're gone? Did my

body stop being something you wanted? But surely you noticed, back when we were young, that age and change waited for us too and that neither one of them was fun or lovely? Nothing is much sillier than t.v. doctors saying "Age is beautiful." What?—speckled old hands and slack jaws, loose thighs, and thick toenails? About as beautiful as dog-do in August on a sizzling road.

I know this much at least, that you'd turned away from me slowly but more and more. You were always courteous about it—but the fact is, you turned. It hasn't been all that hard for me to bear. I've been able to think it was a natural movement of time, working in both of us. But I can't help seeing all these old couples on t.v. saying they've never been happier with their bodies than now, when their children are grown and gone, and they can be alone in the house together. Not that you and I are old, but we turned out not to know what to do alone together. That was one fault at least, and I bear at least fifty percent of the blame.

Neither one of our bodies looks as good as it did back when they were the things that brought us toward each other. Not one single cell, outside or in, is the same as when we met and drew at each other. But in me at least the cells of my mind still look for you. When I walked back into this house tonight just awhile after dark, I prayed you would be in sight in here waiting again. In *sight*, Wesley. But no, here were all the pictures and the big statues of you my memory has carved in all the corners but not you—no part of you I could touch.

Where are you? If you're not with Horace or your mother, then you're not with anybody I know. If you had any private friends, I don't know when you saw them. Except for basketball games at the Coliseum with Ray, you

haven't been out of here one long evening in years. No
successful tomcat ever stayed home good as you.

Any mechanic good as you could get a job for the asking at any crossroads on the moon. So you could be working, and paid fairly, anywhere. But for all your Navy
cruises, I can't imagine you living outside the south. You
always said Yankees all look like they've taken a serious
laxative and are bound for the head. For all I know, you
may just be on the other side of town. Or in Durham.

You may be laughing with some younger woman, way
better built than Rosa now and with new eyes fixed on your
every blink like Rosa's once were. She may be spooning
you constant streams of nourishment your bones have
craved and that I stopped giving or never knew how to
make. But Wesley, you never said you needed that. It was
all I could do to get you to ask for supper if I got home
late.

But now I'm clawing at my own eyes and lips. I never
was that good at manure eating, mine or others'. It starts
my eyes watering, and I'm not going to try tears on you,
even in writing. Words were what I used to try to drown
you with. As much as any Holy Roller at an August re-
vival, I've had the permanent gift of tongues. And now
here again are all these *words*. They're for me—you well
know—much as you. They're to keep my mind from
melting in the heat of all I think and wonder about. You
may not ever have to read one word, but they're helping
me put one foot down firmly and then the other—without
yet needing to scramble and run.

I won't try further to picture you this minute where you
are, alone in a motel watching football with no more company than a cold pizza-box or with some better person. I

didn't try to call or see your mother for fear you might be there with her, though I knew you wouldn't be. *Knew?* What's left that I know now?—not you, never did. Whatever I thought.

LAST NIGHT OF THE YEAR. JEAN AND HAL INVITED ME TO their New Year's Eve party. Like a fool I went. One reason was, I'd already begun to feel what I know you'll feel if you ever read me this far—that I'm talking on way too long about feelings. It was always my failing, and I'm at it again.

I will therefore try to concentrate more on actions, things I do that might be worth reading about. In which case, this whole project will probably end a day or two into the New Year. That still hasn't chimed in yet. It's not but 11:30.

I said I was a fool to go to Jean's party and oh was I. Hal works in the Research Triangle for one of the big microchip outfits, you recall. So the place was full of PhDs in Physics, Engineering, and Math plus their wives, and some of them were doctors too. Talk about practical knowledge! If I'd had a flat tire in the yard, I doubt if there'd have been one volunteer to help fix it. But it would at least have given us something in common to talk about. I got Jean aside after the first awful hour and asked her what she found to talk about—you know Jean is no stronger than us in the I.Q. department. She said "Try sex or food, movies sometimes work, no t.v. except sports. And don't admit it if you're a Christian or a Democrat."

There were a couple of single men that got within firing range of the whites of my eyes, then saw I was old enough to be their aunt if not their mother and retreated. A few of

the wives seemed pitiful and came over saying they heard I
worked with Jean, and wasn't I fine to have made something of myself and learned the English language, implying
of course I'd come from the briarpatch and white-trash
roots in general?

I told them my people were clearing and improving this
land when theirs were still selling scissors in Sevastopol,
and that mine were the people that invented the English
language and handed it to Shakespeare, ready to use. I
overheard more things I knew were grammatical errors at
that party than in any two months at home with our families.

You know I *didn't* say any of the above, just gnawed a
big hole in the side of my cheek and told Jean I'd be
around to help her wash glasses late tomorrow morning,
but that now I had to get my horse-and-wagon on home
before midnight. You and I never celebrated a New Year in
public, and I'm not going to make an exception this time
just because you're invisible.

All the holidays that are important for me happen within
ten days of each other—our anniversary and Christmas
and tonight, except for Easter. I can still actually feel the
old year dragging out the door and the young one drawing
nigh with barely a sound. I'm not even going to switch on
t.v. and watch the ball drop on Times Square. I'm going to
wash my face for bed. With any luck at all I'll have said
my prayers, mostly touching on you, and will be deep
asleep for the fireworks and tears and auld lang syne at
midnight.

Jean asked me, as I was leaving on the doorstep, when I
was finally getting mad with you? She thinks I'm holding

back anger that's killing me and blocking me getting on with my new life.

I asked her who was anger going to hurt but me and the crockery? And I told her I didn't feel the need for a new life—that I hadn't minded the old one, not more than most people.

She said "Ro, that's a sad damned lie."

It made me mad. I said "You're drunk. Go on back in with your smart funmakers. They like your brand of jokes more than me."

Even in the weak porchlight, I could see her go white. So I begged her pardon.

But Jean said "Ro, I *said* 'Get mad.'" (You recall she took that course in Conflict Resolution.)

I said "You can't even guess what you're asking for. Rosacoke *mad* is more than you and any six psychology degrees could begin to tie down." I didn't know what I meant, but it felt true to say.

She cried next of course.

And I left her standing.

She'll be on the phone at midnight now to beg my pardon and wish us grand new heights of mature-woman friendship in the office and elsewhere this whole coming year.

I may not answer.

I DID. THIS IS JANUARY 18TH, NEARLY THREE WEEKS GONE. I was in bed dark but still awake and saying my prayers when fireworks started at the end of the street, and the bedside phone nearly rang off the table. In the silent instant before I answered, I thought it was you not Jean, and then I couldn't speak.

So a strange voice said "Home early, I see."

In the disappointment—and somehow relief—that it wasn't you, I blurted out *"Late."*

It said "Never too late." Then I think it laughed.

I say *it* because by then it seemed so much like a thing, an expensive new machine for scaring victims in the pitchblack dark. Then it hung up hard.

For a minute I prayed it had really been you, that you finally cared enough to check, even mean as that. Then unfortunately I got sensible. I told myself I'd been lucky till now, that I'd finally started getting my share of crank calls after years of nothing but a hot teenager. By the time the fireworks played out, I was truly asleep—the kind of sleep where you keep on thinking "I'm wide awake here. I'm wasting good dark."

I had a long dream about Roger. He had turned into an old Boston bull-terrier. You were gone and I knew I was meant to take care of him, but I kept forgetting to feed him. He was awfully weak and thinning down daily. The neighbors kept trying to remind me to feed him. Then in two or three weeks when I finally got to it, he was too frail to eat. His legs were dissolving to dry little stumps. I tried to force food down his throat with my fist. He still refused and his teeth grazed my skin.

Then I woke up slowly. At first I thought it had to be you, and I tried to be glad. I was on my back on my side of the bed. My arms were up and around a man who had just now started rooting at me. It was hard to believe you'd start like that after so long away, and my hands kept finding clothes wherever I touched—he was dressed in something like coveralls. In all his pockets he wore big objects that pressed in painfully. It dawned on me then that he had

to be armed, that those were weapons. Then I knew it
wasn't you. He was clean to the smell and not really cruel
in the way he moved, not yet anyhow.

So dazed as I was, it took me another thirty seconds to
tell myself "You are being raped, Rose. Now what do you
do?"

I thought if I screamed or started to fight, he'd do nothing but kill me. I thought he might well do that anyhow
once he was finished. But the thing is, I stood it as long as
I could. What kept me lying there was strange curiosity.
The man was trying to talk while he moved, like a speech
he'd memorized way back in school for this one moment,
if the moment ever came. At first I thought if I just heard
his speech, then I'd understand and could talk him down.
But all I got was his main word *help*. If he said *help* once,
he said it fifty times.

The lower half of his body was working, but it felt more
like a dry bumping duty he had to accomplish than any
kind of fun or meanness to me. Wesley, forgive me—I felt
like laughing. Then again I was scared cold, and I made
one mighty roll with my hips.

He hit the floor loud.

I thought "All right. I'll be dead in two seconds." I was
calm as you.

But he stood on up. In the streetlight coming weak
through the blinds, I could partly see the side of his face—
a full-grown serious strange adult, no hungry boy. His hair
was still combed, and he seemed to be thinking.

I knew my time was flying by fast. But for some odd
reason, what I thought of was Rato. I thought how he
would not understand this—how once I was dead, then
nobody else on earth would try to answer Rato's questions.

He'd be left thinking I'd been murdered by somebody crazy or mad at me, not by a man fired up with a fury he could only try to drown in *women*. Then I thought "You sound like Jean or a t.v. psychiatrist. Save your damned life." So I sat straight up and said "Get out of here. I'll give you one minute."

He stood on still, then turned to face me.

That way, the light was shining toward me. He could see me but his own face was dark. Whatever he saw, whatever he believed, whatever he'd *accomp*lished, he said "Please thank me."

I'd better admit that I think I obeyed. I knew I didn't mean it, but the memory of it fouls my mouth.

He was still near enough to hear me, but at least he didn't answer. He bent down slowly to pick up something he'd dropped on the floor, then faced me one long last time. Then he was out the kitchen door, that he closed firm behind him.

I lay back down with both my hands up beside by head, both open and dry. I tried to think of plans for the rest of my life. It seemed important to plan everything now, carefully as possible. I would say a short prayer to be alive, then get up, strip this linen, start it washing, then bathe myself, dress, and *get out of here*. To my continuing surprise, it all felt like a list of things I could do. But beyond the washing and leaving, I couldn't plan. So I stood up in the dark and stripped the bed.

I'd locked the back door (that I'd overlooked—his easy way in), and the washing machine was under way before I thought "Police. I'm destroying my evidence." I opened the washer to stop the water. Then I knew I'd been right. This was my business now. The last thing I needed was to open a hole on the swarm of crows that waited to fly at my eyes and mouth if I touched the phone. I shucked my pants and added them to the sheets, touching them only in two tiny places at the waistband. Then I went to our bathroom.

I remember a movie that nobody else seemed to see in the early sixties, called *Something Wild* with Carroll Baker. She was a girl that got raped in a park while she was walking home from school in her neat uniform. After the man finished with her, she straightened herself up and continued home. Her mother called to her in the hall and asked was she O.K.? She said "Yes ma'm" and went on upstairs. In the bathroom she undressed slowly, then sat down on the tile floor by the commode, took her mother's big sewing-scissors, cut her slip and pants into slow narrow strips, and flushed them away. The sight of her cutting so neat and quiet broke my heart to watch, the first time and now. Then she took a long bath.

I turned on the faucets and made myself examine my gown. It was no more wrinkled than after a normal night's sleep, and there was no sign of stain or damp. But I didn't touch my body, didn't look closer than was necessary to tell I wasn't bleeding.

And I was deep in a tub of hot water before I asked out loud "Now have you been raped?" In legal terms, I guess I'll never know. But after three weeks of thinking it through—and oh I've thought it through, in, out, up, down, back, and forth—I can sure God say this much. I've been used, hard, for some stranger's own secret need or mission. He picked me to prove some blunt point on, and he left me without the least clue of what he meant—whether he proved it or whether I stopped him.

And was he a stranger? One of my tough problems has

been the thought that he must have known me. Surely nobody would pick a name out of a phonebook for such a personal deed. Anyhow the name in the book is ours. Was he a boy from the college? He looked older than that. But with forty years of good nutrition, some American eighteen-year-olds look thirty.

Since he left me, I've read two books on the subject and several articles. And I know that a number of raped women feel like they caused it to happen, that they drew the punishment down on them for any number of reasons. Honest to Christ, I don't. I know I haven't hurt anybody consciously, not any remotely sane man. And I'm not aware of knowing any lunatics. I know I haven't done anything that deserved punishment on the scale I received in those ninety seconds he groveled down in me. Then and since.

I gave up writing here three weeks ago, which speaks for itself. I took a bath a lot longer than Carroll Baker's. I forget how many times I drained and refilled the tub. I dressed in street clothes—no shoes—and lay down in Horace's room on his high single bed. I tried to pray and discovered God was nowhere to be found, not by me. By then it was no more than two a.m. No hope of daylight before nearly seven. So I clamped my teeth, pulled up the afghan that Mama made Horace, and composed my hands to wait out the time. If I'd had any hint on earth of your whereabouts, Wesley, I'd have choked down handfuls of pride and come to you through crushed glass if need be.

Yet I doubt I could have told you. One reason I could start back writing here is, I've given up on you.

Bronnie, at the shop, finally called me two days ago and asked one more time if I'd heard hide or hair of you.

I had to say no.

He said "Mrs. Beavers, excuse my language. But Wesley's the best damned mechanic since Henry Ford, still I got to fill his place. If he does turn up, please God let me know—I'll try to hire him back. But you know I can't promise."

From that minute on I believed you were gone. With God hid from me and you nowhere I could reach in time, I knew there were just two hopes on earth. I had one son, no farther off than Charlotte. He was no tower of strength and anyhow I probably couldn't tell him, just huddle up near him till something better dawned. But then a little snag, that I'd felt before in my mind, stopped me cold—maybe you were with Horace. It didn't seem like you to hide down there that close to Pris, but maybe Horace at least knew more than he'd said all the times he'd called—so concerned and shamed. So I wouldn't press Horace, not till I had to.

Then who but my mother? I had a whole nother week of time off. I'd drive back up there and sit by her, take walks with Rato. The fact that she hadn't asked about you Christmas made her seem like even more of a chance than before. The hope kept me lying there still and covered till daylight started. I'd told myself I could call her at daylight. At maybe five a.m. a car stopped in the street exactly in front of the house and waited two minutes, long enough for me to seize up in a shudder that threatened my teeth. I was frozen down. If it had been that same man, with two more, I'd have stayed there frozen while they did their business. But then it roared off. And I managed sleep, of all strange things.

* * *

THE TELEPHONE WOKE ME AWHILE AFTER DAY, MAYBE seven-thirty. I still couldn't face our room, so I ran to the kitchen and answered. And at first there was a silence that scared me. I thought of course it was my last guest.

But then a man's voice said "Rosacoke?" No man in Raleigh had called me that in twenty years, so I knew I was safe to that extent.

I said "Yes sir."

And he said "Hey." Then he seemed to say "It sounds like her anyhow" and drop the receiver. I was near to guessing I knew the voice, some man kin to me.

But a woman's voice came on. "Rosa, is that you?"

I said something like "I think I believe so."

She said "Make up your mind and let me know. Rosa's mother called to say 'Happy New Year' to her. If she's not there, I'll save my money."

Honestly, Wesley, I don't think Jesus in person could have been more welcome. My mother doesn't call me more than once in three years, and then it's just to tell bad news —some more dead kin.

I said "Oh Mama, it's Rosa—yes *ma'm*. I just didn't recognize Rato's voice."

She said "This foolishness is his idea. He woke up early saying 'Call Rosacoke.' Said he had a bad dream about you in the night, said he'd pay for the call. You're all right, ain't you?"

The fact that my mentally underpar brother had dreamed the painful truth about me and was worried—that was a sweet consolation already. But the fact that my old realistic mother couldn't imagine me being any less than all right was almost certainly what saved my life. But I'd known she could save me; she had before now. I said "Yes ma'm,

I'm truly all right." And then I hated myself and burst out crying. It wasn't really sobs but a block in my throat that shut me up for the next long seconds.

Eventually Mama said "You need me with you?"

Too quick I said "No, no. I'm fine."

Mama said "I think you're telling a lie—and on New Year's morning."

So I said "What if I wanted to come up there and hang out around you and Rato and my old room?"

Mama said "I'd remind you that room is near about a glacier. But it's your home, Rosa—you want it, we got it."

I said "Anything you need from Raleigh?"

She thought a second and said "Is there a Stuckey's Candy Store anywhere along your road?"

I said "Oh yes."

She said "Then bring me and Rato a pound of those pralines. They're good for his eyes, so he claims."

I said "And they don't exactly harm yours, do they?"

She laughed, which is always a shock from her, and said "All right, make it five pounds. I'll reimburse you."

I said "I think I can underwrite that much harmless pleasure." Then I told her I'd be seeing them in late morning. I got my mouth and face ready, then went to the kitchen and fixed the only breakfast I could eat—a cup of tea and part of a slice of dry toast. Then I got the sheets out of the drier and went outside and put them in the garbage, the only real percale all-cotton sheets we had left.

Nowhere in the backyard was there any sign of footprints. The place at least had not been damaged. There was just the big hole in the air that man had made when he slammed through me.

Then I tackled our bedroom—I had to, to pack. It

seemed like a place that might have been hurt beyond healing, though nothing was out of place except that little
throwrug at your side of the bed. The man had skewed it
when he hit the floor. I straightened that slowly, and since
my hands obeyed so calmly, I wondered for the first time if
this whole thing was a New Year's dream.

Now that I'd washed the sheets, my gown and pants,
there wasn't a shred of evidence the naked eye could see.
And I wasn't going to ask the S.B.I. to come in with their
microscopes and tweezers. The only conclusion I could
come to right then was *Yes old Rose, you were hit maybe
harder than even you know. The enemy was a human male,
not a demon. You will very likely never have to meet him
again above ground. You don't yet know what he did to
you, but nothing seems to be badly torn. What's burned is
your mind; hunt something for that.*

So I called Jean's house. Hal answered and said she was
out at the garbage cans. I told him not to bother her, just to
thank her again for last night and to say I'd been called to
my mother's on unexpected family business. I'd be back
well before term began.

Hal got confidential in tone and wanted to know what
had gone wrong last night.

I told him that Rose had never been much of a party girl
at her best and that now I was way under normal.

He said "Do you want us to help you find Wesley? I
know some good detectives right here in town. With com-
puters and government taxes and so on, people can't just
vanish easy like they used to. Wesley's probably already
laid down a trail of canceled checks and charge-card receipts. If you let me approach the right people, I think I
can help maybe more than you know."

I thanked him but said I'd always respected your occasional need to just vamoose. I said I meant to give you room. You'd speak up when you had something to say.

Hal started whispering then. "Tell me to shut my damned mouth if you want to, but did Wesley find out something you didn't want him to know?"

Finally something had made me really mad. I said "Hal Gillam, I'm not a secret poisoner or a millionaire dealer in blackmarket babies."

Hal said "I understand but you know these days women are trying all sorts of things that used to be male property. More than eighty percent of modern divorces are initiated by the wife or the wife's new behavior."

I said "My behavior is the same as it's been. And one thing I'm still nuts about is promptitude. I need to get on the road now for home. Tell Jean what I said." I left him standing with his seminar hat on, that early in the day. Hal has taken more courses than Jean. He's living proof that there's such a thing as pulling your bootstraps so hard your mind just vanishes down in the soles.

I LOADED UP MY BAG AND ROGER AND LEFT BY NINE A.M. The highway was empty as if there'd been a nuclear attack and atomized everybody but me, an old boxer dog, and everything but concrete, trees, and empty houses. Occasionally an ancient black woman would be strolling on the edge of the pavement with a tall walking stick. I'd wave and she'd stop, turn, and watch me out of sight. But you don't see anything like the number of Negro shacks you used to, those tall little huts the wind blew through. A lot of them have just collapsed back into the earth, and the grandchildren have bought themselves "double-wide mo-

bile homes" with decorator-pink shutters and a little packed
dirt yard with not a hope of a flower. Well, they're dry
anyhow and warmer than before.

But the balance of everybody under sixty has moved up
north to stand on desperate street corners, I guess. In all
the sixty miles, I didn't see a soul under sixty years old.
And pretty fast I worked up the idea that maybe God had
finally punished all the descendants of Indian killers and
slave owners by making young blacks vanish, that He'd
driven them all to Detroit and Harlem (does He think that's
a reward?) and left old ladies to guard this gorgeous land
down here. Who did that make me then? I never decided.

But thinking about it, I held up through the ninety minutes alone. All the reading I've done says that rape victims
first go through a bad stage of hating their own bodies. I
felt exhausted that morning. I've faced numerous other
New Year's Days with a lot more to hope for. But I knew I
was right to be going home and changing my scenery.

I didn't hate my body or anything about me. Maybe it
was because I moved so fast to clear out the evidence that I
really didn't know what had happened to my body and still
don't. I think though that what worked, and is still working, in me is the sense that my man was out to harm my
mind. My body was just something he was knocking at,
hoping to find my mind and bruise it, plow it up and leave
the picture of him in the middle of my mind and life for the
rest of the time I'm given. And he may have managed that.

But what I'm planning is that the memory is just of
embarrassment, nothing worse—the embarrassment of
having a dog get excited in your presence and start hump-
ing your leg with somebody else watching. That may be a
serious lie, but how am I going on if I believe worse than

that and let it press on me? Then he *will* have hurt my mind.

What began to hurt, then and there as I came in sight of home country, was all that part of me that's grown toward you and into you. Even if we were married in a j.p.'s office at nine-thirty in the morning, we both knew it was *till death did us part*. I'd come through what could have turned into death just the night before, and I prayed you weren't dead or anywhere near it.

But if not, why the hell weren't you here beside me? Then I could be in our house, *our* home, and not streaking back to my mama—me a forty-eight-year-old woman with nothing more natural to run to than my mother. Why the hell weren't you there a hand's breadth away from me last night to save me from that? At what point in all our years together have I ever shirked anything you asked for? I would die for you every instant of the day, and you damned well know it—and don't forget, I am writing this three weeks after a lunatic fouled me head to foot and in your bed, Wesley, in a house we both paid for but that's in your name and that you left a month ago with no word of warning.

AT TEN-THIRTY ON THE STROKE, I NOSED INTO THE OLD dirt track up to Mama's. You'd think red dirt couldn't hold in place against trucks and every act of God's weather for so many years, but every deep cut and bump that I memorized as a child is still there waiting to hurt you again. I don't want to sound spoiled, but since Rato had dreamed about me so conveniently the night before, I did think he or Mama might be there to meet me. But I left my things and Roger in the car and went inside to see what was what. The

house was empty as home in a nightmare. That was when
the willies hit me.

I stood in that cold hall, calling both their names at the
top of my voice. I felt convinced that the man from last
night and every other body that had ever dreamt of harming
me was hid just yonder behind the room doors. Then I all
but flew out the back.

Mama, as I told you, is more than a little deaf. I had to
go round the edge of the woodshed before I could see her
or she hear me. But oh she was back there, chopping wood
at her age for that little cook-stove she keeps in the kitchen
and won't throw out.

I went up close enough for her eyes to see me, and she
stopped long enough to take a thorough look. For the only
time yet, I thought what a lot of assaulted women seem to
think—"She can *tell*. She's going to mention it, and then
I'll truly die." (Even now I wouldn't be surprised if some
friend's face goes all scared, and I look down and there's a
wet stain of blood in my lap.)

But Mama just said "I do this to keep my arms in practice. I doubt the Law'll let you put a woman in the poor-
house when she still chops every stick of her own wood."
She smiles a lot more than earlier in life, and now she let
loose a beamer that about knocked me over and made me
realize one of the stranger things about recent history—
how much Emma Mustian, this plain country woman with
a tenth-grade education and never more than five thousand
dollars cash-money, looks like the Queen Mother of En-
gland. Just get her one of those ostrich-plume hats and a
satin purse with a modest diamond clasp (say, a hundred
small stones), and she could change the Guard this afternoon and not get arrested.

I said "This may be the best day of my life."

Mama looked at the sky, thinking I meant the weather. "I'm grateful to be here to see it," she said. "I don't know if I grade it that high in history though."

I laughed and said "Let me finish that for you."

She said "You haven't touched an axe this century. Go back in the house and make you some coffee."

I nodded. "All right. But where is Rato? I thought he did these heavy jobs for you."

Mama looked toward the back pines, then took a strong heave at her slab of wood. "Rosa, your brother moves mysteriously. What I ask him, he does. But he's got his own burdens, so I don't ask much. He wandered on off after you said you'd come. I think he's ashamed I told you he was worried. He wouldn't want to be accused of caring, you know, for anything sorry as his next-younger sister. He woke me up though in the dark, about five, and asked could he crawl in the bed with me. It'd been so many centuries since a man asked to join me in linens that I said 'Get warm.' So I lay there quiet by my baby son—what? fifty years old—and waited for his message. Finally he got up his nerve and told me a terrible dream he had about you."

I asked her at once not to tell me please.

She said "He took care of that. He swore me silent." Then she studied me again, longer than before. "I'm proud to see he was wrong to worry. You look some stronger than you did Christmas day, a little tired around here." She touched her own eyes.

"I went to Jean Gillam's New Year's party last night."

"Wesley didn't go with you?"

"Wesley's still missing."

By then she'd gathered an armload of wood, and I stooped to help her. When we turned toward the house, she said "I've been scared to death for you, Rosa."

"Why scared?" I said.

"I know what Wesley meant to you."

I said "He's been gone more than a week. I might have thought I'd cave in too. I guess you're not my mother for nothing."

She gave her old loud hiss at foolishness. We'd got to the back steps. She took the first two, then faltered an instant. I thought she'd fall. But she got her own balance and said "Plan to break. Say when you're going to do it, and choose who you want to watch you." Then she set her wood in the old box on the porch and went to the kitchen.

My mind wouldn't let me believe I'd heard her right. I dumped my own wood though and followed her in.

I walked around the house and let Roger out of the car. You know how the country surprises him. The number of new things coming at his eyes and nose all at once gets him too excited.

He stood there among chickens, the woods, squirrels, and the wayoff noise from a chainsaw. He looked up at me like "You expect me to manage all this?"

I said "Go to it" and waved him off.

He gave me one more slow look, like "I refuse to take responsibility when something breaks." Then he trucked off slow toward the nearest trees. His left hip is getting worse by the week.

Inside, Mama had already started cooking the big midday meal she turns out for just her and Rato. Today it was going to be the traditional blackeyed peas and hog jowl (a little pork roast really, baked in vinegar), stewed okra and tomatoes that she'd canned, little lacey pones of fried cornbread, buttermilk, and a lemon meringue pie.

She tried to involve me in the easy first rounds of the preparations, but soon it was plain that my own three decades of experience in our kitchen still hadn't earned me senior rights here. My hands just will not move like hers.

Finally she said "Don't you need a little rest after your trip? I'll call you when Rato turns up."

So I went toward the living room and stretched out on the old tufted leather nap-couch. And again she was right. I slept without trying.

AT TWELVE-THIRTY MAMA AND RATO WATCH THEIR ONE soap opera, "The Young and the Restless" (the one you call "The Hung and the Breastless"). What holds them is the fact that the actors let the producers make them look so much worse than real people do, what with the wigs and eyeshadow and the uniform Dupont stainless teeth. They keep waiting for some actor to just refuse and walk on the screen one day looking normal and nice like somebody you might know, and they only invest a half-hour a day. They say when you've seen the first half, you can guess the second. Anyhow it moves about as fast as an uphill glacier. You can watch three weeks and they won't even have finished the dinner they started a month ago—otherwise it *is* all very lifelike, provided your income is a quarter-million dollars and you believe amnesia is an epidemic like Hong Kong flu. Then Mama and Rato eat their big meal in the kitchen where, winter and summer, desert plants would thrive. They keep the wood stove fired that high.

I stripped down to my blouse and slacks and joined them.

Rato said his peculiar grace (you remember, "O Lord, I thank you for dinner" or whatever meal he specifies). They both served themselves bounteous helpings and struck in. I did the best I could. Rato wouldn't notice if anybody else above ground ever ate another crumb, but it's one of the main beats Mama patrols.

That day though she didn't say a word. She just kept up a closer watch than usual, even for her.

The feel of her eyes prowling my cheek hurt at first. Then after I warned myself to bear it, it began to seem normal and even strengthening. So much so that when Mama finally said "Rato, tell her your dream," I said "Wait. I'll tell you what *happened*."

And I actually told them. I didn't go into every detail of the man's movements against me or the condition of the laundry, but I let them know that a totally strange man broke into our house just the night before and tried to harm me in my own bed.

Mama's eyes stayed on me through every word. But when I'd finished, the first thing she said was not to me. She said "See, son, your dream was wrong."

Rato said, "You don't know all my dream. I told you she was hurt. I didn't tell all."

I had to laugh. Here I'd confided what was maybe the worst secret of my life, and all I'd triggered was the usual wrangle.

But Mama came back to me. "You seen a doctor?"

I couldn't admit I hadn't thought of a doctor, not to that moment. I nodded. "I'm all right."

She asked me his name.

I said "Doctor Gattis."

"No, the rogue," she said. All criminals that aren't *murderers* are *rogues* to my mother."

"I said he was a stranger."

"But they caught him?" she said.

I had to tell her they hadn't.

"And may not," she said, "short-handed as they are." With television, Mama and Rato know as much about life on a big-city police force as any old cop.

I said "I didn't call the police and don't plan to. The man fled the scene with no real damage, to me or the house. I don't want my name blazed around Raleigh, every sick fool ringing me day and night."

Through it, Rato had sat very quietly. I looked over toward him to check at least. And oh dear Christ, his eyes were full. Next to you and Milo, Rato's always had keys to all my hearts. So I stood and went toward him.

But he waved me off. And when I kept coming, he bolted upright and ran out. The next thing I heard was the back door slamming.

Mama said "He don't understand this, Rosa."

I said "I hope you don't think I do."

"I didn't say that. I see you're here so I guess you're lost. I hope some way I can help you out."

I told her she'd taught me all I knew. It wasn't really true but I don't plan to write her and change the claim. She understands me.

When we'd washed the dishes and got them all put away for the four millionth time, I mentioned Rato not being back. I thought she'd said he spent the winters indoors all day, and that day was cooler than usual.

Mama said "He spends a night out every so often, not when it's quite as cold as this. I worry some but it don't

seem to hurt him. He was always tough but thirty years in
the Army turned him into something that can take what
comes."

"Except his sister," I said.

"Ma'm?"

"Except me, what's happened to me. That's spooked
him."

Not till then did Mama turn, drying her hands slowly.
"Let me just say this—you told him wrong. You said that
man tried to *harm* you. That shied him. That's what scared
Rato off."

Again I all but laughed. "Mama, I was telling the plain
truth. You don't seriously think a rapist means well, do
you? I thought it would help us all to get it out at the start
of my visit so we don't bumble around in the dark knocking each other down in ignorance."

Mama nodded yes but she said "You shouldn't have said
hurt."

I couldn't believe her. "I can't tell a thirty-year Army
veteran that one other person in this world just might in-
tend to hurt somebody?"

"But it was you that got hurt, Rosa. Anybody else, even
me, he would have flinched. You are something he's made
a whole life out of."

Then I did laugh.

But late in the afternoon, when I had managed a long
cold nap up in my old room, Rato still hadn't come back.
Mama was in the front room reading her daily devotional
and *The News and Observer*. Reading is the only surprise
for me in her present life. When I caught her at it, she
almost apologized for taking a quiet half hour in a chair,
and I realized she'd never had time for it till the last one of

us was gone—the last one needing care. I told her to sit still. I was going out to get a breath of air.

Again for the first time, she didn't rise up to be sure I was dressed for my Arctic expedition. I left her looking back at the thin little book, following prayers with her silent dry lips.

I wasn't sure I was hunting Rato, and I knew I could never guess where he'd be. He'd never had personal favorites in *places*, unlike me and Milo. At least he'd never said so. But it dawned on me that I hadn't seen black Mary Sutton in years—the mother of Mildred, my friend that died of the bastard baby shortly before you and I got married. Mary had always been good to me, even if she was tough as whit-leather.

She even gave me the best advice of anybody in the early days when you were the one big problem on my mind. She said if I needed you, then *hold* you in whatever way it took. I've sometimes wondered if I didn't arrange to get pregnant with Horace because of Mary's advice. I know I conceived him within an hour of hearing Mary say to *hold* you.

Now I didn't even know if she was alive. But her ancient shack had stood in a clearing half a mile in the woods north of home, about midway between our place and yours. So I struck off in that direction hoping Roger would find me but he never did. Maybe he was with Rato. Most dumb beasts are.

The path was still clean, and in a minute I was passing big trees that I'd known as switches, individual rocks with shapes I remembered, and the old smells of evergreen and sweet rotting leaves that all came together to remind me of nearly the first half of my life. Some of the memories were sad—our dumb premarital struggles that kept me roaming the woods or trekking to your house with hat in hand—but most of them went farther back than you to a happy childhood. And by the time I broke out in the clearing, I was calmer than I'd been in twenty-four hours at least.

The shack was still there. The ferocious tom-turkey that had always patrolled the place was nowhere in sight, and there was no smoke from the old rock chimney. But nothing else was different. The house was balanced pretty much where it had always been, on the absolute verge of collapse. And the boards had got more than ever like bones or driftwood, leached out nearly white till the whole thing seemed like a miracle of how long a shelter could last just because it was needed. Somebody had to be in it; otherwise it would have blown right to dust. I went up and knocked. No answer for what seemed a month.

Then it opened half an inch. The room behind it was dark, and the day itself was running down, so I could barely see a face.

But I guessed it was Mary, and I risked her name.

The face stepped back and opened the door another two inches.

A blast of hot air struck me. I realized she was saving precious heat, and I rushed to step in. By the time my eyes had adjusted to the dark room, the person had gone to a far corner and stood against the wall.

And it was Mary. She said "Mr. Rato told me he seen you."

"When?—this afternoon? I'm hunting him."

"Ain't you going to speak to me?" Mary grinned, then quickly covered her teeth (or the empty gums).

I said "Excuse me, Mary. You surprised me at the door. Had to get my bearings."

"You been here before. Is it that long ago?"

I told her "At least twenty-eight years."

Mary said "Seems like last Sunday to me."

I looked round for changes. The only thing missing, that I recalled, was the cardboard box she'd kept Mildred's baby in—long taffy-colored bastard Sledge with the serious eyes. You remember he went to the pen ten years ago for killing a girl in Petersburg? I asked about him.

"Sledge own a big car-wash. Doing real fine. Don't send me no money."

I'll probably never know if she was lying. I did ask "Where is he?"

Not missing a lick, Mary said "Newport News." I know Virginia's a peculiar and stuck-up state, but even there can a man go from the pen straight to owning a car-wash in that short a time? I left it right there.

But Mary reached behind her, found a picture frame on a table, walked farther forward, and waved it at me.

I thought at first the man was Billy Dee Williams, the black movie-star—same mustache, same finger-waved hair. But Mary's picture was plainly homemade, a little blurred and faded. I looked for Mildred's likeness somewhere on him, maybe in the eyes. But no, he was just a light-complected man with an empty face. Maybe Sledge, maybe not. Why should I doubt her? I asked did she have a picture of Mildred?

Mary pointed to the dark wall behind where she'd stood. Dim as it was, I made out a whole spray of dime-store brass frames. She said "You sent it to me after Mildred passed."

I'd forgotten. It was one I took with that huge box-Kodak Rato sent me from the P.X. in Fort Sill, Oklahoma. And amazingly, for my skills, it was clear as something from *Life* magazine. Mildred was walking in the road near Delight Church. Milo was driving me to the store. I told him to stop for Mildred. He grumbled but did. By then Mildred and I had gone past the childhood friendship we had. I guess she was nervous about the racial stuff that was already rumbling. Back then I was way too blind or dumb to understand how strange it must have felt for her—her best little girl-friend now a grown white lady. But she smiled and posed, frowning broadside. The frown was at the sun, not me. One picture came out clear, and I sent it to Mary right after you and I moved to Raleigh. How much else of my life—good clear memories—have I sent off and long since forgot? So I asked could I look at the other pictures?

Mary was in my path to the wall, frowning. But then she smiled and stepped aside. She said "You caught me."

I asked "In what?" But I went to the wall, and there were several old pictures of me (all high school pictures with sweater and pearls and those extra teeth I always seem to have in pictures). I knew I hadn't given them to Mildred or Mary. So I was baffled—much more so when I looked down low, and there was a framed newspaper clipping from *The Warren Record* of December 1957 reporting our marriage in Dillon, S.C. and a dog-eared announcement, in my handwriting, of Horace's birth. I was speechless. Why had Mary collected all these, and where from, and why had she first tried to hide them?

She said "Now you caught him."

"Milo?" I asked. I couldn't think who else might have

herded up this little Rosacoke collection in a hot Negro
shack deep back in the woods.

Mary shook her head. "I ain't seen Milo since way before you. This is Rato's place. He begged me for it."

I said "Mary, I don't understand."

She said "Rato came down here ten or twelve years ago
with two pictures of you. He wanted to know could I buy
him some frames, if he give me the money? I told him he
went to town more than me. But he said no, he didn't want
nobody else to know his business. He give me two dollars,
and it was a long time before he come back. I had his
frames though and handed them to him. He sat down
yonder at the table and put the pictures behind glass, took
him best part of an hour. It wasn't till then that he asked
me could he hang them up right here? I asked him what in
the world for? I mean, I knew you—Mildred thought you
were *something*. But I didn't have no call to spread you out
up here like my lost darling baby-girl. Rato just said 'I'm
asking you nice. Rosacoke is the person I miss in the
world. I don't want everybody asking questions about me
and her, if I keep them at home. Down here, I can know in
my mind where she is. I can walk down and see her and
you anytime.' I didn't want to laugh, but it did seem peculiar. So I chuckled. And Rato smiled. But he said 'Mary,
your damned walls are naked.' So I told him 'Sure, hang
all you want.' And in later years he brought all the rest—
the rest of the pictures and that baby card, yours and Mr.
Wesley's boy. I bought some more frames, and he still
comes to see them. Never says what he's doing, never goes
right up to the wall and studies them but sits out here in the
chair. And *I* know. Rosa, your face give that poor boy

satisfaction. Don't laugh at him now. Don't tell him I told you."

I told her I wouldn't think of such a thing. But I did ask had he been down here today? When she said no, I thanked her for the news, said I was home with Mama for a few days' rest and had to run now but that I'd come back for longer toward the end of my stay.

Mary followed me to the door, watched me halfway across the clearing and then called my name in her strong voice. When I looked back she said "You got a secret, ain't you?"

I tried to laugh. But then I had to say "Should have known I couldn't hide it."

"Not from me anyhow. I knowed you too long." Mary smiled again and said "You know where I'm at, all day and all night." Then she shut her frail door.

Secrets *on* secrets—my thrilling life.

THAT WAS THE START OF MY COUNTRY REST. AT LEAST IT gave me another kind of surprise, to spread on top of New Year's night and sweeten it maybe. Maybe. Milo had been the brother I leaned to when we were children. He was so good to watch, still or moving. And being four years older, he could show me signals of the world up ahead where he was already. Rato, with his peculiar mind, was somebody who lived with us a good many nights but said about two hundred words a year—really. The rest of the time, he was off God-knew-where.

For all I knew he was climbing tall pines and launching out high with nothing but his long arms and gliding all day in the summer sun. I knew that, after Mama, I was the person in the family he paid any attention to. Every once in

a while, he would bring me something—a cut finger to
bandage or a rock he'd found in the riverbed.

Seriously, one day he brought me a big damned rock the
size of a coffee can, hauled it upstairs, sat it on the floor by
my bed, and said "I brought you this because I knew you'd
want it."

I thanked him and said I could use it for a doorstop.
Rato just kept staring at my eyes hoping I'd understand, I
guess.

When I didn't, he finally said "It's because it looks like
you." I started to say I was deeply insulted.

But I looked again and yes, there was the line of a nice
girl's face on one side of the rock. I thought he meant he
had found it natural, carved by the water.

Then he said "It *had* the face when I first saw it but hid
down deep. I gouged it some with another rock to find it
better." I thanked him and thought for the thousandth time
my next-oldest brother was bound to be from Space. But it
never dawned on me I was something he thought about
when I wasn't there.

Even now it still didn't matter a lot. Coming on top of
you leaving and New Year's night, it was one more case,
that I didn't need, of how sadly little I know about men—
what they truly think in those calm-looking minds, what
they really will ask for, if they'd ever really ask for all they
want.

I mean you of course. Once my father was dead and
Milo married Sissie, you were the only man I wondered
about and needed to know. And now you've taken your
secret and gone. Call up, Wesley—collect if you need
to—or come to the back yard just close enough for me to
hear your voice and tell me, finally tell me exactly what

you need that I didn't give. What final straw broke our camel's back? It was bound to be from me, right? Who else did you know long enough and hard enough to let them fail you so bad you had to leave?

I know that sounds like Ms. Door-mat of the Ages. I know I'd be drummed out of any woman's-rights club, the biggest traitor of all to my sex. But as much as it's caused me years of pain, I cannot truthfully sit here and claim I'd have changed it any way if I could—my feeling for you. Hard as it was to do, in those days of home—surrounded by our old places—I made myself think back to how it was and where it must have come from in my mind and heart.

First, obviously, it had to come from God. Even if I don't go to church more than twice a year, I'm enough of a Christian still to believe that a woman's feelings for her man and vice versa are put deep into her and him by the Maker. And not just to insure that we multiply and tend to the Earth (haven't we done a grand job of that?). Way past the drive to multiply, for me, has been the way I've seen God's image in you much more often than in myself or any six ministers in vestments and rings.

I mentioned the danger of idolatry here awhile back. It's a danger I haven't always avoided. More than once at important times, you've been a bigger sun in my sky than God Himself. We've both suffered for it. But even when I've kept my worship in balance, I've known that you at your best were just stamped out in God's image and you *showed* it. That's why I was glad for long years to serve you.

After God, I learned it next from my father. Has anybody ever figured out why a big percentage of America's truly lovable men are drunks? Not the kind you see on t.v.

now, drinking a few too many martinis over a business
lunch or an extra bottle of champagne late on a wonderful
candlelit night but the concentrated kind that buys a cheap
pint of antifreeze bourbon, goes in a white room with one
naked light bulb hung from a wire, sits down in a straight
chair at a table painted green, and drinks and drinks till he
pours to the ground like the last tan drop, then stands up,
scrubs his eyes, and starts again.

My father was nobody's genius, I know. He wasn't even
that good a farmer before he took to the bottle in earnest.
His father kept us alive till Milo could take over when he
was sixteen. But from the time I can remember, little
flashes from age three or four, my poor father's is the face
smiling down at me and drawing me toward it. I know
from my years with my own son that Mama had to have
spent endless gentle hours stooped over me doing every
task I needed. So why is it I don't have one single grateful
memory of her, not until I'm at least thirteen? All I remember from her in my childhood is hard words and
switchings, which has got to be miserably unfair.

Calm-headed now, I calculate my father can't have
spent a whole hour doing hard jobs for me. He very likely
never even saw my butt dirty, much less had to wipe it.
Like I said though, his face was what I learned to love on.
Half of what I did awake was to try and please that face
that could beam like the gorgeous sun at Morehead City on
a warm spring dawn. Oh it could beam and *did*, now and
then in my presence but so seldom that I was never sure if
I'd caused it or of how to cause it again. So I told him over
and over I loved him.

He'd say "Sweet Rosie, I may love you," but he drank
on deeper in the bottle till all he aimed at was one great

bottle that could drown him forever till he walked up the road that one particular sweet summer evening and stepped out into Duke Simpson's truck speeding hell-for-leather to a church fishfry with a twenty-five-pound tub of iced coleslaw and a peck of cornbread.

Then there was you in the mile-high fork of that pecan tree the Sunday I found you for the first time ever, thirty-five years ago. I tried to talk at you up there against the glare. You were fixed on something way out past me, that I couldn't spot and you wouldn't speak of—"Smoke," you said. You were watching smoke. I was watching fire.

Everything I've loved in my entire life, I've loved then and there on the spot that instant I caught sight of it. My mind says "*There*" and my heart says "*Hold it*." From that hour on, I held you, Wesley. Or sure God tried to. And thought I'd more or less succeeded till Christmas week when that same smoke you've always watched closed around and hid you, from my sight at least.

Be alive, old friend. Sleep deep. Come home.

WESLEY

WESLEY IS STILL THE KIND OF MAN PEOPLE watch. Even children will stop their urgent business to watch him pass. Though he's fifty he hasn't gained more than ten pounds since his Navy days. His auburn hair is still strong and dark, and his eyes are firm as ever—barely blinking. People always used to praise him as sexy. He'd grin and shrug. But he never refused the tribute due a power he prized in others as much as himself. Before his marriage at twenty-two, he "used himself" (as he thinks of it now) with nineteen women and three men. He still has a clear list of the names and a detailed memory of the circumstances of all those partners with whom he was sober.

Nobody mentions *sexy* much now except occasional women in bars, and he spends very little time in bars. But a good many people still like to touch him. He has noticed

how—in shopping malls even—if he sits down on a bench
to rest and watch the world, some child is likely to spot
him, run up, and (before it can think) grab his legs around
the knees or lay a damp head on his broad thigh, smiling.
If he lays his hand right in his own crotch, within two
minutes at least one woman or man will pause to look. A
surprising number will circle back for a second glimpse.

The fact gives him no special pleasure; it's just one
more peculiar thing he knows about himself. He stirs that
kind of need in others, that curious trust. The men he
works with, and the office girls, are often compelled to
frisk him with quick fingers when he passes—little good-
luck samples of his force and sweetness, his palpable
goodness.

His goodness is his power, which he's never understood. Despite eyes hot as a diving hawk, Wesley has never
intentionally harmed a living soul. Better, he has done several thousand acts of kindness unknown to anyone but him
and his object. Several dozen of them qualify as really
good deeds (he sent a cousin's son halfway through college, and even Rosa never missed the first dollar), and the
goodness shines through his broad skull and eyes like
blood through your hand in a flashlight beam. That light,
combined with his clear regular features and his color and
odor, are what people try to reach inside him.

Wesley has generally walked away from that—though
with occasional women, even after his marriage, he's stood
still long enough to let them express their full intention.
But never for more than an hour or so; the other times he
vanished were not for women. And though he never mentioned those hours to Rosa, he never once thought of them
as cheating. He can enjoy the various facilities and stunts

of his God-given body. He can share those bounties on a short-term basis with, every now and then, a clean kind soul that seems in need.

But he's felt no compulsion to crawl on his knees up a dim church aisle the next Sunday morning groaning in shame and eating tears. It's been his plan since the dawn he was married to go to his grave with the same good woman he met as a boy—the woman that asked for his hand, both arms, and the rest of his life. He's always known that Rosa understood. He's even repeated that pledge more than once on nights through the years when he knew repetition was what Rosa craved. *Forsaking all others till death do us part*—even if it was no part at all of the quick civil wedding he paid for in Dillon.

So Wesley was all but as shocked as she when, in late December, he found himself leave work one afternoon, stop by the bank, and draw two hundred dollars from the stainless-steel computer treasury (they'd kept money separate since Rosa went to work). Then he nosed through traffic to interstate 40 and didn't stop for coffee till five hours later on the far outskirts of Asheville in chill black mountains.

THE WAITRESS SAID "YOU LOOK LIKE A MAN THAT'S BEEN cut at the bone. Let me bring you what's good."

Wesley laughed. "My bone's all here. I just took a look —pink and pretty as ever. But sure, bring me everything you think I need."

It was two chicken-fried steaks, something he'd never have ordered for himself. He took a long look at the battered gray meat, searched the waitress's wide blue eyes, and said "I must look tore up bad. But if you say so, I'll gum those down."

She nodded. "You do. Then streak it to Nashville. Don't stop till you're safe in a chain-locked room."

He obeyed her to the T—ate both steaks, heavy enough for wolves; ate a slab of peach pie with peach ice cream, filled his thermos with coffee. And did not stop till he locked the chain on room 1211 of the Parthenon Motel in Nashville itself.

Then in no more light than leaked through his window from the life-sized reinforced-concrete model of the Greek Parthenon, across the road there in a park flat as Texas, Wesley sat on the broad bed and wept cold tears.

He could not say what had flung him this far. It was nothing he could touch, no word he had said or heard from Rosa. No trouble with his son, none at the shop. And he'd lost all memory of last night's dream. He'd just been working that afternoon and reached for a metric tool from his bench when his hard right hand stopped in midair. Those clear five fingers seemed no more *his* than the car he was tuning. They paralyzed completely and would not draw back when his mind called them in. An instant's panic, then the hand hit his side, and blood recommenced.

But in another minute a voice in his head said "Death is what you just reached for." He laughed out loud, then realized the voice was not his. Wesley had no truck with brands of religion that deal in voices and unknown tongues. Still he couldn't shake the certainty that what he'd heard was a version of God's word, a true special message. What did it mean?

Wesley's own father had died at fifty-six. And once Wesley passed fifty, he realized it wouldn't be long before he'd close in on his father's goal line. But that hadn't seemed to set him back. Except for steady low-grade prostate misery, a common cross of middle-aged men, his body generally worked like always. Not that he did anything special for it in the way of diet or exercise.

With a few exceptions from magazines and television, Rosa cooked pretty much what they'd grown up eating (with bring-home pizza or fried chicken maybe once in ten days). Wesley was convinced that any man over twenty who was jogging in the road or pumping weights at the YMCA with Baptist organists and hairdesigners was ruining his joints and exhausting his chances at that night's sex.

Wesley cared about sex. He couldn't have discussed it for more than ten seconds, wouldn't have given you a key to that urgent private room if he'd been a poet and doctor combined. But from his early discovery of the unimaginable treasure installed just south of his belly, he had been a desert saint of desire and performance. By now he had spent thousands of hours of his life far out on the tether spun by his ample well-made genital. Rosa had been the partner of at least half of those times (the others were with himself and virtual strangers)—generally willing and sporty, though less than eager for the repetitions his mind required. He thought of it always as fire and light, he knew it kept him alert and young, he suspected he'd done more good that way than with ten years' gifts to the damned Red Cross or Community Chest.

So he turned to it now, high up in Nashville by the Parthenon's shine. Even after his wedding, masturbation had been at least half his sex life. Good as Rosa could be if he got her attention, nobody knew the exact rate and grip as well as he. In five quiet minutes in a locked storage

room or a clean toilet, he could take himself to the true
outer limit, glide in that glare, and come back strong and
calm and ready for hours more of work. A whole morning's defeat could be glazed and soothed off that easily and
cheaply. And he never needed the aids that so many of his
friends laughed about—magazines, head-movies, dreams
about strangers. He even had a rule that he couldn't imagine sex with any person who hadn't, in actual life, given
him sexual permission. Anything else would have been
rape by Wesley's rules.

But that first night in Nashville alone, he labored a
quarter-hour with no result but exhaustion. His body
seemed willing but the mind wouldn't focus down to that
white final moment of laser light that triggered reward.
Finally his need was so real that he chose a face off television and worked himself through a quick tale of access to
her body—a girl in a parking lot at dusk, he helped her
with her groceries, she asked him into the back seat beside
her, and from there on (as night fell down on them slow) he
gave every service she dreamed of and more. The eventual
hard knots of semen tore out of him like dry barbed-wire
and pelted his chest with the sour stench of humiliation.
But they let him sleep, half-dressed on the covers.

HE'D REMEMBERED TO HANG THE *DO NOT DISTURB* SIGN
outside, so it was nearly noon when he woke. His hands
and chest were still crusty; his hair was damp and moldy.
But he kept the habit of a lifetime and, before he went to
the shower, he cleaned his teeth with his tongue, smoothed
at his hair, buttoned his trousers, and lay back to pray.
Most days he leaned on the Lord's Prayer, with just the
added names of his family and a few friends, any particular

problems of the coming day. That one morning he tried to state his problem and request specific help. He said "Merciful Lord, I am one scared man. If You've told me I'm bound to die soon, then let me face around and take my due on home ground with my kin. If I misunderstood whoever spoke to me in my head yesterday, or if it was the Devil, still lead me back home now and show me how to act."

BUT HE LIVED IN THAT SAME AIRLESS ROOM DAYS LONGER, right through Christmas. He didn't behave like a frightened or depressed man. He kept his curtains open all day, he joked with the maids and waitresses, he drove downtown several nights and went to the movies or to bars near the original Grand Ole Opry auditorium. He struck up conversations with numerous women, but none of them rang back to his voice with the sound he needed to hear—the chime of his mother's old cutglass ice-cream bowl. So midnight after midnight he returned to the motel, renewed his reservation, honored his cock, and tried to sleep.

Many times he picked up the phone and tried to call Rosa, his mother, the man he worked for. He even rang Rosa's line eleven times on Christmas afternoon, but of course she was gone and the phone bell sounded like dying cries from a virgin child left hungry and lonesome in a big dark field. If she'd answered though what in God's name could he say?

So he stayed close in his room, talking to nobody but the black man that brought him the one room-service meal he ate all day (a hot turkey sandwich on untoasted white bread with cool tan gravy and a sad little white-paper cup of warm cranberries). That night he took his first steps of the day—just out and around the parking lot. He didn't have the energy, not to mention the heart, to walk two hundred yards and see the Parthenon all high and bright. Three other cars were parked near his—the only other guests tonight and all with license plates from the upper Midwest, retired old couples fleeing Minnesota snow toward the Florida sun (or new grandchildren on down the line).

BY THE TIME HE GOT BACK TO HIS ROOM THAT SAME AWFUL night, Wesley knew this much. He was not as afraid of the actual death that awaited him as he was of being dead at heart now, of having been dead the past twenty years. As a boy he had dreamed of a world in which his own life meant a good deal. He'd been seven or eight years too young to serve in the Second War. But the war had given him the vision of boys mattering outside their own houses, their own mothers' hearts. One single boy—Eddie Steer from near Manson—had been a fighter pilot, won two or three medals, and got his big picture in the Warrenton paper and several store windows. That one face alone (broad, grinning, blond-haired) had meant a world to Wesley in what it said about where plain American boys could go, what they could bring back, and what it would mean to the people they knew and rank silent strangers.

When he'd pitch baseball at John Graham High and head back to class from a victory game, he could glance at every face around him (younger boys, teachers, the tipsy damned principal, not to mention girls) and get an even bigger idea of life—he would not only matter here and now to a small-town school, but one year soon he'd matter to the crowd. Always, even after now, there would be crowds of people calling Wesley's name in genuine need and with thanks to give him. In particular there would be one fine woman, loyal for life and keeping her looks, plus three or four children that would grow up polite and count for something and tend to him and their mother in old age.

Rosa had volunteered, hard and steady when they were both in high school (she was two years behind him), to be the woman. And she had been interesting—the smartest, best-talking girl he'd seen outside the movies and no pain at all to watch, with her long live yellow hair and blue eyes that were the only ones in the world steady enough to stare his own down. But then he'd joined the Navy to begin his big life, sailing out of Norfolk.

It had been a grand hitch. He had missed seeing guns fired at real human foes (since they'd sent him in the opposite direction from Korea); but he'd been to Gibraltar, Naples, Rome, and watched wild horses from the rail of his ship as they flanked the sandy bright Azores. Four of his nineteen women spoke no more English than it took to make change; their moans in the dark were a universal tongue. And it lured him on in his faith that he—this one lean boy—would soon do something the world would love, and discover it had always yearned for.

Nobody'd ever known a word of this. Wesley hadn't mentioned it, not because he doubted his mission and his power but again because words wouldn't support him. Rosa had dreams enough to bypass the damned Queen, and couldn't she evermore hang them out to see?—bright in the air before her till her own eyes burned and Wesley wanted nothing as much as her, her entire body in the clasp of his hands and her secrets touched.

Frustrated as she made him feel, when every dream had

to be hers to the letter and go exactly her way, he consoled
himself when pregnancy trapped them in a premature marriage that his wife anyhow was well-endowed in mind and
body and was going far too. So maybe their strengths could
join together. Together they could amount to something,
which was more than you could say for anybody else in
either of their families since man left the caves.

THAT WAS THE LIE THAT POISONED ALL THE REST—THAT
he and Rosa would thrive together. Sure as rat bane it poisoned them both, their pitiful son, and the roof over their
heads. Once married, they lived in Norfolk for two years
—Wesley selling and fixing motorcycles. Then Rosa
pressed down powerfully, and they came with the baby to
Raleigh and dug in there. Dug bottomless graves. Wesley
had decent jobs all the time—always somebody else's best
mechanic—and Rosa had improved herself with courses,
starting at the YMCA and moving on to N.C. State till
she'd got her respectable job typing for a building full of
college English teachers (no two of which were smart
enough to change a sparkplug). They made enough money
to pay a mortgage, run two cars, and put Horace halfway
through college till the poor boy decided he'd already
learned more than any living teacher and dropped out (with
no offer to refund any money to his parents).

But money had never been it—not for Wesley, not the
prize he was after. Money was something you took in with
one hand and passed out with the other, something that
might help oil you forward but was never your goal. And
what it was had died of suffocation or disappointment before their son could spell *hippopotamus.*

It was hopeless of course and had always been. It was a

dream Wesley had made from the sight of his own good
face in mirrors and the things riled women said about his
soul and body. Surely God didn't build such towers to
burn? Surely they were meant to be true lighthouses, guid-
ing others to joy—or safety at least. What Wesley saw
now though (and he spent a good part of the nights reading
the Gideon Bible in his room) was the fact that had stove
him up. He was meant to have lighted his own light. The
tower and the spiral ladder were provided, the mirror was
polished in place, he had never lit the fire.

Wesley didn't think it out in those exact terms. But they
came close as any to what he felt. He had been created a
special soul. If nobody else but his mother had known it,
then he at least had. And the way Rosa hunted him, she
must have known too. Yet they never asked him to do
anymore than sit still and let them twine him in vines
strong enough to lock elephants. And soon he'd consented.
And now it was too late.

At Judgment Day a few women might stand up and
mention a nice quick generous time he'd showed them.
Rosa might testify to how much information and poetry
she'd got from studying his face. Horace might say his dad
had never denied him any reasonable thing he wanted. His
various bosses would be forced to say Wesley Beavers
could repair the *Titanic* after all this time under miles of
water with his eyes blindfolded. But when God got to
Wesley himself, Wesley would have to say "Your honor, I
just didn't understand. I wasn't smart enough. I thought
You'd done it all. I waited too late for You to start me." He
wouldn't expect or ask for mercy, and he had no reason to
think he'd get it.

So why not pick up the phone, tell Rosa he was on his

way home, and hit the road now? (it was the last afternoon
of the year). Because in his mind now, Rosa was the cause.
She'd fed him the main lie—how grand he was—and had
devoted the past thirty-odd years to blinding his eyes to
outside duties. As women went, she was nearly first-rate.
But now he felt certain he never should have married.
Damned if he'd swallow the little pride left and let Rosa
lead him blind to the grave. Where else though? And who
with?

All his life Wesley had surprised himself by how much
he liked loneliness. Three-fourths of his boyhood was
spent alone or with dogs in the woods. That was when he
formed his conviction of a kinship with all of life. He
never spoke it out to anybody. But by the time he was
fourteen, he was convinced forever that natural living objects were all aware and wished him well. He suspected
them of powers of communication, different from his own
but aimed at him. When he was alone he stood a chance of
hearing them—short clear sentences about courage and
generosity, their own demands for respect.

So another of the big mistakes of maturity was letting
too many people into all the rooms of his life, then leaving
the wild country for cities where even the finest ear
couldn't begin to hear natural signals, even birds couldn't
sing. That was another reason sex had stayed so important
in Wesley's mind. It was the last line he kept to the secret
world where angels spoke in silence and brought their gifts
back and forth in relays—self-respect (for your body's
power), the sight of your goodness in other creatures' eyes,
and oh the chance to make those other creatures happy as
you and as ready to shine.

*   *   *

So New Year's Eve in Nashville, Wesley decided to celebrate by going downstairs to the motel bar and seeing what happened. He had spoken to nobody yet but maids and waitresses and desk clerks, the occasional drunk. There was bound to be a New Year's crowd gathered. Let whoever was there set the course for his next outward move; he'd gamble that far. Resting and thinking and reading the scripture had shown him nothing but how balked he was, what a sad cold corpse.

The bar was crammed at ten o'clock. As he plowed his way through the swarm, a man put a drum major's paper hat on Wesley's head. He wore it as far as the mirror, saw it looked about as appropriate as a toupee on a moose, and handed it to the nearest woman.

More nearly a girl. She was barely five feet high with baby-fine blond hair. And she was dressed all in pink wool that made her seem nested, a safe young rabbit almost asleep. What kept Wesley from laughing was her eyes. He'd never seen deep brown eyes on a blond before, and these eyes were big enough and serious enough to stop a hot bull.

She thanked him for the hat, then dropped it on the floor, and went back to her glass—one of those foaming milkshake contraptions that Wesley scorned as "candy drinks."

He ordered straight bourbon and asked her if she had a name.

She said she had till some fool stole it from her. She meant the husband she'd recently left. Her maiden name was Joyce Wilson. She had married Tim Hunsucker but would soon be Wilson again. "Just call me Wilson now," she said.

So Wesley called her Wilson all that night and the rest of the time he knew her.

She was twenty-six years old, a radiology technician at Vanderbilt Hospital, and when after an hour of noise and two more drinks, Wesley asked her to come to his room, she laughed. "Hold on, Pop. My mother said there'd be geezers like you."

It hurt Wesley, which he showed as fury. Women had called him a good many things but never old. He emptied his glass in one long swallow, gave a silent bow, turned his back, and left her. He headed for the parking lot and his car—surely some place in town had to have better company—but halfway there he decided "Hell, you *are* a damned pop. Go watch t.v."

AND HE WAS LYING ON HIS BED, WATCHING THE TIMES Square mob of soused fools all dreaming better luck, when his phone rang and nearly threw him to the floor (it hadn't rung once since he'd been there).

She said "This is Wilson and I'm still downstairs."

Wesley said "Happy New Year from here then. I'm too feeble to climb back down."

"How about me climbing up?"

He said "You sure you're twenty-six?"

"And a half."

"Then suit yourself."

Once he'd hung up, his first thought was to run. To lie here and wait for her was plainly risking adultery. And Wesley felt that by his own lights, he'd never committed adultery. There was no way he could be locked in this tight a space with that fine a woman and not try to eat her. And being this far, this long away from home, it would be a real cut in his promise to Rosa—it might open out before him like a permanent road and he never go back. He thought it through for several minutes, and Wilson still hadn't knocked. She'd probably lost her nerve. So he turned out his light, switched off the television, and lay still and quiet. He even napped.

He was anyhow dreaming of an almost endless fall down a black-glass chute that led to the end of the universe when somebody tapped on the door. He rose in the dark, zipped his fly, and opened on Wilson.

In the half-dark of the hall, she looked smaller and younger. Twenty-six, a year younger than Horace—Wesley could easily be her father. He said "You ought to be somewhere better."

"You too," she said. "Look at pitiful you, holed up on the road while the old year ends. You're asking to die of a bad broke heart."

Wesley nodded. "I am."

"I ain't going to let you." She stepped in past him, went to the toilet, and shut herself in.

He locked the door, smoothed up the bed, and sat in one of the two easy chairs. Only then did he see that he had no bottle, not even a Coke.

Wilson took a long time in absolute silence. But when she came out, she looked even better—some mysterious work around her eyes and cheek hollows. She laid her big purse on the floor by the chair and sat down slowly. Then she studied his eyes for what seemed the better part of two or three hours. Finally she laughed. "Now tell me I've picked the Louisville Slasher. You're wanted for fourteen women and a dog, all headless but grinning in Dempster Dumpsters from here to Ohio."

Wesley nodded. "You've got him." No trace of a smile.

She waited that out. "Can I have your autograph, darling?"

He said "Can't write. Never finished first grade. I'm mainly pitiful, is what I am. Dangerous of course."

Wilson said "I'm sure you are. But tell me this—what's the thing you've done that you're sorriest for?"

"I can tell that," he said. "I've thought that through. I killed myself at age twenty-two."

"To be dead that long, you smell good from here."

Wesley said, "Old Spice. It purifies."

"Tell me more," Wilson said.

"I was one fine boy. God had plans for me. I was meant to spread joy. People smiled at my face on more than two continents. Then I let my high-school sweetheart trap me and that ended that."

"How?"

"You've heard about marriage! It's not exactly *freedom*. Both of my feet been nailed to the floor since 1957, Christmas week."

Wilson asked "Where was that?"

"Dillon, South Carolina—our shotgun wedding. We've lived in Virginia and North Carolina ever since, Raleigh most years."

"Then you've done a powerful ripping-loose job, to get those feet tore up and brought west."

Wesley said "That was easy. But now I'm stuck here."

"How's that?" Wilson's legs had curled up beneath her, and a shawl-necked sweater nestled her breasts like the duty it most enjoyed (more than warmth).

Wesley fought a great rush of need to hold her, to drown his eyes and mouth in her neck—the lovely deep bowl at the pit of her neck, lilac-colored and warm from a distance. Not a mark on her visible skin anywhere, from damage or age. And no cheap whorehouse make-up or smells. Just a whole grown woman that trusted her gifts. "I'm scared," he said. "I've ruined so much. I'm scared if I move, I'll crush something else."

"What's left?"

"My wife."

"She know you're here?"

"No ma'm," Wesley said. "She's worried to death."

Wilson asked, "Do you love her?"

"I must not," he said. He'd discovered it that moment. Cruel as it seemed, and whether it was true or not, Wesley's sudden doubt set free that instant in Raleigh the one living man who meant to harm Rosacoke's own body (Raleigh time was an hour ahead of Nashville).

Wilson said "Be sure. Cause if you love her, I'm clearing out this minute. I'm no kind of thief." When Wesley didn't speak for a minute, she reached for her purse and gathered to stand.

"No God," he said, and waved her down.

"No what?"

"Don't go."

Wilson said "Why not?"

"I'd probably die—be found by the maid on this sour bed with my clean hands folded and my eyes rolled back. Ruin her whole new year."

"It *might* set her back." From that instant on, Wilson's body—with no special knowledge from her—hurled millions of fine silk threads toward Wesley, grappling cables too frail to catch moths but, coming as steady and fast as they did, sufficient to draw him in and helpless. In a while she checked her watch and said "Happy New Year, sport, six minutes ago." They'd heard the noise outside but not noticed.

It seemed to Wesley he was back on the rails, that something (surely this small girl here) had lifted his capsized old engine and set it square and firm on the track. Rusted maybe but stoked again and aimed. His heart filled so full and fast with thanks that he had no choice—if he meant to keep breathing—but to stand now, hold out his right hand, and say "Let me thank you please."

"How would you manage that?"

"I'll know," he said, "if you give me time."

Wilson thought a moment, then took his hand, rose up beneath him, and said "I've got till six a.m. day after tomorrow."

THEY USED IT ALL. WESLEY HAD LONG SINCE GONE PAST the starved-bunny leap-on-roll-off tactics of famished youth. Most of the first night in fact, he never hardened stiff. In the early hours, that worried him—more for Wilson's sake than his own. But when he eventually apologized, she said "Man, I'm as happy as a bee gargling honey. You have learned some things about women, let me tell you."

So Wesley took heart, got up and turned off the one bathroom light, then came back and worked on, chiefly for Wilson's benefit. Finally a little before three, a big tunnel opened in the black dark above him. And Wesley saw that his luck was renewed. He had a fresh chance to give somebody the thing they'd missed—their body worshiped (Rosa had long since declined to accept that).

He turned then to Wilson with new intent. His faculties pointed to a white-hot focus. He entered her body and let her know how one grown man could search a woman from crown to toe and use each atom of her precious skin—or so it seemed to Wesley (he also sank in a flood of pleasure that threatened to kill, that strong and fast).

At first it frightened Wilson. She'd known a few boys, a few grown men but nothing like this. This fellow was in it for something even she couldn't guess. And while he didn't exactly hurt her—she could feel how steadily he tried to honor her—there was something more than a little scary in being at the mercy of someone this big and strong who seemed to need precisely *her* and *now*. It felt like a need that couldn't be fed, not permanently ever. A need that could swamp any boat ever built, not to mention her cute little spanking-bright rowboat.

BUT AFTER THAT, THEY BOTH MANAGED SLEEP. BY THE time daylight woke Wesley, six hundred miles east Rosacoke was climbing the track to her mother's. And he did think of Rosa in the first conscious moments—with a sudden rush of thanks for the times they'd laughed, several million jokes between them (mostly started by Rosa). This afternoon he would somehow call her and find words to say all the questions he felt. Not that he suffered bad guilt about the night, or about Wilson sleeping here bare beside him, but that he couldn't imagine beginning a year without letting Rosa know Wesley was alive, remembering her, and planning on her always if she still cared to know him. He didn't think about it beyond that point—Wilson stirred awake.

Wesley naturally wanted to continue where they'd stopped in darkness.

But Wilson was firm. She wrapped strong arms across her chest and said "I'm black and blue now, buddy. I need me some aspirin and a quart of hot coffee."

That trusting banter was almost as good. They showered together like brother and sister (that might need to spend several weeks in jail) and went downstairs to eat breakfast for six.

FROM THEN ON THEY LIVED IN WILSON'S TRAILER. IT WAS brand-new and she owned it outright. It was parked in old cedars on the edge of a big pasture that belonged to her brother on the Franklin road thirty minutes from town. She had bought it with the money from her second divorce. The son of a bitch had beat her badly, then repented of his meanness—Tim Hunsucker, a pitiful drunk (her failing till now: drunks had somehow impressed her but never again). And when she left him, he'd come to her begging—let him set her up in a nice dry place to show his regret. It took her no more than fifteen seconds to tell him where he could buy a new trailer, to her specifications, and where they could park it.

Wesley took to it at once. It was more like living on a ship than anything he'd tried since the Navy. Space was at a premium, so you didn't save any junk that might not matter in the next three days. And even if the built-in furnishings were ugly and looked like they'd melt if one match was struck, you could all but hose it out when it got dirty. Not like a house with brick foundations, where decades of dirt silt up and multiply under your feet. And the

rooms were so small you could make a real impression on
them. In a bigger space your actions might lose themselves
in the excess air before they reached their target.

IN THE FIRST FEW DAYS, WHILE WILSON WORKED, WESLEY
went to town, bought a minimum of clothes, and cruised
the countryside thinking. He had set a date—January 11th,
his dead father's birthday—to decide on his future. To return to Raleigh and his old home, or Raleigh and not Rosa,
or to stay here with Wilson, or some fourth place. The
happier he felt with Wilson, the more he knew that Raleigh
and Rosa were all but surely where God meant him to go.

He'd make a pledge there (Rosa had made them recite
the Baptist marriage vows, just between themselves, the
week after they finished their civil ceremony); and Wesley
never broke sober sane promises he could keep. What if he
went to Rosa, explained to her as best he could what had
scared him, and asked her to join him in pulling up stakes
and going somewhere new—that they both could like and
start over in, getting old wrongs right? What place though
and what were the old wrongs and what would *right* be?
And how would Rosa replace in his heart the things he'd
be giving up if he gave up nights like these with Wilson?

AFTER SUPPER ON THE TWELFTH, HE DISCUSSED IT WITH
Wilson. She asked if he'd thought anymore about hunting a
job? Up till then he'd been living on credit cards. Her
question hit Wesley wrong at first, but he held in his
temper and told her that he'd be deciding two days from
then what his whole future was.

She looked down steadily at her wine and then said "I'm

glad you warned me. It'll be my future partly too."

"How's that?"

"Jesus, boy, I've brought you right to the core of my life. I've set you up like the big Buddha here. If you don't want any part of my gifts, then give me the satisfaction at least of running you off the lot like a dog. Don't get up in two days and say 'So long.'"

Wesley smiled. "Run me off. That'd make it so easy. And it's what I deserve."

Wilson shook her head hard, and her eyes filled up. Till that one moment in all their time, she'd been dry as a boy.

Wesley said "No, really. I abandoned my wife. I cheated with you. I've sat here for days now letting you serve me like a coal-black slave. I haven't so much as washed a cup."

Wilson said "You've made me feel like a *soul*."

Wesley laughed. "Beg your pardon?"

"You've made me feel like something that mattered for more than flat-fucking."

He frowned. "Words like that ruin your face."

She smiled. "See, every other man I've known has all but begged me to talk dirty to him."

"I like words too much. My wife taught me that."

Wilson said "Whatever else, you're a gentleman."

Wesley thanked her but stood. "What's your vote say? Which road do I take?"

"You told me you didn't love your wife. I've leaned on that."

Wesley said "Stop. I'm not saying you're a liar, but I don't recall saying any such thing. Maybe you just gathered it from my general actions—I couldn't blame you.

But I know I haven't thrown the word *love* around. Don't think for a minute I understand love enough to use it that freely."

Wilson waited a moment, then smiled. "Do you like her?"

"Better than anybody."

It hurt Wilson bad. She waited to ask "Then why are you here?"

"I'd run out of hope."

She said "You haven't exactly come to the hope chest. I've tried two times to kill myself."

"That's what I mean," he said. "I've got hope to bring." Standing in the midst of Wilson's private paid-for living room, Wesley believed himself. Even more, he felt fulfilled for the first time in years in his life's old aim—other people's happiness, caused by him.

NEXT MORNING HE STOPPED AT THE CLEANEST GARAGE BEtween Wilson's and town; and in half an hour, he had a decent job repairing foreign automobiles. When he got his first check at the end of the week, he would send half of it to Rosa with word of his whereabouts and what he planned. As he walked from the garage back to his car, he caught his face in the outside mirror by the driver's door. He had never spent a whole ten minutes of his life in studying his face, but he held still now long enough to think "This boy'll live."

THE NEXT MONDAY NIGHT WHEN HE'D PUT HIS CHECK IN A new account, Wesley sat down at Wilson's dining table and wrote to his wife.

January 20, 1986

Dear Rosa,

I'm alive and sorry I couldn't tell you sooner. Nobody harmed me. I just spooked that one afternoon driving home from work and wound up in Nashville, Tennessee for no good reason except that a waitress in a truckstop mentioned Nashville. I appreciate you not reporting me to the Law. Nobody has stopped and questioned me. That's not all I'm thankful to you for.

Rosa, I don't know how much of this is about you. What it got down to was, I was a dead man. Everything I had ever loved to do, everything in me that I ever respected, seemed long gone. After we got married you were the only person I could test myself against. Your face would tell me whether I mattered in the world or not. But with all the years and your new life, I couldn't read much news off of you. That doesn't have to be even half your fault. Don't punish yourself too much.

Not to hurt you but so you will be free to act your own way from here on in, I need to say that I am living with a woman that works as a radiologist at the Vanderbilt University Hospital here. I didn't meet her till well after I got to town. She wasn't my destination, no part of it. But she doesn't smoke at all or drink to excess and for now is keeping me fed and safe.

What it means for me and you in the long run, I can't say. If you want to act against me with the Law, I won't stop you. But now that I've told you this much, I certainly can't expect you not to seek help and company of your own from wherever you find it. It hurts me a lot to come out and put that in writing all of a sudden. But I'm aiming to be fair, and I figure that's fair—mean as it feels.

I've got a decent-paying job and will be sending you half of my pay every week. That will take care of my share of the house expenses. If I've calculated wrong or if there's anything else unusual I should know about, say so. I want to be fair, like I told you.

Rosa, you have given me your whole life up to now, I realize. I've never been sure I asked you for that much, even when

*we were children and couldn't begin to guess how long time
would be. But I sure God know you gave it and gave it from a
full heart without stinting. I hope you aren't looking back now
and thinking Wesley just took and took and never tried to give.
I did try and a lot of the time I wanted to try. It's just that one
day in December something in me gave up wanting to try any
of the old stuff in the old place.*

*I don't feel like I never want to see you again. It may work
out that way. You may want it that way. But for now I've got to
do what I'm doing.*

*I'll let Horace and my mother know as much of this as they
need to know. You can tell or not tell anybody else. I think
about you a good many times a day, especially when I'm
laughing. We are better at that than anything else, remember?*

*Love still and always,
Wesley*

By the time he finished that and sealed it, his watch said
a little past one in the morning. Wilson had been asleep
two hours. Wesley felt like going to the little guest-bed-
room (the size of a steamer trunk) and sleeping just that
one night alone on top of the cover. He brushed his teeth,
not facing his own mirrored eyes anymore than was necessary. Then he went to the cubicle and lay down quietly. In
under two minutes he'd amazed himself with tears in his
eyes. Too tired to ask why or for what, he dried them deep
in the hard rubber pillow and seized his shoulders in both
broad hands. But in his still head, the voice said "Now
you'll never sleep again." It seemed too true to doubt or
regret.

Then Wilson came in and sat by his waist. Silent as they
were, his tears had waked her. She knew not to mention
them. She said "I wasn't all that deep asleep. I'd have
welcomed you, son."

"I felt like I ought to be in here tonight."

"What's wrong with tonight?"

Wesley didn't want to tell her, but he had to be fair. The one thing he didn't mean to do this time was tell a real lie. He said "I just now wrote my wife the truth."

"Which is what?" Wilson asked.

"That I'm staying put here with you for now."

"You sure about that?"

"If you'll have me," he said.

"You know I will. I've said it before."

"You never said *why* though. I doubt I believe you."

Wilson waited a minute, then struck him hard beneath the ribs.

Wesley flinched and rolled to his back, face upward. "You'll have me dialing that number for help, a beat-up male."

Dark as it was, Wilson kept her face grim. "I'll keep on beating too, long as you spit on my deep feelings. You've already given me more than I've had in twenty-six years, from anybody else."

"Tell me one thing," he said. He couldn't believe her but needed to.

"You know I can't talk. You're the good one with words."

Wesley said "Christ Jesus, that's a new damned note." And because by then her face touched his shoulder, he fell straight down into sleep like a stone.

Wilson couldn't let him go off unassured. So there, on a cheap bed wide as a plank and hard as the road, she stripped them both with two swift hands. Then boarding his long body low at the knees, she bent and set her mouth to say in a silent prowl up and down his limbs, his hard torso, the sweet white bowl of his thrusting hips, that no one man of all she'd known (and she'd known some) had come anywhere near matching the way he made her know she mattered on the crowded ground like a rare snow leopard or the shining dove.

Wesley lay flat still and let her speak, meeting her silence every three or four minutes with honest thanks—aloud in words—and more hot tears. Dark as it was, he knew he was climbing again and upward in her strong light.

ROSA'S DIARY

WHEN I GOT BACK FROM MARY'S THAT AFTER-
noon, Roger was worn out asleep on the porch.
When I spoke to him, he looked up a second.
But I doubt he recognized me—he was that tired. So he
must have been out trekking with Rato after all. Inside, I
saw right away that Rato had beat me home and was
watching television in the front room with Mama. Poor as
they were, they keep that one room hot as Brazil. They
could start a rubber plantation in their spare time.

So of course Mama dozes through most of their pro-
grams, but Rato sits upright believing every word. I
thought my nerves were still not safe alone and that I
should sit with them, but by then my lack of sleep was
clubbing me down. I said my New Year's party had wiped
me out, so I was going upstairs to rest. I'd be down in time
to help with supper.

Mama said she'd made up my bed this morning and lit the oil burner, but she followed me up to the steep steps anyhow.

And the room was preserved as perfectly as the Wright Brothers' bicycle shop in the Smithsonian. Anything I've ever owned (and haven't burned or taken to Raleigh) is up there right now, and Mama dusts it all. I don't think it's any kind of shrine to me like that spread of pictures at Mary's house. No, in Mama's mind it's just a real living part of her house. The person that used to stay there may be back any minute, so it needs to be clean and ready for occupancy. And isn't Mama right after all? After nearly thirty years, hadn't I just this minute climbed up there, in serious need of a familiar safe place?

Her pale strained face seemed to say that much and a good deal more. I dreaded what she'd ask when she finally spoke, so I stretched out fast with my face to the wall.

She took her time spreading the afghan over me and then sat by my feet. "Are you too sick to talk?"

I didn't meet her face, but I said "No ma'm. I'm just dead tired."

She said "You are telling me two different things. First, that a man broke in your house this morning and raped you. Second, that there's nothing wrong but your lost beauty sleep. Even you wouldn't come all this way for a nap."

I had to laugh. "I'm very much afraid you're right. It hasn't hit me yet though. I dread when it will. But now I'm telling you the absolute truth—I'm three-fourths asleep."

Mama said "Have you checked yourself real good?"

I told her I wasn't bruised or bleeding.

"Did you get you that 'day-after' pill?"

It's something else she's learned on television, a pill to neatly flush out any child you may have conceived in a rape—that easy.

I told her I hadn't.

"Then tomorrow you need to go get one of those. Drive to Henderson and see Dr. Drake. He's kind and smart and he'll *talk* to you." (There are no doctors left in all Warren County. Imagine that. In our childhood there were four white and at least one black. Not enough money up there now, I guess.)

I told her I was past that worry, thank God.

It surprised her. She said she menstruated till she was almost sixty.

The last thing I remember saying was "I won't envy you that."

I WOKE UP IN THE DARK PRAYING. SOMETHING MUST HAVE scared me toward the end of my nap because I was out of breath and praying hard for safety. At first I thought I could hear somebody working in the kitchen, but then the house went quiet again. I suspected they'd let me sleep through supper, and now I had a long night to face alone. It didn't seem possible. If it had come to that, I'd have no choice but to stumble down and crawl in with Mama.

But no, I couldn't start sleeping with my forebears. Mama couldn't come back to Raleigh with me. So I couldn't use her now like a shield, however strong she was. I lay flat out then facing the ceiling—trusting it was there (it was too black to see) and planned my future.

My husband was gone, probably alive but maybe gone for good. My son was married to a social climber and gone forever. My other kin were too old, too strange, or too tied down to help. What it was, was me and a middle-aged boxer dog against the world. And the world that night seemed mainly to consist of one man—surely real, surely nothing I'd dreamed up for fun—that had apparently meant to harm me.

But the fact was, he hadn't done serious damage. I knew enough about my body to know that no, he hadn't even bruised me. My mind might turn out to be a little jostled, but the rest was intact.

The scary thing was, he was still on the loose in Raleigh, N.C. He was somebody I could cross up with at the grocery store smiling. Or he could be back in my bedroom any night he chose, next time with maybe no intention to run.

That sent a chill through me like I hadn't felt till then. More than my body, he had raped my *place*. I'd blinded myself to the worst he'd done. With Wesley gone, the thing I needed most in the world was a safe place to be. And all I had was a strong dry house with a hole stove through it by, for all I knew, a lunatic. A hole he could use to go and come at will. What was the answer to that? Nothing I could think of. So I lay there shivering hard in the dark.

Then at the foot of the steps a voice said "You still up there?" At first it sounded so much like my father that I was scared worse than ever. Rato, like Horace, is named for Daddy. But it had never crossed my mind that he bore him any likeness. It was so close though, I couldn't reply.

He said "Rosacoke."

And I said "Yes sir."

He said "I'm nothing but your next-to-oldest brother." Still he started to climb.

Rato had switched on the light at the bottom of the steps. So by the time he got there, I could see a little of him. And he did look young. He never has had much of a beard, you know, and now he's begun to soften in the jaw and neck. But in most men that just makes them look like their mother. Rato looks more and more like his early self, the one that hung around my childhood like an occasionally friendly but mostly wild yearling—the one whose thoughts were no more likely than a deer's or a colt's to be on any subject you might share. Now he stood in the midst of the door and waited.

I said "Step in here and sit down a minute." I turned on my little weak bedside lamp.

He said "She took your chair away" (you recall he will not call her *Mama*).

I told him I hadn't been using it a lot.

He said "That wasn't enough of a reason. The room is still yours."

I said "Old darling, I'm glad you think so. I may be needing it any year now."

Rato shook his head hard. "Don't ever come back here."

"Why? It's home."

He said "It's the most unprogressive spot on earth."

It hadn't occurred to me that progress mattered much to Rato and I laughed.

He shut me up with a strong palm outward. "This county used to be rich and famous. Old Nat Macon, the Speaker of the House of Representatives under Thomas Jefferson, was from right up the road. The Alstons and Eatons had several hundred slaves each. And look at all those grand homes in Warrenton. Now though it's nothing but fallow fields and Mexican migrant workers in whatever fields are working and miserable Negroes on welfare—did you ever think our family would quit farming and go to selling trucks? I could have killed Milo when he quit."

The fact that Rato even knew history existed was a lightning bolt. But I passed over it and told him "Be merciful. Milo was tired."

"Hell, I'm tired. The *world*'s tired. That's a piss-poor excuse. Everybody's meant to work till they vanish."

In spite of his thirty years in the Army, I'd never thought of Rato as that hard a laborer. But I didn't mention it. I just said "I feel like I'm doing my part."

He nodded. "You are. I want to come join you."

I must not have heard him or understood. Anyhow I didn't answer.

So he walked on forward and sat on the absolute edge of the bed beside my feet. "I asked could I come live with you."

I said "You know I may still have a husband."

Rato said "I doubt it, not after this long. I'd leave if he came back."

Something deep down in my heart spread open. I wanted Rato with me. But that would be theft from my mother. I said "What would Mama do without you?"

He said "She's wanted me gone for years."

"That can't be true."

"She wants me married."

I laughed again. "When was the last time she mentioned marriage?"

"Two weeks ago when she had a heart spell."

"What exactly did she say?"

"She said 'Son, I'm going to be dead soon now. Get you somebody.'"

I couldn't doubt that but I said "She didn't mean leave her now, not out in the sticks alone with her angina."

"She does everything that's done around here. I can't even drive."

I said "No but you're on hand. You're company."

Rato said "I'm about as much company as the ceiling."

It was true and also the closest he'd ever come to a joke or to showing any sense of what he might mean to others. So I was amazed but I said "She wouldn't be safe."

He said "You sure God ain't. Somebody's out to ruin you, and he knows where you sleep."

If that's not the scariest sentence anybody could dread to hear, I don't know what would be. Even with Rato there in the room, cold fear slapped up against my teeth. Foolish as it sounds, it hadn't really crossed my mind till then—how open to harm I was in that house. I had gone through life thinking the worst that could happen was feelings, some resentment from you or Horace. All the wars on the edge of my life, all the crimes in the next block over, hadn't convinced me of the fact that one or two people in every handful are ready to kill you or pare your face to the slick wet bone and pass on forward. By then I guess my eyes had watered. The little light showed it.

Rato said "Now ask me to join you."

I tried to gather my wits and protect Mama, but he'd caught me in the quick, and I couldn't deny it. I said "For a week or so, sure. Till I get new locks. We can take Mama with us."

"I won't go then," he said.

"Don't be mean, Rato. Why not?"

"Because of Wesley. If he turns up one night and finds just me, it'll be all right. I'll pack in two minutes and climb on the bus. But let Wesley find Mama with that heavy-duty heating pad and all the rest of her rheumatism stuff, and he's liable to look in the window and run."

There seemed to be a sizable truth in that. Old-lady equipment has always tended to shy you. Remember when I bought that cream for the liver spots on my hands? You'd barely go in the bathroom for the whole next week. But who could I get to stay here with Mama? Milo and Sissie might stay a few days but not a long stint. Any special arrangements would mean explaining something incredible to the world—that Rato was going somewhere. *Why? Well, his sister got herself raped in Raleigh the other day; and she needs a bodyguard.*

But I said "Thank you, sir. I'll make us a way."

And Rato cut loose a smile so broad it burned out whatever dark was left in the room.

THAT WAS THE NIGHT OF THE FIRST DAY OF THE YEAR. I stayed on through the first three days, trying the best I could to fit into their quiet ways. What I always forget about my mother and brother is how much like animals they are. I don't mean I feel like any kind of human superior to them, but I sure Lord feel different. They move through their days like self-respecting horses, taking a lot of careful time with things you and I hurry through like eating three meals or arranging to sit in a chair to watch the television news.

At first it made me jittery to watch their slowness—*For Christ-in-Heaven's sake, you don't need to take four minutes to butter that one slice of bread!* But I told myself to hold back. And even with the immediate worries I had, in a couple of days I'd gotten a good deal calmer myself just from adjusting to their rates. Rato and I didn't speak again of any plan to take him to Raleigh, and I didn't plan ways to break it to Mama.

She and I spent a lot of time alone in the same room together, drying dishes for instance. But she never again mentioned the rape or the morning-after pill and never mentioned you. I couldn't decide if she was being tactful and yielding to my maturity or, what I suspected was more likely, that she was too old now to care all that much about her children's lives. She wishes us well but secretly prays we won't tell her too much. She's got other thoughts and we don't need to know what those are yet (I mean is it all just death and regret or some brand of happy relief?)

So it was a big surprise to me when, on the second night as I was undressing in my room, Mama heaved herself upstairs and sat on the foot of my bed and said "I want to ask Rato to go back with you. Is that all right?"

I admitted at once it was fine by me, but what was she going to do for help?

She kept her face serious. "You don't think Rato's a whole lot of help, do you?"

"He's protection," I said. "And company."

"I've got a good rifle and your granddaddy's pistol. My hearing's not what it was. But if they just give me a minute's warning, I could hold off a big squad of rogues. And company! Rato hasn't said five hundred words to me in all his grown life. Don't forget, he was the only one of my four children that refused to breast feed." Finally she laughed.

I told her no, I'd never heard that.

She laughed "No ma'm, after four weeks passed, he rolled down off my nipple one night and never came back."

"Didn't he get hungry?"

"He did, by dawn, and it's lucky I had some bottles left over from Milo's last feedings because when I offered Rato this beat-up old tittie again, he spasmed out stiff as a board in my arms and wouldn't come near me."

I said "You're joking. That can't be true."

She raised her flat right hand, an oath. "Never again— four weeks old and swore off."

"What's wrong with him, Mama?" I'd never quite asked it plain before.

"I know the whole world's always thought he's backward. Your granddaddy used to say 'Nothing wrong with Rato but he's a little backward in coming forward.' Even the Army never pushed him past corporal. I'm just his mother and no great scholar myself, but I've always thought Rato was smarter than the rest of us put together. He figured out at one-month-old exactly what he wanted in life, and he's calmly gone about getting it and doing it from that day forward."

It seemed honest enough for a mother's explanation, so I thought I'd risk a little more. "Mama, do I mean anything special to Rato?"

"You're his sister."

"Beyond that, I mean."

She waited and studied me slowly. "If you're meaning any of this mess they talk about on television—brothers and sisters, fathers and daughters." Her frown was as deep as I'd seen it.

So I laughed. "Calm down. I meant no such thing, I just

wondered if there was anything I ought to know before he comes to Raleigh, if he's coming."

"He's coming if you ask him. He's aching to get out of here. I've known that ever since the Army turned him loose and he couldn't get a job anywhere round here. But special? No, I can't think of nothing. He loves his privacy but you know that. He eats all of anything you set before him. Sleeps nine hours every night that comes. He'll tell you every detail of every dream he has the next morning at breakfast. And that's all he'll tell you from that mind of his, night or day. Otherwise, he's as much trouble as your Roger or any other good dog—none at all. You do have to get used to him being there. His soul takes up a lot of room in a house, like having a hot brown racehorse in your sitting room. He's kind to be sure and housebroke and clean. But he's thinking his own thoughts night and day, and Rato's thoughts are the last thing you'll ever guess."

I nodded, "And what happens up here if you fall off that step-ladder you're always climbing and break an ankle or have a little heart spell? You want to come with us?"

Mama shook her head hard. "First of all, I'll be fine. Second, if I'm not, whatever happens will be something I'm responsible for. Plenty of women older than me are out in the country here working full days with no better company than squirrels in the yard. Nobody's been killed since the Civil War"—she still says *Silver War*.

I suspected that wasn't quite true, but then I couldn't think of any exceptions—not white ones anyhow. So I thanked her as sincerely as I ever had (and she's been one of my two main receptacles of thanks since birth).

She surprised me again. She said "Besides, you may be doing me a favor. Here lately I've been wondering what

lonesome *is*. I haven't been alone ever in my whole life—
oh, a few minutes in childhood. Maybe I can finally fulfill
myself."

I hoped she wasn't serious, but I wasn't going to be the
first one to laugh.

Then, thank God, she did—a low easy chuckle.

That was the Thursday, as I said. On the Friday evening
I phoned Milo in Henderson to let him know the temporary
arrangements. Rato was coming to Raleigh with me.
Mama would be out here alone. I could tell right off that
the news upset him. Milo has always dreaded change. He
rightly wanted to know who would be taking care of
Mama. I told him the whole thing was her idea (not quite
the full truth), that he was not more than forty minutes
from her, and that I could get there in exactly an hour.
Milo said, "The world can end in under an hour, once it
starts ending."

I thanked him for the warning.

Then he got mad. He said "Why the hell have you got to
upset the whole damned family's applecart now just because your husband has flown the coop?"

It wasn't till then that I realized he didn't know a thing
about my New Year's night. I thought Mama might have
tipped him off somehow. So I chewed on the lining of my
cheek awhile, then went on and gave him a short true account. At the end I was proud of telling the whole story
with not one tear or even a frog.

Milo let me finish the whole thing without interrupting.
Then he waited a good long time. Finally he said "Have
you all finished supper?"

I said yes, an hour ago.

So he asked could he come and take me to ride?

It sounded so old-fashioned, I'm afraid I laughed.

Milo said, "I'm glad somebody thinks it's funny. Please show me how."

I told him to come on.

IT WAS DEEP DARK AND FREEZING WHEN MILO GOT THERE, but a ride was still what he had in mind. He pecked me on the cheek and made polite greetings to Mama and Rato. Then he said "Rosa and me need to catch up on some business. We'll be riding around."

Mama said she hoped his car heater was working.

He reminded her that few people ever asked for a heater when *his* heart was present.

She said "That was true, oh, thirty years back."

Milo didn't try to trump her but took my elbow and led me out. At the door, Roger made a big play to go with us. But Milo said "This is going to be dog business enough without you, son. Go eat a Gainesburger and trim your nails" (on Mama's bare pine floors, Roger sounds like Fred Astaire in ski boots).

At first it was like so many dozen nights from childhood and just after. Then it had seemed like Milo wanted nothing but me dark and an arm's length away on a car seat saying nothing till he asked me to—and us forging on in the old pickup like there were no oceans and we might pull into Peking or Lhasa for breakfast tomorrow. Plenty of nights he never asked a single question, and never once did he try anything funny (in all our lives, he never has—though there have been times I more than half wanted him to). For years I'd been honored just to be there waiting to be asked and to think I was some kind of help, whether or not he ever said so.

Wesley, before I found you that first day, Milo had after all been my first sight of glory. He was my brother, that could drive me crazy ten times a day, but also now and then he was a mirror of the angels. Anybody as fine looking as Milo and you both were when young is bound to know it, bound to realize that their faces and bodies are gifts of God to help other people bear their days. I can look back at photos of me then and see I wasn't all that much of an eyesore myself, but you and Milo were better. No question at all you were heaven-sent blessings. And Milo came first in my acquaintance.

But once we'd threaded through Warrenton and were on the Macon road, he said "I guess I better hear it."

And again I had to laugh at how *my* assault—my big recent chance at a personal tragedy—had become my family's property. I said "Milo, it's not the end of the earth or even of Rosa. Some fool desperado couldn't get through New Year's on his own resources and had to come banging on mine. I threw him out before he got really dangerous." I realized it wasn't all that true a description, but Milo's attitude had forced it on me. Maybe it would help us both.

He asked, "Was it somebody you know?"

I said "Sugar, it was so dark and late, it might have been *you*. No, I don't know but I seriously doubt it."

"None of Wesley's friends?"

I said "Wesley is gone and Wesley is strange in all sorts of ways, I'll grant you, but he'd never send anybody to harm me."

Milo said "I didn't mean that."

I said "Good" which helped clear the air.

But we were halfway to Vaughan before he could finally say "Rosa, you've got me confused. Everything I hear and read tells me that rape is the worst thing that can happen to a woman."

I had to stop him. I asked "What is it?"

"Ma'm?"

"Rape—what is rape?"

Milo turned to me slowly like I'd gone wild right then on the seat beside him. "Rosa, grow up. Every four-year-old knows what rape is."

I said "I honestly don't think I do, not anymore. Tell me what you think."

"It's when a guy holds down a woman against her will and comes inside her body."

"All right," I said. "That's what I mean. It was a man. He held me down long as he could, and against my will, but I'm not sure he came—not inside me at least."

"What did the doctors say?"

"They didn't. I haven't told anybody but my own family—Mama, Rato, you."

"You didn't call the Law?"

"Milo, the Law was the last thing I needed. You know how famed for gentleness they are."

"Then it's too late," he said. "You'll never know his name."

"I wasn't wanting to call up and thank him," I said. "He can stay unknown."

Milo said "*He* knows who he is. He knows where you are—"

"—And how to find me next time. I've been through this. Don't bother to scare me. It's why I'm taking Rato back to Raleigh."

"Rato's about as much use to you as a French-speaking flea."

"Rato's who I've got. Nobody else offered."

Milo said "I never got a chance."

I thanked him. "But you've got a wife and a job."

"You could stay with us."

"Thank you again but I own my house. I can't leave that. My Christmas vacation ends next Monday, and anyhow you know Sissie and I couldn't go half-a-day without starting the Great Sister-in-Law Massacre of 1986."

We had turned around by then and were halfway back to Mama's. But Milo slowed the car and pulled off the road in a wide spot in the pines. He lowered his window an inch, and cold air was quick to hit us. But he looked me over carefully. "Rose, I'm as sorry as I've ever been on this earth."

"For what?" I asked him.

"That this hit you."

I smiled. "It did. But thank you."

Milo shook his head. "What can I do to make it up?"

For one quick instant I wanted to say "Just run with me now, hard and fast far from here. You and me like in childhood, us two together forsaking the rest." But you know I didn't. Too much else, too many more, had come in between us and had their claims. I said "You and Sissie come see us soon. Meanwhile, keep a good eye on Mama out here." When I reached over to touch his face, his whole left cheek was wet with tears.

I thought I knew the answer but I asked anyhow. "What's the real trouble, Milo?" I figured it would be something about Sissie, his sad old marriage.

But he waited a good while, gnawing on the heel of his hand. Then he said "None of it was supposed to turn out this way, was it?" It seemed like a genuine urgent question.

I had to say, "What's *it*, Milo?"

"Jesus," he said. "—our lives, all these awful futures."

For a boy born to dirt-farm every day of his life, Milo always had more dreams even than me. I figured they'd died long since though. He hadn't mentioned them, to me at least, since he was sixteen. I thought he'd just agreed to die from the neck up like the rest of us. I mean, how long can you sell pickup trucks and dream about truth and light?

So I told him I thought we'd done fair enough. We all had our health, good jobs, good dry roofs over our heads, kitchens full of the latest. None of us had served any time behind bars.

He suddenly struck the steering wheel with both fists. "Tell the truth, goddammit! Your marriage is finally ruined. Mine's been a cold junkyard since day one. Your son is a pitiful poor excuse for a new generation. Sissie and I got scared and quit after one dead baby. Now we're all bearing down into late middle age. Death could strike any minute, and what would any of us have to show? A few thousand paychecks, an unretired mortgage—damned little else."

I said "Who do we know that ever had more? Look at our people."

He looked out the windshield like they might have been in the woods all around us. Finally he said "You and I are bad enough, but our people are too pitiful to think about."

I said "Milo, I had dreams too. And I know neither one of us has made it to the White House yet. But we're middle aged now, not dead and gone. We may have thirty more years to live through. If we bend double in pain this early, I don't see how we'll make it to the end."

He said he wasn't sure he wanted to make it.

I said in that case I was sorry I loved him—I'd try to withdraw.

Milo said "Please don't. I count on you."

I nodded again and we went back to Mama's.

Wesley, one thing I want to do right now is break down and bawl. But every time I get my body fixed to do it, somebody walks up that I've loved always and breaks down *before* me. I'm left running to get the cool compresses. Am I going to have to make reservations, say, thirty days ahead? Please book me in, if you have any pull—one big howling white trash breakdown.

IT'S FRIDAY NIGHT NOW, JANUARY 24TH. WHEN I GOT home from work, your letter was waiting on the hall table. Rato had laid it there on top of a stack of junk, and at first I didn't recognize your hand. It had been a lot of years since I'd seen that much of your writing in one place. And a Nashville address wasn't quite what I was expecting. I'd somehow got used to the idea you were closer by than that, like the east edge of town with your hair parted on the opposite side maybe. But when the name itself bore in on me, there in the upper left-hand corner of the envelope, I went straight up to our room to read it. Once I was on that bed, I couldn't. I had to go in the bathroom, lock the door, and sit down before I could even cut it open.

You haven't left me a whole lot to say. You've even made it all but impossible for me to go aiming this diary at you, like you'll ever read it. But it's too soon to make any rash decisions, I guess. I'll try to go on living the way I always have and hope that time will clear a path day by day, the way it usually has.

When I've got my thoughts together, when I've got some

thoughts at all, I'll draft a letter to you here and then decide whether to mail it. After that I'll try to decide whether there's any point in keeping this sad record alive.

January 26, 1986

Dear Wesley,

I'm relieved to know that you're alive and working, and I thank you for the check. I've done all right with everything but the mortgage, so this is a real help.

I won't pretend to understand any of the rest of what you say, about why you left your home and family and job or how you are living with somebody else in the face of the vows you and I made to one another personally twenty-eight years ago (from the week that you left). That is not to say that I believe I've been anywhere near a perfect wife or to blame you with not being a better husband than I could have dreamed of most days up till the day you left this last time.

I just want to say that I don't think I was living in a cloud, and I thought we were anyhow doing as well as any two people I've watched in all our same time.

If there is any one thing, or any twenty, that I can change to put us back together in better shape, please let me know what it would be. The way I feel now, there's not much I wouldn't do to fix us.

A lot has happened here since you left. If and when we meet again, I can tell you as much as you want to know. In the meantime I will try to hold on in the hope that the good things we had will come clear again in your mind, clear enough to blank out whatever and whoever else may be blinding you now.

Love,
Rosacoke

I mailed it and a month has gone by in silence here— just two notes from Wesley with checks, all on time and honest as far as I know. Precious few words in the notes, no more real news of him or his new friend (if she's still there). And no whisper of a hint that I should ever expect to see him alive, in this world anyhow.

I can see—looking back through this in the past few days, debating whether or not to recommence it—that I haven't said a word about how much it has hurt me. A stranger finding this in the twenty-first century at some flea market or yard sale might be excused for thinking that this marriage broke in two after nearly three decades without hard pain on either side.

I can't speak for Wesley's side of course. But me, I hurt so much right this minute—two months after the last time I saw him—that if you could hook my hand up to a circuit that ran on nothing but pain for fuel, you'd have an arc that blazed in the night like phosphorus you throw off a bridge in the river, phosphorus enough to burn till Judgment.

I really did think I had got past that. Not that I've suffered nearly as much as some people I know. But I have had my father's death to live through and my grandfather's, all mine and Wesley's long courtship miseries, the agony about Horace when he was conceived and I was deciding whether or not to get married, and then the normal hourly pains of a wife-and-mother's trip through all but thirty years.

So I guess I'd fallen back on unearned pride, the belief that I was too strong to be hurt by anything but Wesley's death or maybe Horace's (I hate to sound unloving of my only child, but I'm trying to be honest first). All the more surprising then, how bad off I am now—even this long after the event. You'd have thought a rape, if it was a rape, would have hurt deeper. Certainly all the articles and television prophets claim so.

But right this evening—the night of Valentine's Day—
all I feel like is the grown woman who wasn't good enough
to keep her place in the heart and mind of the only person
alive on earth that she hoped to please and hold to the
grave. Was that so foolish of me? Did I stumble this blind
into this harsh a punishment? I am a strong unusually
healthy woman for my middle age. With the example of
my mother's strength in front of me, I can imagine staying
on upright with my feelings intact for at least another thirty
years. How in the world am I going to do it? And why
should I want to?

—Just go on typing neat letters for a university English
Department and bringing home a check that would insult a
woman much dumber than me? Or fielding phone calls of a
son who checks in every Sunday night, in duty not enthusiasm? Or cooking two meals a day for my dear extraplane-
tary brother till he and I both have lost the teeth to eat with
and the eyes to see a plate?

THIS EVENING, A MONTH AFTER HE LEFT WESLEY'S FIRST
letter waiting in the hall for me, Rato asked me about it for
the first time. We'd finished our supper and were watching
the end of the national news. The last story had been about
hungry children in South Carolina (of course—why is it
never Boston or Ann Arbor, Michigan?). And when he
leaned forward to switch it off before *P.M. Magazine*,
which Rato calls *B.M. Magazine*, he said "Poor old
world."

And I said "Poor old me." I was just tired, nothing
much worse than usual. Get me tired and you've got self-
pity on your hands.

That must have given Rato the opening. He came to me

over by the dishwasher and put his left hand on my shoulder from behind.

It almost scared me out of my skin. I don't think Rato has touched me more than twice in our lives. I'm afraid I jumped back, put my hand up to my face like a shield, and said "Jesus!"

Rato takes the name of Jesus very seriously and hates more than anything the way people use it today as an all-purpose substitute for "Shit!" in polite company. Rato said "I'm sorry. But don't say that, please ma'm. He don't need it."

I had to laugh and beg his pardon. I explained it by saying my thoughts were miles away and he'd surprised me, that was all.

Rato gave it a few seconds to settle through his mind and then said "I know you're sad. I've been waiting for you to tell me."

"Tell you what?" I asked, though I certainly knew.

"Where Wesley is at."

I asked "Will you drink another cup of coffee?"

He said "I wouldn't sleep till Thursday-week, but I'll watch you drink it till you turn beige and faint."

So I poured a mugful and went back to the table and Rato joined me. I said "He's in Nashville, Tennessee with a working woman. He's got a good job and no plans for home."

"Is he crazy or sick?"

I smiled and said "Thank you. Neither one, he says. He says it had got to where his life felt dead. He doesn't blame me."

Rato said "Sure he does. You're the one he's left."

"That's a big help. Thank you."

He said "No, it's true. And you know it."

"I'm not sure I did, not in that hard a way. But all right, what am I meant to do with the news?"

Rato had gone past the point of timidity now, and he strode right ahead. He thought he knew his ground. "You need to know what I've known all my life—how to live by yourself."

"I don't want to. Nobody else does either."

Rato said "That's a lie. There's a few other people in the world with sense."

"And good sense means everybody holing up, alone as bones, and banging on their bare walls for company till they finally wear out and die with no heirs? How would you arrange for the human race to continue?"

He smiled. "I wouldn't. I think the sooner we give up the ridiculous job we've made and turn the earth over to dolphins and penguins, the better off God and the universe will be."

"I thought it was *all* God's plan."

Rato said "When was the last time you asked God how He liked it?"

"I'm not in all that regular touch with Him."

Rato said "I am."

Coming from Rato, it didn't seem crazy or scary but the simple truth. I'd waited for it all my life. And I said "What am I meant to do then?"

Rato said "Whoa, you're jumping over a few steps here. I'm not saying your whole life had been wrong or wasted."

I said "No, you're the one in the family who came closest to persuading me to marry Wesley back when I was pregnant and in such bad trouble."

He nodded. "I remember. And I don't take it back. There's nothing wrong with Wesley."

"Then it's all my fault," I said.

Rato shook his big head. "It's nobody's fault but the whole human race, except me and a few dozen others that know."

"The priests and nuns and weirdos?" I asked.

"And Ratos." Luckily he was able to smile.

"And what is it that you all know?"

"—What you and Wesley are just finding out. What you call *love* is something that can't last many years past high school, and then where are you?"

I told him you were where we'd been for at least twenty years, two people sharing a roof and a bed with a lot of mutual company and comfort, a son to raise between them, some real good times.

Rato said "And now this awful bad one."

I said "All right but, since we couldn't foresee this, were we still supposed to dry up and stay home frozen in childhood just out of fear of thirty-years-hence?"

Rato said "I didn't freeze."

I said "What did you do?" I'd never before asked him the first question about the life in his head and had never heard anybody ask him. For all I knew, he might stand up now and walk back to Mama's. But I felt like he'd at least given me the right.

He said "I've had the best life of anybody I've watched" (I already knew Mama agreed with him). And that seemed the end. He grinned to guarantee it.

I said "I'm glad to know you. Tell me what was good."

Rato asked me if I didn't think that called for a hot fudge sundae? One of the main joys of his life in Raleigh is the old fudge maker you gave Horace a century ago, that made his pimples so much worse. Rato keeps fudge steaming round the clock. And it's all I can do to convince him that, if I followed him scoop for scoop, I'd be bigger than Two-Ton Tessie tomorrow (he never gains an ounce). I told him to be my guest, which he proceeded to do. But once he had a platter of several million calories before him (he arranges them very artistically with the walnuts and cherries), he was ready to fill me in on his life. "This is America, right? Land of the free? I've been the only free man that you, or anybody else, knows."

I asked how was that?

Rato leaned far forward and tapped me hard twice right between the eyes. "Use your bean, sweet thing. I don't owe a cent, in cash or love, to any live soul. I've had twenty years in the world's greatest Army, and I've seen half the sights worth seeing on earth. Plus I estimate I had all the pleasures a man's skin can feel. I can still walk into any PX on any continent and buy the world's finest goods for next-to-nothing prices—cameras or cars. And I've got a lavish pension and that big veterans' hospital in Durham, when the time comes and parts start falling off of me. All that and never once, not one single time, has nobody ever turned to me with hurt eyes and said 'Rato, you have cut me to the quick, and I can't forgive you. I'm leaving *out* of here.'" He downed a big spoonful of fudge. "If that's not freedom and a happy life, then I *am* the half-wit you've all thought I was."

I said "I never did and you know it. But let me ask you this. Haven't you missed not having a regular mate through the long days and nights and no children to watch grow up through the years?"

"No ma'm, not a minute. I swear my Bible oath." And he swore it right there with that flat palm the size of a paddle for the biggest rowboat.

I said "Excuse me, Rato. But to me it looks like a desert life—the diet for a damned horned toad or a gila monster."

Rato said "That's because you're brainwashed. You believed in movies and songs and t.v. Somehow I knew it was all popsicles, cold sugar and water and then a dry stick."

"What told you that?"

"Maybe Jesus in the night."

I had to say "Rato, now *you* spare Jesus."

"No," he said, "I may be serious. Something told me to go my way."

"When and where?"

"Long before I was grown. Something out in the woods. I could talk to trees. They'd answer me back."

I had to smile. "We were scared of that."

He shook his head. "Get serious, Rosa. I was a perfectly real child with a working mind. I just didn't want to run with you and Milo and make all that noise. I wanted to be by myself, be still, and listen."

"So you listened to trees and they said what?"

"Not words. I didn't mean that. I'm not a damned simpleton or Walt-damned-Disney. I mean they taught me things about living on my own, finding my own nourishment in my own ground—not leaning and leeching on other poor souls."

"You had Phillip, your old dog. You leaned on Phillip."

"No, I didn't. We also talked to each other a lot, laughed a lot. But it wasn't leaning. I knew Phillip couldn't outlast me. I knew he'd die before he was fifteen and he did."

"And you grieved for him, I remember."

Rato nodded. "I did. Not ever again."

I couldn't stop myself. I had to say "Wouldn't you grieve for me?"

He said "Where are you going?"

"Nowhere tonight. Or I very much hope not. But you know I've got to someday, and lots of women die younger than I am now. Wouldn't you mind that?"

Rato had finished dessert by then. He didn't have anything else to face but me. So he faced me, not blinking till it almost hurt. He said "Rosa, you could get cruel here in a minute."

But I kept going. I told him I'd been down to Mary's house while I was home.

He said "She told me."

I told him I was honored to see his pictures of me.

He looked miserable as a turtle jerked screaming out of his shell. Finally he said "Those are souvenirs."

I nodded. "Everybody's got souvenirs. Mine are all around me here. I'm glad you've found your place."

He said "Mary's good to me."

I said "She gets lonesome."

So he saw his chance at last to laugh. "You don't have to be lonesome to like Rato."

I told him I'd understood that right along. If I'd offered him a whole nother sundae, he'd have eaten it.

I HAD GONE ON TO SLEEP WITH VERY LITTLE TROUBLE, thinking only that the biggest surprise of the last two months had not been desertion or rape but hearing Rato say his skin had *felt every pleasure*. I'd just thought Rato's idea of pleasure was endless sundaes or, at the most, daylight on his hair. Was there any way to ask him more about that without opening too weird a door on too big a room?

Then at ten minutes past two in the morning, the phone rang by my bed. I answered it first-pop and the one voice in the world I'd prayed never to hear again said "I hope you've had a nice rest."

Some awful bred-in courtesy—plus grogginess—made me say "Yes, thank you."

So he knew he had the right woman. Then he said "I may be needing to check that soon."

And I hung up.

He may be there still.

I LAY BACK A GOOD WHILE, WIDE AWAKE AS A SCALDED child. For the first quarter-hour I tried to pray. Prayer had been some help to me in childhood and the early years of marriage. It really had seemed to do what Jesus promises in the Gospels, change things. Jesus says "Ask and it shall be given." But as Wesley and I got older and began quietly to go our separate ways and our son went on down a third way of his own, I must have begun to think prayer changed precious little. I mean, I've asked for a thousand pains to turn aside, and to the best of my knowledge I've yet to turn one.

Of course it had begun to dawn on me lately that when Jesus said "It shall be given," he didn't quite say what *it* was. He didn't say it was the exact thing you asked for— money or healing or that your lazy son pass his algebra test. Maybe it's just peace of heart, the peace of knowing you've talked to the center of things and He or It has said "No" or "Not now."

Anyhow I lay there trying again to talk it over with the center. I did have one big request—that I not be killed in my own bed or maimed. Otherwise I asked for the strength to see this whole business through. And by *whole business* I meant everything that's hit me since the end of the year, the end of what I had thought was the rest of my life.

Toward the end of what I had to say, a patch of nerves the size of a half-dollar in my right shoulder began to sizzle like bacon. I thought "That's not too promising an answer" so I said "Amen" and stopped. What was left but to wake up Rato, make a gallon of coffee, and wait for day with every light in the house blazing? I knew it was weakness. I knew my mother wouldn't have done it. She'd have crept downstairs and got the butcher knife and lain in her dark sheets waiting, not asking another soul to bear her trouble, least of all her pitiful husband or her four children drowned in the sleep they needed. But I was Rosa. And Rosa stood up then, put on yesterday's dress, and went to Rato's door.

For somebody as private as Rato, it's always strange to me that he sleeps with his door open. But he does. And anywhere within twenty feet of his door feels and sounds like the path to a stable. Again I don't mean to say Rato is some kind of dumb beast but that he doesn't put the usual human brakes on the sounds his body wants to make— snores, belches, and long speeches in the night. I've more than once, since he's been here, heard him sit up in bed and say a whole paragraph of sentences—all clear in their wording and a lot more correct in grammar than he is when awake. In the night I always promise myself I will re- member and understand him better. But then I don't. So whatever message he's sent me turns out to be in vain one more time.

Now I waited at the door a minute for some sound that he was asleep or not. But there was nothing coming through but a silence so deep it scared me. I called Rato's name more than once, no answer. I stepped on forward in the pitchblack till my knees bumped his mattress, and then I bent down to feel in the sheets. They were cold and empty and I froze. It seemed like any second a bat the size of a big dog would flap down from the ceiling and claw my eyes. I even covered my face with my hands and called "Rato" loud. But there was no answer.

And speaking of dogs, there hadn't been a peep out of Roger anymore than there had been at New Year's. As a watchdog he's roughly in the Helen Keller class. He either sleeps through enemy visits, or they throw him a soup bone that buys him off. From the upstairs hall, I even called his name too. Still nothing.

Two possibilities. Stay upstairs, call the police, and wait till they arrived creating a mob scene in the neighborhood for no cause probably. Or risk going downstairs and trying to act like a normal grown person. From the top of the steps I couldn't see or hear anything unusual. I always leave on a lamp in the front hall for just such emergencies, and it was burning calmly.

So down I went. From the dining room I could see that the kitchen was brightly lit. I had heard how intruders sometimes cook themselves whole meals before leaving. I also knew it was where burglars always go first on breaking in since it's where people keep the *cutting* equipment. Knives are the second most popular thing they steal, after firearms. I picked up a heavy brass candlestick and pushed open the swinging door. And of course there was Rato fully dressed eating Cheerios with extra raisins and honey.

He said "Good morning" like it was.

I said "Don't apologize. You have only scared ten years off my life."

He said "Thank me then. That's ten years less in the Old Folks' Home not knowing who you are."

I thanked him and asked what he was doing having breakfast in the middle of the night?

He said "I was getting my strength up to deal with that creep on the phone." It wasn't till then that I noticed how, sure enough, he did have a respectable butcher knife and the biggest hammer out by his plate.

I asked how he knew about my call.

Rato said "Not a lot of calls at two in the morning are legal, are they?"

I asked "Rato, who is it?"—not imagining he knew.

He said "Lady, I'm a stranger here myself. They're not hunting me."

I asked was he scared?

He said "You forget I served in Berlin in the early sixties."

So I had. Not that I thought Rato had personally been eyeball to eyeball with Khrushchev at the Berlin wall, but he did have a point. I thanked him for reminding me.

"What did he say?"

"He asked me if I'd been resting. When I said 'Yes' he said he might have to end that soon."

"He just meant tonight," Rato said, "—were you sleeping tonight? He knew he could ruin that and he has. That's all he can do now with me here. He gets his little pitiful pleasure from that."

I said "He seems to watch me. He's bound to know you're here."

"Sure he does," Rato said. "Why else would he call tonight? If I wasn't here, he'd have just come without calling. Now all he can get is a telephone thrill. Tomorrow we'll get the company to put one of those tracers on the phone. Next time he dials you, bam—he's behind bars."

What my brother learned in the Army and on television continues to surprise and amuse me. I was impressed and grateful but felt the need to cool him down a little too. "Remember though I've never reported any break-in here at the house, so we can't mention that to the phone company or anybody else."

"Don't need to. Just tell the latest truth—you've been getting a bunch of sick calls. You're losing precious sleep and you want them to stop."

Rato was getting more excited than seemed like a good idea for the hour, so I went to work to calm him down and get us both back upstairs. The usual way to do that is to start remembering our childhood good times together—like the day when he, black Mildred, and I started digging to China deep in the woods where the earth was softer. I told him the whole story again this time, and he enjoyed it as always. Especially the part where Mildred and I give up and quit at supper time. But Milo finally has to go find Rato long after dark and bring him home to bed. He had suceeded in digging himself in knee-deep at least.

Still when I stood up and said "I'm going to go stretch out on top of the covers and get a little more rest before time for work," Rato just shook his head and said he'd stay on down here an hour or so longer.

"You sleep all you can," he said. "Be sure I'm your guard."

I'd no more than pulled up a quilt, touched my head to the pillow, and smiled to think how well my weird brother's visit was turning out, and then I was sunk deep as I'd been in many long years.

TODAY DURING LUNCH HOUR I DID GO DOWNTOWN TO THE phone company and sign the necessary papers that license them to put a machine on my phone which might catch a nuisance caller. I didn't have to swear (but almost) that if and when they caught somebody, then I'd prosecute. My old dread is that it'll turn out to be somebody I know, some student from school or some old friend of Horace's. Or, pray God no, some friend of Wesley's that knew he was leaving and thought the friend might pick up the slack. It'll be Monday before they can install the tracer, but Rato's looking forward and will be here to let the installer in. At least he's got me doing things, not sitting still waiting for things to be done to me. That can't be bad.

The one thing Rato hasn't mentioned doing yet is buying a pistol. I wondered about that myself, before he came. Oddly enough, Wesley would never keep firearms here, saying that if anybody broke in the house ahead of us, they'd just kill us with it when we walked in—which still sounds sensible to me. But I suspect Rato feels differently. I won't deal with that, yea or nay, till he brings it up though.

IT'S NOW MARCH 12TH, 1986. TWO WEEKS HAVE PASSED since then, and wouldn't you know it? The minute we installed the tracer, the phone went quiet and has barely rung once. More than ever I think the culprit was somebody who lives near enough to know what the traffic in and out of this house means. But like most Raleigh citizens these days, I don't know the neighborhood well enough to guess who's who. There is a big rowdy houseful of fraternity boys three blocks north, but somehow I think I'm dealing with something besides being rowdy and spring panty-raids.

What else to mention? Life otherwise has been very quiet. Rato spends his days apparently happy to be shut up in this house with the television and all my old detective novels. I've never known him to read before, but he's knocking them back now like popcorn—sometimes two a day. Occasionally he and Roger go for a fast walk around the block, and I've tried to suggest that we go to a movie some night or out to a restaurant or even to a mall, just so Rato can stroll a little and see some new faces. To the best of my knowledge, he hasn't met a new soul in Raleigh. Or since he left for the Army for that matter. But I honestly begin to believe that he's happiest when I leave him to do exactly what he's doing, what he's always said he wants to do. Of course on almost all the weekends, we drive up to Afton and buy two boxes of pralines and check on Mama.

We generally go early on Saturday afternoon, after I've folded the laundry and laid in the week's groceries. She's always there to meet us smiling but not panting with her tongue hanging out for hunger and joy to see her beloved offspring. I think it's begun to sink in, even with Rato, that our mother's relieved to be there alone—nobody to cook for, nobody leaning on her mind even as silent as Rato. It's even surprised her. I can see her working overtime to con-

vince us she's glad we remembered her and turned up one
more time.

She tries to make her new duties sound like chores—
that she's taken on the nursery class again at Sunday school
and has good stories from there every week, that her new
young friend down the road (a Limer woman) has started
gadding her about to shopping centers as much as an hour
away where she even broke down and bought one new
dress. It's navy blue to be sure—the same basic model
she's worn for sixty years, and she wears it with those
same pearl earbobs she must have found in the pyramids.
But it *is* brand new and two inches shorter than anything
she's worn since leaving high school, so that all but quali-
fies as a *People* magazine cover-story.

They even came to Raleigh one day last week and didn't
even try to call us, just got their feet worked over by the
last old chiropodist in existence—their ingrown toenails
trimmed and their corns whittled. Mama said "It killed me
to spend twenty dollars on feet as ugly as these, but it sure
was worth it. These ten toes think they died last week and
waked up in Heaven." Her feet have always been her personal crucifixion.

We usually spend Saturday night there, and I make Rato
chop a week's supply of firewood (not an easy thing; he
thinks Mama needs the exercise). I check on her oil and
groceries and touch up anything she's short on. I snoop
around the house for fire risks and other dangers. But I
seldom find any. She didn't run the place all those years,
and raise four children plus a drunk and a cantankerous
father-in-law, on harum scarum principles. She sees me
checking behind her and never tries to stop me, though I
can tell she's amused.

The only real difference is, she's losing weight. Mama's never been really fat, whatever she's said, but she's surely always been well-upholstered. Those layers are quietly peeling off her now. I've asked her about it. She says "Rosa, your mother is an *old* woman. If people don't die in their seventies from bad hearts or kidneys, then you'll begin to notice how they just start vanishing into thin air. It can take another twenty years, but they're on the way. After a while you can all but read the newspaper through their hand. I think it's kind of pretty. Just get used to it anyhow and don't worry me about eating. I eat everything I want. And everytime I think about it, I take that vitamin pill you gave me for insurance."

I know she's right and I believe her. I also know if anything happened to her right now, on top of all this other, it might be the straw that brings my poor old camel right down. (If Mama saw me writing this of course she'd say that the biggest shame I could bring her, as a mother, would be just that—not being strong enough to bear her death.) But late on the Sunday evenings when we pull out of the drive and leave her standing up alone there on that porch—that's always been swarming with people before, people that she *brought into the world*—and that big body now shrunk in like a dryfly, then my callused heart hurts a good halfway down the road to Raleigh.

Rato never speaks of it. It's not that I think he's hard-hearted. I just think he can discard parts of the world that won't directly press on him, the way I manage to disregard the starving masses of Ethiopia. I suspect Rato thinks he lives with me now, and I'm his main concern. And maybe he's right. Maybe one of my big mistakes has been diluting my feelings by trying to care too much about too many things.

Anyhow I've got no real complaints against him so far. He's as quiet as a bale of cotton. He lives as neat as a snake, no mess of any kind behind him. And he's as easy to feed as a baby. If I let him take his walks when the need strikes and give him control of the television at nights, then he's the easiest-to-please friend I ever had. And why not another thirty-odd years of it?

Even down into my early womanhood, in Afton and Warrenton and all out in the surrounding county, there were dozens of couples stranger than me and Rato—old brothers that had been together since the cradle with nothing but a Negro woman or man that came in to wash and cook for them (that much at least and who knew what else?). Old-maid daughters and their fathers. Lots of bachelor brothers and spinster sisters.

Everybody thought they were doing fine. I never remember one word of unkind rumor or criticism against them. This whole idea that the purpose of the human heart is to make hot love on the even nights and think about it in a warm sweat on the odd nights is sadly lacking in imagination, to me anyhow. I think those old Victorian Baptists were a lot smarter and sure God more tolerant than us with all our smart ideas and laws that say this one can't touch that one—no no no!

It was just a more sensible time, I guess, back then before Americans got this present idea that life without a richly contented marital love-life is worse than being staked down to the jailhouse floor in a banana republic in the worst month of summer with roaches big as pancakes. People, even in my childhood, used to be trusted to find their own nourishment like dogs in the woods—the right brand of grass or herbs to eat that would heal their pain.

If you didn't want to set up in the babymaking business, fine—just take your favorite sister or brother or parent and set you up a household in a nice cool oak-grove and live till you both had your fill and quit. And if either one of you decided to reach out and touch the other one—well, who'd ever know what the response would be and who the hell's business was it anyhow?

When did marriage get to seeming so unrealistically important? Maybe when big families broke up and there was nothing to life but Rosa and Wesley and poor little Horace, no deep cushion of aunts and uncles and cousins around you to help absorb all the million daily shocks of life. Nobody but your sworn wedded mate. And good luck, by the way, when your mate decides he's been dead from the neck-up or waist-down ever since he met you, or two weeks after the honeymoon (if you ever had one, which Rosa and Wesley didn't).

If you arranged in the fifties to be a pioneer career-woman, then you'll have that wheel to push your new-found energies against. But who arranged for that? Not me. I type letters, mimeograph exams, Xerox everything from Shakespeare sonnets to directions for jumping a stalled battery. It's hardly soul food though, believe you me. I could quit tomorrow and, except for the salary, not miss an instant of it ever again.

But even with Wesley sticking by his share of the mortgage, I couldn't begin to think of quitting work. So I'm expected to spend another twenty-odd years at a keyboard typing other people's thoughts eight hours a day just so I can come home and sleep warm and dry in a house that no

longer has anything to offer me but protection—and in fact
has already failed at that. *Expected by who?*

God is something I guess I've pretty much left out of
this diary. And out of my life more and more in recent
years. Even in adolescence, when a lot of the boys got
religious, I could quietly take it or leave it. I mean I've
never considered for ten seconds being an atheist. I'm sure
there's a divine being that created it all, me included, and
is watching me and it sympathetically at least—however
many babies get born with their bellies outside their skin
and with tumors the size of children's beach buckets. In my
experience though He sure to goodness keeps His own
counsel.

Maybe I've just been too involved in my own thoughts
and hopes to take the time to learn to sit in silence long
enough to hear His version of what comes next, any questions He may have of me. When I found out I was pregnant
in 1957—and me no more married than Mother Teresa—I
tried to pray, as I said. Well, I got as much answer as if I'd
prayed to rocks in the road. A direct answer that is, in
words or music. Then at the last minute I had to stand in
for the Virgin Mary in Mama's Christmas pageant at Delight church (with Wesley as third Wise Man), and the
sight of real live little Frederick Gupton tuning up to holler
there in my lap—and wasn't *he* my answer? *Rosa, help
this present needy child. And all other children placed in
your care.* So I picked up Frederick and married you and
had Horatio "Horace" Beavers and our long life together.

Since then though I've barely said a prayer. During bad
times I have occasionally said "Take me where I ought to
go" and then just waited to see where my feet went next.
But very little else. And look where the feet have landed.

So that's been my philosophy here these past months since Wesley left and I got slammed down. I don't know any other way to act. I guess I could try going back to church, meeting the new minister, and seeing if he has any help to offer. But church too long ago lost its shine for me. Even Wesley kept going to services longer than I did. And when Horace got into his teen years, he went through a deep time of needing to be religious. I'd find him on his knees in his own room, praying for whatever little sins he imagined he'd committed (or so I guessed—I never asked and I doubt he ever saw me at the door). It touched me at the time, but it never made me want to follow suit.

The real problem was, I worshiped Wesley—didn't I? I've said here somewhere else how I learned to love men's faces from watching, first, my father, then Milo, and then Wesley. Needless to say, I hadn't ever really touched my father and Milo—their secret bodies, I mean (though I'm not sure it would have been the world's biggest sin and crime; it might have helped me love Wesley better and more sensibly).

So when Wesley and I finally got down to serious business, I just started transferring everything I'd ever felt about God and Jesus onto one human boy from down the road. Wesley's good frank face, his mysterious eyes, and everything strong and lovely and sad in his long clean body—for me, all that just turned into God and Christ and Heaven. And when we brought our separate bodies together and made them one (and they did become one—I can take a solemn oath, even here now alone—more times than a few in all our years), then I had even more of a reason for thinking one *man* was the whole point of life—my life anyhow.

It didn't have all that much to do with personal fulfillment, actual orgasms, or any of that woman's-seminar stuff you hear on t.v. I sure never counted the number of orgasms I had in Wesley's presence and with his assistance —maybe not more than a hundred. What it pertained to mainly was my own deep happiness, my best satisfaction. Being bare, with Wesley bare and striving in me—it just came to mean I had a big purpose, secret, known to no one but him, still the thing that justified my life. My tiredness and boredom, my failure to be the kind of woman I'd been as a girl—somebody admired by her family, her teachers, and the damned county paper for general neatness and excellence.

It wasn't that I grew up like some girls I knew to become a common whore and sex-junkie. Some smart decent girls from near us in the country—girls that I've laughed and primed tobacco with—had themselves six children by the time they were twenty-five just because they couldn't stop their bodies from climbing aboard Spencer Scott or some other hot-eyed boy with straight teeth and a nice mole there to the left of his right eye.

Me—I can look at most men, and sex will be the last thing I see and want. It was just—just!—that Wesley didn't do anything for maybe the first ten years I knew him but go on getting grander in my mind (in the night, bare inside me). He seemed more and more like Rosa's only goal. Love Wesley, serve him, give Wesley all you've got.

Then about the time Horace began to have a pre-teenage life of his own outside my kitchen, and I left the house and got me a job, I began to suspect Wesley didn't need me all that much either. He sure never told me otherwise at least. He'd roll over on me several nights a week and kindly but silently gouge down in me the same as before. But it wasn't the same.

Either I'd changed somehow and had less to give him or that, however hard Wesley dug down in me, he couldn't anymore find the stuff he'd found—the sweet and nourishing best heart of Rosa, that had fueled him on through so much trouble.

Maybe that's why he left last Christmas week. It's anyhow all he left me with. And what it brings me down to, here and now, is the least helpful thing imaginable—*me*.

I am all I've got. And it's some kind of lonesome in here where I live, where I'm nailed up lonesome with the little bit Rosa knows and dreams of still. Wesley talks about feeling dead. When he first wrote it, I laughed bitterly just to read the one word—what on earth could he mean?

But now I think I understand perfectly well and agree. I can easily imagine, a year or so from now, just being one of those hollowed-out women that goes to an office job five days a week, types thousands of words a day, files the product, then slides back home on a slick conveyer belt to drink cheap vodka and watch television till two in the morning, then four hours' sleep. Then eventual retirement, with a farewell luncheon (baked chicken, Waldorf salad, and a gold-plated pen and pencil set to write your thrilling memoirs with), and twenty more years in a grimy cheap apartment watching t.v. and thinking how fast time had run and worn you out.

Join the human race, Rosa. Be a normal cold uncomplaining zombie. You had nearly fifty years awake as a woman with feelings in every damned cell—more feeling than any two average others. It's begun to cool now. Little

nerves are dying off from exhaustion and old age. Thank
your stars and shut up. Lie down and just rest. The human
race mainly consists of citizens such as you—people that
had a nice few years of life, then consumed the fuel (like
natural hair-color before you go gray), and are making cold
time till death stops by one night and says "Now." Two
mornings later there's your obituary in *The News and Observer*, three inches long. Some old boss of yours says
"Dear old girl" and kisses his wife an instant longer as he
leaves for work. Some English major from way-back-when
(now a forty-five-year-old advertising man) says "Old Ms.
Beavers, she was one feisty lady." And that'll be *it*, except
for God—whatever He thinks and awards you in Heaven.

It will after all be the first day of spring in no time now,
if the world lasts till spring and Rosa's here to greet it.
Some little cell hid deep down in me may still be breathing, may still sprout green if daylight strikes it.

Do. Amaze me. Sprout and thrive.

WESLEY

LIKE EVERY DREAM WESLEY EVER HAD, THIS ONE was real as a normal day. That was why, all his life, he'd counted on dreams to help him onward. His were never foolish or dumb. Even the ones that left him nervous, especially them, were gritty as newsreels. So when this one started outside Nashville just before sunrise, his mind braced itself for whatever would come. From the start though it promised to be long and happy.

The girl was maybe seventeen years old. He must have been somewhere near that age himself since it seemed very natural that they should sit here together, near the surf but warm and dry. He was not in the Navy yet. Or at least he wasn't in uniform, just starched khaki pants and a polo shirt. They were both barefooted. She wore a pale dress. Otherwise all Wesley saw was her eyes. They were fixed right on him in a way that, in any other girl, would have been odd or dirty. And for once that seemed sufficient to him. His hands stayed calm on the sand between them. His mind didn't think of moving elsewhere, to hide in the dunes or even to touch a girl as fine as this.

So he stayed on, peaceful in her nearness and glad at least to find one girl that could watch him and yet not draw on his strength or stroke his body with those eyes, strong as the moon at full. He remembered his mother's training enough to think he ought to say some kind of thanks.

But when he tried it, just the first few words, the girl smiled, touched her own silent mouth, and shook her head. So it was perfect, right?—the day, the place, his mind, the company.

No, he needed to know her name. Unbelievable as she was, she didn't seem strange—no haloes or organ music. He even wondered why he couldn't relax and let her just be here. If her name came to him in time, then good. If not, well, there must be worse fates than a happy life with a flawless Jane Doe. Still in another minute of watching, he felt his mouth go to work without him. Over the surf, he heard his own voice say "My name's Wesley."

The girl waited, then laughed. "Of course it is. That ocean's the Atlantic too."

He actually blushed. "Have I lost my mind?"

"How so?"

Wesley said "Beg your pardon if this makes you mad but who are you?"

It wasn't anger on her face but surprise, then maybe regret. She said "This is like soap operas—amnesia. I'm Rosacoke."

* * *

SOON AFTER THAT HE WOKE UP IN NASHVILLE. AS ALWAYS, he was alert at once. So he knew his surroundings—the master bedroom of Wilson's trailer, her sleeping body beside him.

The sounds from Wilson began to reach him. Nothing you could tape-record or describe, except maybe the rush of blood through her skin or the growth of her hair. Maybe the solemn push of her kindness against the whole world, the big steady trust she'd offered from the start to a strange man old enough to be her father.

In another ten seconds, that was all Wesley knew. The strange dream was gone. Superstitious as he was, he had to gamble that he was lying on the edge of a lucky day— treading the warm and buoyant knowledge that a woman this good would join him in a moment.

He also knew it was the first day of spring. The sky was still dark, the air in the trailer was still dry and crisp, and Wilson's flank—a thumb's reach from him—was chill to the touch. But Wesley's heart lifted at the thought. Content as he'd been in recent months, winter had kept a thick film on his eyes. The past two weeks though, the sky had arched up higher at the spine. The light was healthier, stronger, and seemed surer of lasting. More than ever before in his life, Wesley took the annual blessing of the day as confirmation of the rightness of his place. The sun itself was confirming his choice to be here now, beside this girl.

He lay absolutely still, not touching her, and watched the porthole above her shoulder. Behind the thick curtain it would still show daylight the instant day broke. From the shine of his watch, he knew it would be another few min-

utes. Whatever came after that—the first glow that said
dark had ended again—he'd wait for day.

IN THE WAIT WESLEY SAID HIS USUAL PRAYER, ASKING GOD
to give special care to the leaders of the world and to his
own family. He named them as always—starting with the
president, then his mother, his wife in Raleigh, Horace his
son and Horace's wife Pris, this woman asleep with him
now, and his own sorry self. In prayers, since the day he'd
run from home, he thought of himself as sorry and sinful.

Unlike Rosa he'd never really doubted that the world
itself, not to mention his loved ones, was held in shape and
suspended from harm partly by his prayers. Once in the
Navy he'd got in an argument with a Catholic from Provi-
dence, Rhode Island. Wesley had attacked the idea of nuns
and monks—grown strong people (that could have been
farming or painting ships) sitting idle in monkeries and
convents, not even plowing or childbearing.

The Catholic had let out a stream of profane abuse more
startling than any southern brand; but then he'd said "You
ought to fall on your hillbilly knees now, Reb, and thank
your stars those sisters *are* praying. If they weren't locked
up—peaceful and pure—praying for your spotted ass,
God would long since have melted your shit to tar."

And ever since, Wesley had agreed and joined his own
daily voice to the silent choir of all those pale pimply
ladies kneeling on stone floors behind blinds and bars.

AND AS HE GOT TO THE END OF IT, THE PORTHOLE GRADU-
ally glowed. One more weekday, a whole nother spring. It
didn't seem sacrilegious in the least to roll with the next

breath up against Wilson and start, with his right hand, to rousing her. They had half an hour before the alarm, sufficient time to honor the occasion—spring and its goodness —and both their good bodies.

Wilson mumbled "I need my sleep now, Wesley."

He laughed. "You slept like a puppy on drugs." He knew. He'd waked up twice to pee, and every time Wilson had been thoroughly drowned. His hand went out again, gentler this time. She let him work and in another half-minute he began to think he'd won. The old moist findings of his blind hands—perpetually the same, miraculously new—lured him down that dark hall in his mind that led to perfect repayment, entire reward. Today like all other days, it seemed incredible that so much could be got for so little —no money, no hard work, no pain, just mutual patience and courtesy, *permission*.

Without a single word suddenly Wilson was bolt upright in the sheets, then standing, then pounding the linoleum toward the bathroom door.

For a few seconds Wesley could hope she was fitting in one of her several brands of sex gear (he still knew less about birth control than the average high-school boy). But really he knew better. And then the shower came on. Oh Jesus, she'd started the day without him.

She was one of those modern kids that spent a whole morning in the shower, so Wesley knew he was high and dry. Mad enough to turn the trailer over and leave but still hot and hard as a wombat, he rolled to his back, threw off the cover, and tried to love himself. In the dim light he could see enough of his cock to admire. It was straight and stiff as stainless steel, the hair was still dark—no wrinkles or gray or other sign of age.

But oh the old bright focus was gone. With all the thick spit of morning in a hand trained for forty-five years, his mind couldn't help him. That one mad girl, by turning aside, had the strength to cut Wesley's power at the source. In twenty more seconds he'd lost his will. What he hated most was the fact she'd won. And he didn't know why. How had he harmed her? He was gentle as a pet. He'd only meant to give her the best he knew.

BY THE TIME SHE WAS READY TO SHOW HER FACE, HE HAD made fresh coffee and was half-dressed, drinking it. Wilson walked the length of the kitchenette silent on her pink chenille scuffs and found her own cup. When she'd sugared it precisely, she joined him at the table in the living-room corner. She looked young and fine, in her white slacks and figured smock for work, not a hair out of place.

But Wesley's mind couldn't think what to say. He couldn't smile either. He stared out the one big window and said "First day of spring."

Wilson said "Don't I know."

That came as a surprise. He felt even madder. Finally he could say "Then what did I do wrong?"

Wilson looked baffled. "Nothing. When?"

"Don't be childish, Wilson. I'm too big for that. You goddamned well know what I mean."

"At dawn in the bed? What *you* planned to do? It just didn't happen to be *Wilson's* plan. You hadn't asked Wilson."

Wesley said "I hadn't understood you took written applications. Is that the new procedure?"

She laughed a little but then she got earnest. "It may need to be. I been thinking it over. The problem is, Wesley, you need more of me—of sex anyhow. All men seem to, the ones I've known."

"And you've known a cast of thousands, I'm sure."

"Don't be mean now. You were no virgin boy."

"No, ma'm. I'm married. You're shacked up—remember?—with a long-married father in a field near Nashville in a mobile home ugly as a mule with mumps. It's adultery, lady. You're a tax-paying grownup and you're sharing the crime."

Wilson finally asked "You know that too?"

"Yes ma'm, from the start. I'm a Christian boy."

She took a good minute to blow and drink her coffee. Then she had the strength to face him, eyes to eyes. "Then let's end the crime."

Wesley asked "What's your plan?"

"Well, there's two," she said. She had plainly thought through it. "Either you get divorced or we split up."

He said "And either one's fine by you?"

"Maybe so. At first I hoped for plan A. Here lately though I've got some questions." The seriousness invading her face was aging her fast. She suddenly looked like somebody's wife, some teenage boy's mother lowering the gate.

Wesley hated to watch but he had to push on and know where he stood. He said "Let's hear every question you got." He never thought he'd be in a place like this—some young girl holding his life in her fingers and turning it over like a frog in a lab (in the Navy he signed up for an improve-your-mind biology course till they had to cut frogs, and then he quit—not seeing the point).

Wilson said "Let's wait till we're home this evening. It's early. We're mad. I'm not thinking plain."

Wesley shook his head. "There may not be an evening. This ain't my home, not yet anyhow. And I ain't mad. Tell me now or never."

She felt the knife-edge of hurt in his *home*. And she heard the sweep of his ultimatum in *now or never*, but she held her temper. "We're way apart in age. You know a lot I just don't know yet. You've raised a family. I've yet to have mine. You won't want to go through that again surely."

"I never said so."

Wilson said "You want to discuss it?"

Wesley said "The discussion can wait. I just meant I hadn't ruled kids out."

"But a marriage would need to come first," Wilson said. "You haven't really mentioned a word about divorcing Rosa."

The sound of Rosa's name in another woman's mouth, even this far away, still shocked Wesley. It even surprised him to realize Wilson knew it—her name, his loyal wife's name. Had he just let it slip or had she read his mail? He wouldn't fight that now. He might need it later. He said "I don't know I'm getting a divorce."

"Then how can you ask for this much of me?"

"Because you've given it, Wilson—open-handed till just now. You've give it by the *ton*."

"—In hopes of much more. You don't think I want to be 'shacked-up,' as you say, for the rest of my young life, do you?"

Wesley said "I thought you were burned bad as me. I

didn't know you were rushing back to nobody's damned altar."

"I'm not, no. But we've been together nearly three months now, and I'm thinking it's time we knew what we mean."

Wesley said "I've been meaning I'm *happy*."

Wilson smiled naturally, then pushed it aside. "I'm saying I'm not, I guess. Not now anymore. I just can't keep talking about it this morning. I'll be glad to go right on after work, but now I've got to run."

"You do that," he said. "I may be here."

WHEN WILSON HAD PUT ON HER COAT AND WAS READY TO leave for the hospital, she stopped by the table. Wesley wasn't due in as early as she and was still drinking coffee and watching the news. She didn't say a word but waited behind him and then bent slowly to kiss Wesley's head— the crown of his skull, still densely covered.

Wesley waited too. But then he leaned back on the pressure of her mouth.

She stayed there to meet him and waited for help— some opening word.

He couldn't find a word though, so he had to let her leave.

ALL THAT DAY AT WORK WILSON THOUGHT OF NOTHING but the evening, what she'd say when they sat down finally to talk their way through this mean log-jam. As she X-rayed her fourth patient of the morning—a handsome and valiant twelve-year-old boy with leukemia and a possible broken arm (from school basketball)—she had the closest thing to a vision in her life. Behind this child's threatened nearly transparent skin, as if her own eyes were X-ray, she saw the young Wesley. Though Wilson didn't know it, he was the same boy Rosa had seen in actual flesh, up a pecan tree all but forty years ago gazing off at smoke. The simple condensation on earth of God's love of things, sent for all to see and honor as they could.

Wilson saw it now in those same terms, almost those words. It made her think she would be a big fool to lose Wesley now. Thickened though he was with flesh and years and boredom, the present man who asked for her body— her steady companionship—was as good a soul as she'd ever get a chance at, the only one so far to promise to use her. Stand him beside the rest of the men she'd been through till now, he shone like a torch on a dark hill at midnight.

She'd read enough in women's magazines to know such thinking was old-fashioned and dangerous. It had landed her mother in a marriage as fruitful as frozen sand. But the chance had never come Wilson's way before. She'd about given up hope of that brand of luck, a run at someone genuinely this fine. Calm and grown-up and gentle and *there*. If she drew back now, in fear or self-love, she felt convinced she'd be cursed for life. Meanness, hot hands, hard dirty mouths, blind cocks poking at her in dry cold dark. Sixty more years in howling solitude, strapped down to a relay of pitiful failures till she herself was one more failed woman—grinning too much from a face that looked like a burnt-out trailer, missing a few back teeth and dye-haired, begging all passers for any kind handout.

As the boy with the hurt arm left her room, Wilson heard herself say the sudden kind of sentence she never said—the kind of thing technicians learn not to say. She offered hope. She said "You'll live to be a strong old man." No sooner had it passed her lips than she thought "Damn. That's a lie." But as quick again, she knew the whole truth. She had been shown the future and licensed to tell him. So she sent him a big smile—"I know I'm right."

The boy's name was Travis—Travis Todd. He stopped and stood straight upright in the door. He turned her promise over in his mind, one more claim in the thousand he'd heard since learning of his affliction. Then quick as Wilson said it, Travis knew to believe her. Never having met an angel before, he nonetheless accepted the message. He said "You sure I can hold you to that?"

"Absolutely."

"Where you live?"

"Out the Franklin road—Route 4, Box 40. Big double-wide mobile home on high cinder-blocks. Ugly as a mule with mumps, my friend says, but warm and dry. Stop by any time."

Travis gave a deep laugh, which was startling for his age. "In about sixty-five years I'll be there, you watch. Have a big supper ready. I like everything but liver."

It fueled Wilson's day right through till five. And all the way home, she bore traffic gladly.

But Wesley wasn't there and wasn't there at bedtime.

HE'D WORKED TILL AFTER SIX ON A BMW THAT BELONGED to a man who taught Law at Vanderbilt, a man maybe ten years younger than Wesley but single and sporty. He was one of the scarce customers that liked to watch Wesley work and talked to him like an equal. Wesley had soon figured out from his well-fit clothes and slow needy eyes that the fellow had to be queer, but that had just got Wesley interested. From his first days in the Navy in Norfolk, he had been a steady queer target—sailors in general were, back then.

Nobody seemed to know whether it was the tight uniforms or their tendency to be knee-walking drunk or shore-leave or the fact that—being generally so horny by the time their feet touched firm ground—they were liable to say yes to the first offer they got for a good meal, some warmth and comfort, some kind personal attention, and relief. At first it had shocked hell out of Wesley, even hearing the older sailors discuss it as calm as they did. He had said right off that if a man ever touched him below the waist, he believed his skin would crawl right off his bones and head for home if he didn't kill the guy first. Or both.

But neither one had happened. He'd been out at a beer joint at Ocean View one Saturday night when the girls were extra awful. They were the kind you couldn't imagine handling, even with the recommended sack on their head. And he might have known, from the bathroom wall, he was in strange country. Over the urinal in neat handwriting, it said *Blow job $5.00. With lipstick $7.50.* After reading that Wesley was ready to thumb on back to base. But when he had paused long enough to button up all those complicated sailor-buttons and then walked back out into the big dark room, a normal-looking guy in a Harris-tweed jacket walked right up and handed him an open giant-sized can of beer. Wesley had grinned and said "How do I know this ain't poisoned?"

In dead earnest the guy said "You don't," took the can back, drank a long swig, and returned it to Wesley.

So Wesley laughed and said "Now how do I know *you* ain't poison?"

The guy said "Oh *I* am. I'm as queer as Uncle Harry's hatband. But I don't think it's catching unfortunately."

The guy looked about as queer as General MacArthur, so Wesley waited awhile to laugh. Finally he did. Then he drank the beer, felt calm, and a half-hour later was sitting in the guy's room at a swanky beach motel five miles farther south with a magic-fingers mattress and a framed picture of James Dean on the bureau (Dean had got killed just a few weeks before, so surely the picture didn't come with the room).

There they switched to harder stuff, the first bourbon of Wesley's young life. It tasted scary but he never showed it, never got drunk, never passed out anyhow, never reached a point where he lost control of his will. It surprised him more than his host, who had hoped for at least some signs of slackening. What Wesley was mainly conscious of was that a series of fences in his mind just silently fell down in lovely slow motion, like in a horserace movie, as the guy tried to jump them. Wesley watched it all from as far away as the guy himself—and both of them watched smilingly. Finally Wesley was naked as a peeled tadpole and stretched out grinning in the cool dry sheets. The guy kept his own briefs on but joined him enthusiastically for all the rest, the remainder of darkness and a fair part of dawn.

Wesley's later memory was that he'd lain on his back looking down through the hours as, by dim light that filtered through a crack in the bathroom door, the guy prowled and grazed over Wesley's body like something gentle but almost starved. Wesley estimated that he'd met the guy's every hope and need; the guy had anyhow kept saying "Incredible. Absolutely incredible." Wesley also knew that he personally had never been more thoroughly or skillfully pleased and honored than by that particular stranger's hands, that tireless mouth.

What he didn't remember was that, toward day, he'd gathered the guy—a smaller man then Wesley—into both his arms and held him near while the guy moaned and kicked toward his own destination in his own quick hands. Then they slept an hour. Then Wesley woke up entirely sober, and dressed, and left for base. He'd long since forgot the guy's name or home but could still hear his grateful moan toward daylight and see his dazed grin as Wesley waved goodbye and said again "Thanks."

The rest of his years in the Navy, Wesley had been with two other men. One was a five-hour stand in St. Tropez, France with a cheerful French picture-painter that didn't speak one single word of English (which proved no problem). One was a long cool weekend in Baltimore, completely indoors like something in a test tube but safe and with peaceful background music (the guy was an English teacher). Neither was as strangely peaceful and kind as the one near Norfolk, but both were still good enough to keep Wesley from joining his working mates through the years in their meaner queer jokes. There'd been no reason, in his years with Rosa, to turn back to men. The roar of his early manhood had cooled enough to let him focus fine again.

And women were the natural target of his aim—the harbor of his trip. It was mainly with women that he'd sometimes get the chime he aimed for and worked to hear, that thirty or forty seconds at the end when you've come on off and you know you've showed her your own big secret and witnessed hers. All it is, is everybody's same average secret—a sweaty thrill, eyes clenched, and some panting (though a good deal nicer than baseball for instance). But *average* doesn't mean that it's not worth striving for, not worth any decent form of chase.

Tonight though, March 1986, he'd toiled through a day with the gall on his neck of Wilson's refusal, her problems to discuss in one more session like those Rosacoke had made him dread—"What *you* don't notice, what *I* have to bear." So when the law professor pulled up in a cab to collect his car, Wesley went out to meet him with an open-faced grin.

They discussed the repairs, seven hundred dollars worth, in considerable detail (the fellow knew a lot more about cars than Wesley had guessed). Then the welcome fact of spring, then the lengthening days. Then Wesley had noticed what he'd noticed so often when queers came at him, the man's quick check for a wedding ring. Wesley had never worn one despite Rosa's urging. And when he caught the look, he frankly extended his left hand and spread it. "Nope. No more."

The professor said "Let me buy you a drink."

Wesley said "Thanks, doctor. I'm dirty as a dog."

"My friends call me Stanley, and I've got a shower." The absolute centers of his eyes were empty as some old open well in the country with a magnet buried deep in its heart, the kind of dark you could fall in forever.

Wesley saw that and heard him asking—dignified, brushed and combed but asking. When had anybody last asked for Wesley? Fifteen years maybe, more like twenty. So it cost Wesley little to say "I hope your water heater's set on high."

Stanley said "Old Faithful. Vesuvius."

Wesley said "All *right*" and felt two whole skins of

deadness slough off him. He had no idea what would break next. Going with this guy just meant *going*, one good drink of liquor at the absolute least. Not going back to Wilson's yet, that was the main thing. Wesley was running his own life again, which was two-thirds the reason he was out here at all in middle Tennessee—as poor an excuse for human habitation as he'd run up on in a traveled life.

SO HE FOLLOWED STANLEY TEN QUICK MINUTES IN HIS OWN car—a condo spacious enough for four, every wall hung with antique maps. Wesley took a long shower and, to his surprise, stepped readily into the clean jeans and shirt laid out on the bed by his old work clothes. Stanley was Wesley's exact size and was nowhere in sight. That by itself was the first surprise—he'd fully expected to be interrupted in the midst of his shower with a new bar of soap, some corny reason. Wesley whispered to the mirror "This dude *is* a lawyer." Then dressed and combed, he went out to find him.

Stanley had already poured two bourbons on the rocks big as baptismal pools and was waiting in the den. "You look like a bourbon man."

Wesley laughed. "I'm not a drinking man. But sure, tonight bourbon sounds like the ticket."

Stanley said "You celebrating something tonight?"

Wesley thought it out, then laughed and said "Abandonment."

"You or somebody else?"

"Let's just say both and quit while we're grinning." Wesley chose a deep white chair facing Stanley and managed not to panic when the cushion swallowed him.

With the born lawyer's deference to private rights,

Stanley nodded, then raised his glass in a toast and settled in his chair.

They drank bourbon for three quarters of an hour and listened to Barbra Streisand records in chronological order. Or so Stan said. Stan loved her but Wesley had always thought her outsized nose acted like a megaphone at unexpected wrong places in songs. So he didn't mention that, to him, they sounded more like whooping and hollering than actual music. He just kept thinking "That girl's mighty lonesome. Somebody go squeeze her." But it wouldn't be him; he was glad to sit quiet in a safe clean house and be his own man.

By the end of the Barbra stack, Stanley had worked his way through all the basic questions about Wesley's past—a good legal work-up, Wesley could tell.

And Wesley had answered honestly, amused to be asked. Everything—his parents, the Navy, Rosa, Horace, his jobs, his flight, right up to Wilson and this morning's quarrel. Nobody he could think of had ever taken that close a personal interest in the surface of his actions, not even Rosa. One more thing about these fellows, he thought—they can make a straight man feel dignified in a way few women even aim at. Since they aren't trying you out for the role of Prince Valiant or nest builder and daddy, they can afford to notice the more here-and-now parts of your life, like your hobbies. And they can sure, without ever mentioning it, make your face and body feel important again—more even than women in bars, who are much less concerned with sex here and now than in watching men spin at the end of their string.

Also Wesley had finished his third straight drink. He set down the glass and patrolled the inside lining of his skull to check was he drunk. Soft on the surface and his skin was beginning to burn all over but no, not drunk. And when Stan rose to refill the glass, Wesley said "No sir, you sit back down."

More than a little startled, Stan obeyed.

Wesley saw the perplexity and laughed. "Whoa. I ain't the Nashville Strangler. I just meant I've got to drive home eventually. If I stop now, I ought to be ready in an hour or so. If you got plans, go right on your way—I can sit out there in my car till I'm ready."

Stanley said "Not a plan in the world. Stay put. How would a two-inch filet mignon sound, about half an hour from now?"

Wesley waited to be sure firm ground was still under him. Then he met those eyes head-on and said "I bet it'll sound like my favorite hymn. But Stan, let me tell you—I'm an old ladies' man; you'd be wasting your money." He sat forward quickly and his eyes stayed clear.

They didn't do business this fast in law school; the need for lawyers would quit if they did. So Stan said "Can you wait while I pour some bourbon?"

Wesley said "Am I that hard to lose—old gator like me?"

That relaxed Stan some. He sat back and said "You're a breath of fresh air."

"*Fresh* I'm not but thanks for the compliment. I've just been a sailor and a strongly-built man for most of my years. I've met a few guys that liked my faculties, and I didn't see any cause to start slugging or call in a preacher and strike out for Hell. I'll be honest with you—I took two or three of them up on the deal, and I won't lie and say my life got twisted. I thanked them all; they were gentlemen

—though whether they were Christians or not, I can't say."

Stan smiled. "Episcopalians."

"Are you one too?"

"A Whiskeypalian?—no, God and I called it quits years back."

Wesley said "You still believe in Him and all though? I mean, you like pretty things too much to be an atheist." He looked round the room again—maps, books, antique chairs, a black statue of God's head and neck (or somebody bearded and equally solemn).

Stan smiled again. "Never heard it put that way. No, I guess you're right. But the church ships men like me off in flames, every Sunday on schedule."

Wesley said "Me too. If church calls the shots, I'll be in the sub-sub-basement of Hell. God's name though is Mercy; I heard that in vacation Bible school before I was ten. The lady that told me was a smart old maid; she'd read the Bible through three times, so I bank on that."

"You go every Sunday?"

Wesley said "Lord no, maybe once in two years and then just a funeral or wedding or such."

Stanley said "Then you think all the Bible is right?"

"I guess you don't."

"Saint Paul is the block in the road for me."

Wesley said "Which is he?"

"You know, all the letters—Thessalonians, Corinthians, the laws against everything—women, hair, gays."

Wesley said "I got Saint Paul's number way back when. See, he never met Jesus like Peter and them. So he had to pedal extra hard to make up for that. And me, I'm happier than most grown men; but couldn't you fellows let us have *gay* back? We haven't got all that many words left."

"But you just said you've gone with men."

For a moment it seemed Wesley couldn't remember. Then he said "That was back before steam."

"Never too late again."

Wesley said "*Me*? I'm old as your daddy, stringy and gray."

"More like a brother. You're doing all right." Stan smiled and left to refill his glass two whole rooms away.

Alone, Wesley shut his eyes and at once saw himself upright on a prairie, though he'd never been any place west of Kentucky. He saw no other live human being. He was in khaki pants and the dark blue sweater he'd won in high school; it seemed to be winter. The sky was tin gray and a cold hard wind blew through his dry hair and left his skin tight and sad—how sad? He sat on, blinded, and wondered at the vision till he knew again what he'd felt this morning, with Wilson at sunrise. Every pore in his skin was yearning for touch, some human brand of courteous service with a few quiet jokes. His own shut mind spoke silently "This skin is lonesome, son."

Stanley was back. He went to his chair, set his drink on the table but stayed upright; Wesley's face had changed in the absence. Stan said "You sure you need to leave?"

That somehow shook Wesley; he felt caught out. An instant later he felt a sick guilt, though guilt was as rare in Wesley as Spanish. Every minute he stayed on here was a lie to this kind gentleman, a regular customer. But the way it came when he finally spoke was "What would a fellow, not forty like you, see in me? You can do far better on the downtown market."

Stan said "AIDS."

Wesley said "Beg your pardon?" (he'd of course heard

the word; but as late as that a spring, it was still not a term on everybody's lips).

"The plague," Stan said. "Anybody like me on the downtown market is begging to die. A clean straight man with standards like yours and eyes that dark with a human I.Q. is a spring in the desert—simple as that."

The candor brought Wesley back down fast. He pulled in his gut, thrust his chin forward, and then said "Doctor, you got me wrong. I was all but a virgin till late December. For going on thirty years, I'd been with one woman—give or take a misstep. But here since New Year's I've been, like I said, with a Nashville girl that has had two husbands and isn't a tramp but is no nun either. I haven't been tested so I can't guarantee I'm not strowing death every time I grin."

Stanley smiled. "You've got a big grin, I agree. But everybody says now that smiles don't spread it or sneezes and coughs, just contaminated body fluids in the blood."

"And you gay fellows are dropping like doves."

Stan smiled. "Many thanks—for the doves anyhow; most people say *flies*. So far I've just lost one old friend—died in New York six weeks ago, his brain reamed out by a cat parasite that almost every child's had and thrown off. In the first few weeks, he kept calling me and saying that maybe a trip down here would bring his strength back. I hemmed and hawed and he got the point. Or had gone past knowing my number and name."

Wesley's head was clearing by the minute now; he sat well forward so his voice could keep low and still be heard. "And you still brought a strange crossroads mechanic back to this handsome spread and hoped he'd help you? Christ Jesus, Stan." Wesley didn't sit back but stayed there nearer.

Stanley stayed deep in his chair. "You found your woman, knowing she'd been around. Am I all that strange?"

Wesley said "You're the one with the well-trained mind, so don't hesitate to say I'm wrong. But here this minute now, for the first clear time, I feel like the world's in for some grade of Hell worse than we've ever seen, and I've seen whores in North Africa eat *out* with maggots—I mean blind maggots boiling in sores—and them still selling their ass half-price. Something right now, since you mentioned your friend, just speaks down in me and says we'll be there in a New York minute."

Stanley said "Worse" and waited to drink, then said "And it may outlast us both."

Wesley sat back, heavy as if struck down. One thing about him had outlasted time—Stan mentioned his eyes; they'd stayed that keen, no glasses ever. From there, ten feet away, he saw Stanley's birthmark—the first time yet. It was almost down in the collar of his shirt, the color of walnut and hen-egg size. And seeing it there did less for Wesley than the sight of a mile-high bird on columns of heat in a summer day. But he thought "He's despised that mark all his life. I can reach out and touch him, right there on the place. It won't cost me a thin red cent. He might just be my brother or cousin; he won't misread me. I can do that much." Wesley didn't think why and he stood up to do it.

But Stan held his palm up. "You know you got to eat. Let's cook those steaks."

Wesley said "You may not believe me now; but country as I am, I eat steak rare."

Stanley said "I believe you. Come and tell me when it's done."

Wesley said "That's easy. Just listen up close, then when it barely stops mooing—"

THEY ATE AT NINE WITH A BOTTLE OF CALIFORNIA BUR-gundy and talked like members of the same old family—long quiet minutes with the clink of silver, then brief remarks on food or weather or the world and local news. Then they went to the den again and watched the first half of *Gone with the Wind* on television. At the end, when Scarlett tried to eat the radish but threw it up and then vowed endurance for her and hers, the camera flew back; the music swelled up, and Wesley's eyes opened (he had snoozed off and on). He said what he always thought at that point "If Scarlett O'Hara had been Jeff Davis, we'd be free now."

Stan was from smalltown northern Ohio so he withheld comment, but he was tired too. He got to his feet and said "Are you welcome at home tonight?"

The word *home* almost made Wesley flinch, and he said "—Welcome to a razor fight."

So Stanley offered two simple choices—sleep with him in the king-sized bed or alone in the guestroom, small but clean. He also said "Either place, you're safe—I don't sleepwalk or haven't yet."

Wesley smiled. "Don't worry. I got my brass knucks." He didn't of course but it helped him to say so.

In the guest bathroom Stan laid out towels, a new toothbrush still sealed in a box, and a clean black comb; then went his own way.

Wesley focused his mind the best he could on the here and now—this well-kept place and its kind proprietor. Imagine keeping a backstock of toothbrushes; this man had to be desperate or a saint. In under ten minutes Wesley shucked his clothes and, naked as ever, was asleep on the wine before he finished the whole Lord's Prayer. From somewhere farther off than Mars, he thought he heard Stan's voice say "Night." He knew he should answer and he earnestly tried, but no words came—just deep brown rest.

Sometime after three though his eyes clicked open, wide awake. Stan had left on a light far back in the house; it crept round the half-shut door and told Wesley where he was. Thoroughly sober, he asked himself was this a mistake? Would anybody hear about this and misread him? To hell with anybody; he was now his own boss. So he lay on easy and listened to the space. Was Stan up walking; was that what had waked him? Nothing but the normal sounds of a building breaking apart by millimeters. Should he rise now, dress, and creep on out? If Stan woke up, he could just say thanks. But where would he go this late?—not to Wilson's and risk finding her with somebody else or locked in with all her deadbolts and chains.

The thing that bothered Wesley most, lying there quiet, was the sense that any instant now the black net would close on his face and mouth—the terrible sadness he'd known here lately. If that should land on him now, God help him; could he stand it alone? Till now he'd never had to. *Head it off*. How? Leaving meant riding around in the dark or finding an all-night cafe open or renting a room in some motel.

He stood up quietly and put on everything but his shoes. Then he took one pillow and the heavy spread and walked up the hall to Stanley's door. It was fully open and the sounds that came were all but snores—good. Wesley crept on in to the foot of the high bed and laid his covers on the floor beneath it. Fine—he'd managed without waking Stan. But when he knelt, both knees cracked like rifles. He winced in the dark but covered himself.

Then Stan said "Is that where you really want to be?"

"Absolutely. Thank you."

"And you're feeling all right?"

Wesley said "No I'm a miserable worm."

Stanley said "I'd apologize for all that bourbon but you're twenty-one."

Wesley nodded in the dark. "You've been good to me."

"Anything I can help with?"

"Thanks again, no sir." Wesley waited a long time. "Unless you're some brand of angel in disguise."

"It's really that bad?"

"Yes. I'm scared."

Stan said "Not of me. Forget it."

Wesley said "I'm not scared of you, just my whole life. I'm a man with too many problems here now. You don't need to know everything, not yet. See, I've been a boy with no more troubles than a rock in the road, but lately the rock's been learning to worry."

Stan said "Isn't this about normal for the course, men past forty? I'm moving in on it, not many yards behind."

"And you're this lonesome here alone. Doesn't this lonesome life get you down?"

Stan waited to think. "No more than yours, I guess. It's just a real life—same troubles, different names."

"You never been married?"

Stanley laughed. "That was one disaster I somehow missed."

Wesley said "It's got its points."

"Like what?"

A real wait and then Wesley laughed. "I'll think of one soon." Another wait and then Wesley asked "Ever think you'd just as soon *pass* on the rest of it, sit it out?"

"Not but once a minute," Stan said. Then he said "Say your prayers."

Coming from a lawyer, that raised a laugh but Wesley obeyed. And when he'd finished he was worse than before. He got up, went to the single window, and tried to look west toward Wilson's trailer. Whatever he expected, he got no strong transmission through the dark. If she missed him, Wilson was blasting no wail. He even faced round the opposite way—Rosa his wife. Nothing again.

In his whole life till now, had it ever been worse? He'd torn up every root of his past and run, and now where was he all these months later? Great God, in a room with a lonesome lawyer trained to the ears and hungry for men when men were illegal and might well now be poison and death. Another fine life. Wesley stepped closer to the window blinds and tilted them wider. In the thin starlight he could see a stretch of thick grass below. Grand!—if he jumped to die, he'd land in soft grass.

Stan understood from that far away. He said "We could get up and drink some milk. Or I could lie down there near you, in sight. Would that help any?"

At once Wesley said "You get your sleep. You'll need it tomorrow." And then in the silence, he thought of lying under sheets next to Stan—not touching but there. The thought wouldn't work; he was aimed at women. And even though, years ago, his firm brown hide had not been allergic to any well-meaning earthly touch, women were the only real magic for Wesley, in the visible world (he hoped to see God, though he'd never realized it).

So asking for help from a grown man this late in life seemed stranger than trying to understand your bird dog by learning to bark. He actually shook his head and smiled, then quietly counted Stanley's breathing. Under the numbers he kept on thinking of Stanley's life, guessing at its particular trials. Another pitiful fool like himself, old enough to have good sense but down in the dust still grappling for food.

Every audible voice in Wesley's world had told him to run from any such nearness—or stand and fight it. But here again he'd come this close. No one could see; no one would know. So what did he feel? The count of Stan's breath had got to three hundred. Stan was plainly out but Wesley kept thinking.

What did he feel? He tried to think a clear path back to his times with men—like silent wrestling in a dark sack not quite big enough—but no feeling came. Past pleasure is gone as fast as pain; in his own way he knew that and thought *Thank God*. Why would anybody ever reach out again, if all the good past could still be enjoyed?

Wesley's count was up around four-eighty-five when a voice in his mind again spoke clearly—"Nobody you love will pay for this." Till then he hadn't really known such a worry—or owned up to it. But whatever spoke the calm assurance spread down on him like a warm blanket, and he sank on into the same deep solitude as Stanley beyond him.

BETWEEN THEN AND DAYLIGHT WESLEY WATCHED A LONG dream—a world where nobody ever touched again, for bodily pleasure or in hopes of a child, never again from birth to death. All were locked in permanent transparent armor as tight as natural skin so that everybody still looked normal but could never step free. That way they were safe, and though it kept them from talking or smiling or eating their meals, the world kept on otherwise the same. The sight didn't wake him, so he rested till sunup—one more whole day and Wesley still upright.

WHEN WESLEY GOT TO THE TRAILER THAT EVENING, WILson wasn't in. But the bed was unmade from the night before, so he knew she'd slept here and would no doubt be back. When she still wasn't in by dark, he broke out the fifth of bourbon he hadn't touched in weeks and poured a stiff drink. In his life till then, Wesley probably hadn't drunk ten ounces alone. And he promised himself it wouldn't be a habit. But tonight it felt like a useful companion. It got him through the televised news and the first dumb hour of comedy.

Then he thought he heard a car pull up. He waited for a hand on the door. But nothing, false alarm. Five minutes later he pulled his hand back from the telephone, dialing Rosa's number. Why be mean to her just to soothe his nerves? But then he dialed Stanley. Three rings, four—

what on earth would he say if Stan answered? He couldn't go there two nights in a row. He hung up fast.

THREE HARD HOURS, THE MOST TIME ALONE THAT WESley'd had since Christmas week before he met Wilson. The worst time maybe of his life till then. But he took it sitting down, knowing that was the way—not twiddling or running. At eleven o'clock he finally said a prayer. Still seated firmly in the La-Z-Boy rocker, he said "Lord, I quit. *I* don't know how." He stayed in place, head back and eyes shut. He hoped he could weep and bleed off the pressure. But too many dry-eyed years stretched behind him to make tears easy. So he tried press-ups on the arms of the chair, imagining he'd lost the use of his legs.

Like Willis Shearin, the old shortstop on his high-school team, who'd been in a car wreck; his spine had been crushed. He couldn't feel anything below his two nipples and not one cell in his legs or feet worked. Not for motion at least, though they sent pain through him like squirrels through a maze. After a minute of such self-deception, Wesley felt panic seize him. Stop this right now or you'll scream pretty soon.

But he didn't. He went on pressing up faster and faster, his legs *were* dead, pain raced through his trunk like squirrels on an interstate. Now his lungs wouldn't work. He tried to scream but no air came. Nothing to do but work on alone. When he'd done a strong dozen more press-ups, a car stopped. Then the car door slammed—no doubt this time.

Then Wilson stood there, still in her work clothes, her work badge on. Her face was tired and two shades paler, but oh she looked fine. He'd forgot how fine. He was still pressing up. So he paused in midair.

"You lost it?" she asked.

"Yes, lady. I'm a sad lonesome cripple. I've lost my legs." To Wesley's amazement, tears sprang up. He flopped back down in the chair and laughed.

Wilson held her ground by the door, ready to turn and leave. But it was her home. So she came on toward him and sat in a straight chair. "You look all right otherwise. What hit you?"

Wesley forced himself not to wipe his eyes. He said "Nothing really. I was just exercising. You caught me at it."

"But you're crying too."

"I been missing you."

She smiled and sang a little bar of music to match their rhyme. But then she went grim again. "You let yourself in here knowing I was gone?"

"I did, yes ma'm. You hadn't changed the locks."

Wilson thought, then nodded. "Fair enough."

"I took a night off. I think you know why."

Wilson asked "How many more of those you planning to take?"

Wesley said "Can't say. It depends on a lot."

"Then you better head out now for good. I can't have no part-time man, let me tell you. I've told you already—I'm all or nothing."

"I understand that. But maybe we could talk?"

Wilson said "There's not a whole hell of a lot to say, if you don't want to be here."

"I never said that. I said I'm somebody with a lot of

trouble to get through. That shouldn't be news to anybody near me."

Wilson said "It's not. But we'd agreed to talk last night, I thought. I came here and waited and you never showed. So guess how I felt—guilty as sin."

Wesley said "You weren't. Shame on you."

"Want to say where you went?"

He said "No ma'm, I don't. It was not to hurt you or make you guilty."

"Won't you want to know where I've gone, if I ever fail you?"

"Wilson, if we ever make each other the big promise, then sure. Till—and if—we do, you can plan your life however you need to."

"And that won't hurt you?"

"Sure it will. I'm a person, not a stainless-steel wrench. But when I left my wife three months ago, I gave up my rights to make such a claim—on her or anybody."

"You like this life?" She waved around her. "Us here, like this?"

"I loved it, yes ma'm, till yesterday morning. I thought we were fine. It was you changed the tune."

Wilson said "I had to. I waited too long."

"But you let me think you enjoyed my body. It was one big part of what I loved about us. Women need to understand that about men."

"And vice versa. Women need different things, this one at least."

Wesley nodded. "I've watched television—I think I know. And I mean, I haven't brought you home any Cold Duck or cut flowers for candlelight dinners, but I've done

all I could imagine to let you know you've been a big help
to me at this time of life."

Wilson nodded but still couldn't make herself smile.
"Everything but the one last promise I need."

"To move here finally and marry you?"

"That's about it."

Watching her still face, expectant as a dry field in a hot
day, Wesley suddenly knew his answer. The last two days
had formed it in his mind with no help from him. He said it
straight out. "I'd be glad to stay on like this indefinitely,
like the life we had till yesterday anyhow. But if what
you're calling for is a divorce and a wedding, then I can't
help you right now. In the first place, a North Carolina
divorce takes a year's genuine separation. In the second
place, after so many years of goodness, I owe my wife at
least a face-to-face visit to tell her my plans and see to her
future. I need to see my son. I've got a few things back
there that matter to me; I'd need to rent a truck and bring
them here."

Wilson waited to be sure he was finished. "Then can't
you say you plan to do all that and set a firm date?"

Again he knew the answer. After the early evening
panic, it was cooler than he'd guessed. "No, Wilson, I
can't."

She could meet his eyes, but she couldn't find words.
Finally he said "You want me to pack?"

She looked at her watch, honestly unsure. It was too
close to midnight to throw him out, and she didn't know if
she wanted to risk a second night in a dark field alone. So
she said "It's too late to find a motel. Stay in the little room
and then go tomorrow."

Wesley thought again of calling Stanley but then decided no. That could have its own troubles big as any here. He knew it would be hard to sleep separate from her, but he had no choice. She was offering a kindness. He couldn't make waves now and try to swamp her. He thanked her and stood up. "You sleepy?"

"Ought to be—I worked a double shift—but no, I'm not."

"Me neither. We could watch a movie."

THEY WOUND UP MAKING A BUSHEL OF POPCORN AND watching *The Three Stooges' Greatest Hits*. The ninety minutes of head-bonking farce eventually broke through their mutual blues and had them finally laughing like children. Still at the end Wilson stood up quickly, washed the empty bowl, and went to her room. Not so much as "Good night."

Not till he went to the tiny guest-cubicle did Wesley realize that his clothes were Stanley's. He'd put them off and back on at work without thinking. Wilson hadn't mentioned them; had she noticed the difference? Was it some secret plan of Stan's this morning—to let him wear them knowing he'd have to call and bring them back? Never mind; he could leave them on the porch some day at noon and just abandon his own to Stanley.

He laid them neatly on the one folding chair and, naked, climbed in the narrow cot. The wall between him and Wilson was cardboard; he could all but hear her breathing, then sleeping. He nearly prayed that she change heart and join him or call him at least. But it seemed unfair to try to set God against her. So he blessed them both and again all his family and this time Stanley. Then he waited for sleep.

It didn't arrive. Instead came a long wave of pictures of

Rosa. Still not recalling his earlier dream, Wesley would
no more have bet on that than on late snow. But here came
a chain of memories of Rosa, all clear silent pictures. All
moving backward more or less through the years from this
past December to the first real meeting with her he remembered (not the one she remembered, with him up the tree,
but almost two entire years later at Warrenton in school
with her stumbling into the football fieldhouse by mistake
—looking for the home ec. building—and seeing him
upright there in his jock).

Wesley had quickly covered his crotch with big hands,
but Rosa held her ground in the dim doorway and said "I
always catch you wrong."

He'd said "Lady, ain't nobody *caught* me yet. When she
does, it'll be the rightest catch of her life."

And she'd said "Stuck up" but apparently believed him
and set out to catch his soul and body then and there.

What waylaid him tonight, in the time it took, was the
discovery of Rosa's early beauty. That child had been special—and not just her long straw hair and blue eyes so big
they threatened to fall right out of her face but the power
she gave off steady as voltage. There were some boys who
did not see it at all. More than one of them made fun of her
for being a solemn sort of Pilgrim mother and smarter than
any three of them. But Wesley saw past that plainly to her
real power and felt it from the start.

That first day when she said "Stuck up," he went
straight over to her—still in his wet jock—and said "Take
me down a whole notch then, lady. See if you can."

She'd said "Shoot, Bo, I got better plans" and walked
off pretending not to know his name or anyhow not to be
already dreaming his face and voice four nights a week,

her entire future, the thing she intended every day of her life (once that life began, which now it could).

Could Wesley use that at all, here and now in this spot? Unlike Rosa and every other woman he'd known, he couldn't linger long in memory for its own sake. Memory had to tell him something he could bring on forward and make work now for good sense and present help. It was one thing to realize your wife had been special thirty-odd years ago; what good was that now?

He didn't know a lot about archeology, but he suspected he was stuck on a kind of ancient dig—sweeping off layers of sand or barnacles, hoping to find a firm core left in an old thing he'd honored and used but that now was near ruined (by him, he granted). Could he find anything deep down in it that he still felt a present need to know and tend? Or sound fiscal practice—why in the world walk off for good from an investment as big and long-standing as his and Rosacoke's?

Only if it gave him new life again. Only if the core of the dug-up statue still showed enough of its old strength and draw. How could he gauge that from this far away? Was it time now to hit the road back east and check out the air? Would Rosa even see him, much less take him back if he wanted to come? Should he get up right now, go to a pay phone and call her up, ask permission to visit? Should he wait till daylight and then write a short note asking the same? It was his own house too. He still paid half the mortgage every month. Why the hell not drive up and unlock the door?

By then Wesley had thought his way through the hours till his watch said two in the morning. So much reasoning, on top of the outlay with Stanley and Wilson, had finally sapped him. If he hadn't already been laid out flat on a decent mattress, he'd have fallen far from a dangerous height and crushed every bone. As it was, he slept like a child—that desperate, sucking up every instant of sleep like the food of life itself and hope.

BUT THE NEXT AFTERNOON WESLEY PACKED UP HIS FEW duds at Wilson's, took her out for supper at Bar-B-Cutie, didn't say a word about sadness or permanence, kept her smiling, and delivered her safe to the trailer at ten.

Wilson didn't say "Come in" or ask another question or flinch even once.

Wesley honored her style and stood up outside the driver's door as she walked away. He waited till she found her key, stepped inside, and lit the porch light. She didn't look back to smile or wave, but he waved once and heard her lock the door inside before he drove off.

On the way into town, he waited for the hurt to start. Apparently something real had ended, some way toward life. But all he could feel for Wilson was thanks. So what if she'd slammed him hard this week?—back at the start of this new year, she'd shown him again how much he could mean; how good he could feel in the right arms saying the few right words. If he'd found Wilson easy as that, in a downtown motel lounge stuffed with drunks and hookers, then wasn't there all the more reason to hope life still had Wesley Beavers in mind with some better women?

For old time's sake he went back into the same motel and had a drink in the lounge, all but empty tonight. Nobody looked his way; nobody came over. And when he ordered the second drink, he thought he'd finish that and, if nobody good had turned up, he'd rent a room upstairs and sleep again in the place where he'd started this new life.

But the drink ran out and nobody came, and Wesley couldn't make himself register here. He paid his tab, walked out, and wove a careful way through traffic across the street and a block ahead to the reinforced concrete Parthenon. Wesley knew very little about the original building or Athens or Greece or the virgin goddess of wisdom herself, gray-eyed helmeted daughter of Zeus with owl and spear.

But he had good eyes and an ample but wary supply of awe. And this full-scale replica of the great temple— brought down from its native granite mountain and westward five thousand miles to be set up on a green flat lawn in Nashville, floodlit now on an early spring evening— was sufficient to confirm the gradual happiness that had crept back through him these past twelve weeks.

He was more than half sober, but he wanted somehow to express his gratitude. He'd never been all that good in the past at offering thanks when thanks were due for life's better times. He didn't want to let this night go by without a way to speak what he felt—that Wesley Beavers was *coming through*; that whatever person or place lay before him, Wesley now believed it was all for the best. He knew he'd, some way, tie it all up and make it work from now to the grave—a long way off with him an old man.

With that grand building glowing above him the color of honey on a purple sky, those high bronze doors like gates to Heaven (or surely not Hell), he suddenly regretted how bad he'd been in the seventh damned grade when Miss Jennie Alston made them memorize poems; and he'd hung back and mumbled smiling nonsense to deceive her. Something like the one about World War I, "In Flanders Field," seemed the ticket here tonight (it had always moved Miss Jennie to tears, and she was as tough as a lightwood knot)—

> To you from failing hands we throw the torch;
> Be yours to hold it high!

But he couldn't say the rest. So he waited five minutes in the far rim of trees, queers, and whores circling round him in cars with their windows rolled down. And finally he knew it, a way to speak.

Wesley climbed straight up the steps toward the doors (three times his height), slow as any actor to the stage or killer to the gallows. He turned toward the floodlights. Then blinded by glare and what may have been tears, he said the thing he knew by heart "The Lord is my shepherd. I shall not want"—all the way through to "I shall dwell in the house of the Lord forever."

He faced back and wondered if in any useful way an imitation concrete temple like this was a house of the Lord. But he didn't feel wrong in his general purpose or the text of his thanks. He touched the flank of the nearest pillar and then kissed the hand. As he stepped back down to the warm damp grass, from one of the dark circling cars came the clear noise of two hands clapping and a whistling cheer. He bowed and grinned to whoever praised him.

WHILE WESLEY WAS SLEEPING PEACEFULLY THAT SAME night on the east edge of Nashville in a mom-and-pop motel called *Quo Vadis*, Rosa woke up in Raleigh, crept downstairs in her blue nightgown, and wrote this letter that she mailed the next morning.

March 22, 1986

Dear Wesley,

It has been over two months since I wrote to you last time. In the meanwhile you've been loyal with the checks but of course no news. I've had a lot of news here too, that I've kept to myself. Every woman I've talked to says I'd be a big fool to break down now and start talking to you again.

But the simple fact is you're about the only friend I've had since I grew up, and just in the last week I've felt more and more like if I can't talk to you then I'll likely bust. I've long since gone past being mad at you or constantly asking why? What I mainly feel now is how much I miss you.

Maybe one of your problems here was the way we had got to being like two old dogs in the same yard bumping up against each other at feeding time and curling up together in the cold night for warmth, not much else. Maybe it's not enough to live like dogs, even after nearly thirty years. Still it was a lot more than most people have, to my eyes anyhow. And I'm aching, buddy.

So here is some backdated news from Raleigh, N.C. It's sent by way of filling you in on friends and family, not as a set of warnings or threats or even prayers.

On New Year's Eve I got home early from a party at Jean and Hal's and turned straight in. A few hours later a completely strange (I think) man broke in, found me upstairs in our old bed, and was hacking on me before I really woke up. —With his body, I mean, not any kind of knife.

My mind ran through all the possibilities. Was it maybe you? Anyhow when I couldn't stand it an instant longer, I tried to throw him and succeeded. At that point of course he could have bent back down and strangled or stabbed me. But after he paused to look, he ran. Since then I've had a weird phone call or two, a couple of stopped cars outside at four in the morning, but nothing worse.

For good reasons of my own, I didn't call the police. And I still haven't told anybody but Mama, Rato, and Milo. Rato then volunteered to move up here awhile and live with me—which is what he's been doing ever since, to my considerable relief. We have worked out a right good arrangement.

And Mama, even at her age, seems none the worse for staying out there in the country alone. Your mother does the same and thrives on it. Maybe we'll all have to eventually. I'm thinking it'll be time soon now to get Rato moved on back to the country before he gets too used to city life. We've had one of those phone taps on the line for weeks now, and no other weirdos have called, so I begin to feel like I may be safe again.

Otherwise that's about it, no more big events. I haven't so much as had a date and don't especially want to. I don't say that to punish you. I'm assuming you're still there with your new friend, and I guess I can try to stand straight here and pull my collar up neat and wish you luck with whoever helps you onward. It's either that or "Screw you, you vicious ungrateful thieving hound," isn't it? And since I don't remember ever saying that word in public before, I won't start now. Also I don't really feel it—not yet, not more than one or two minutes a day most weeks.

I'm trusting you haven't run up against anything as rough as I did. (Do men, outside prison anyhow, ever get raped?) Now that I've written this far, I can look back and wonder why and whether or not I'll mail it. I don't honestly think I'm asking for pity or to make you feel guilty—I know you are not to blame. I really do think it's what I said first, that I can't help believing we were each other's oldest closest friends. And I just want my few friends to know the best and worst about me.

So now you know the worst. "The best is yet to be." Or so I'm leaning on. I don't even try to think back to the last time I was thoroughly happy, for more than two minutes. But then they never guaranteed joy, right? Anytime I feel like throwing my head back and howling at the moon, I can flip on the evening news and watch a few hundred thousand Ethiopian children starve in the comfort of my all-electric clean formica

*kitchen or another whole block of houses in Beirut crumble to
dust with all hands aboard.*

You ever do the same?

Want to be pen pals? You know my address.

An old friend,
Rosa

Two days later at lunch time, Wilson stopped by the
service station and delivered the letter (the only address
Rosa had for Wesley was the trailer).

He thanked her and offered to buy her a Coke.

Wilson flashed her best smile but said she had plans.

Wesley asked "You all right?"

She said "Bet on it."

Wesley laughed and told her if anybody came around
offering odds, he'd take her tip. And she roared off. So he
bought himself a drink, sat down in the Volvo he was fixing, and read the letter. Much as he disliked reading, he
didn't budge till he got to the sentence where Rosa exoner-
ated him of all responsibility for her rape. He'd read all he
could for the moment at least. He folded the letter, hid it in
his pocket, and stepped back out into full sunlight. In another minute he walked over to the Exxon sign by the road
and flopped down there on the ground at its base.

His boss, a kind old giant named Buster, shambled over.
"That gal must of sawed you off at the knees."

Wesley said "She'd like to but no, not today she didn't."
He stopped there, hoping Buster would leave. What he
needed this minute was time to crank his brain; it had
stalled just now. He was blank as if a crowbar had leaned
from the lowest cloud and struck him.

Instead Buster pulled out his thirty-eighth Kool of the day and lit it. "You need some time off?"

Wesley thought "That's bound to be God" (meaning Buster's offer). His brain caught fire. He said "Thank you, yes."

"You'll be leaving town?" Buster vaguely knew Wesley had ties in Carolina.

"Very likely, yes."

Buster said "All right. Draw a week's advance pay. If your business takes longer than that, call and tell me. You're as good a mechanic as I've ever known, and I'd sure hate to lose you. Can you work through till six?"

Wesley had worked for good bosses before, but nobody else ever went far as this. He reached up for Buster's right hand, shook it, then let Buster help him to his feet. Then Wesley said "Nobody ever outbid you. If there's any way on God's earth I can live here, you'll see me in a week. If not, I'll repay you."

Buster said "A deal."

JUST AFTER SIX WESLEY DROVE TO THE QUO VADIS MOTEL, showered and shaved again, and paid his bill. As he walked out of the office, he thought "I should have called Wilson and let her know." He could go back now and do it on the pay phone; she'd be home. But what could he tell her for sure? And since *sure* was all she wanted to hear from him, then he had nothing for her. He drove on to the first gas station, filled up, checked his oil and tires, and wove his slow way to the interstate eastward.

As he came off the ramp into speeding traffic, the clock said 7:05 p.m. There was still a weak wash of lilac in the sky low down near the ground. With any luck at all, from

God and the humans and this car beneath him, Wesley ought to be home before Rosa woke up. He thought the clear word *home*, then changed it to *there*, then changed it once more to *Rosa's house*. Wherever, he was moving. It didn't feel bad. If he got tired he'd stop and sleep a few hours or days or weeks. Nobody expected him, free as a bird.

Then Wesley thought again *Rosa*. Raped in his bed in the house he'd deserted not three weeks before, a woman who'd done him not one bad turn in nearly forty years— not purposely at least. He suddenly felt responsible. His abandonment of the woman he'd promised to guard had set the world free to turn on her with its own vile plans. He'd said more than once to boys at work that if his wife should ever get raped, he doubted he'd want to touch her again.

It hadn't crossed his mind that he'd be the cause, that his own fear of death and a cold soft peter might flush him off his sworn place strong at Rosa's side and leave her open to any hungry boy with the power of hate. Now it struck Wesley with the weight of a cold steel office-safe dropped on his head from a building at dawn. Blame and guilt were not Wesley's suit. He could accept blame whenever he saw he'd caused a fault, but then he wouldn't spend five minutes howling. He'd concentrate on finding the way to prevent a repeat.

HE WAS ON THE WESTERN RIM OF THE MOUNTAINS WHEN HE saw that the only hope this time was to park up next to Rosa again and literally shield her. Rato was all right for short spells of duty. But Rato had never sworn to stay for long years of this. And anyhow Rato's pitiful brain couldn't handle something complicated as a felon in the shrubbery, not to mention the bed.

Was Wesley ready for that much again? Had a little more than three months out on the road been enough to revive him and strengthen his soul to stay the remainder of a life with Rosa? And if he could, then what about her? She'd written that letter not a whole week ago, warm and open. But one letter wasn't face-to-face forever.

He replayed his memory of the first nights with Wilson, the bones of his mind truly pulverized by thanks for her goodness. The strength she restored to his arms and legs that truly had been at the door of death. The picture was still bright and dark enough in memory, still rank enough with odor, to bring him quickly to readiness here on a black highway with trucks roaring past him the size of bombers at the near speed of sound. No fourteen-year-old kid in bed in the distant cabins beyond him on the highway, locked in with inflamed *Hustler* girls to the sounds of Mama downstairs in the kitchen scraping dishes for the sink, was primed more hopefully than he was now.

As Wesley entered the long slow first mountain-climb then, he set his automatic pilot for sixty, opened his jeans, gently freed his cock from the clean tight drawers, and met its need as only he knew it—grinning at the cheap but complicated thrill. He hadn't done this since leaving the Navy, he was almost sure.

As he got near the ridge, of the rise and his joy, he thought "If women knew how many grown men are out here stroking their lonesome dicks—and all but losing control of their cars just past the speed limit—they'd stay home baking those good cakes and pies, not risking their necks on personal fulfillment."

When he came, he bent low over the wheel to watch the seed bloom up in his fist by green panel light—the beautiful calm that spread up through him from heels to head like cream in coffee. Then he cleaned himself with a warm bandanna, turned on the radio, and sang for ten miles— Kenny Rogers, sad and sweet.

You picked a fine time to leave me, Lucille—
With four hungry children and crops in the field.

Since Wesley had never had a moment's uncertainty about his own gender, he imagined he was Lucille trucking back home toward four wormy kids and one sorry man. She was glad to oblige, having had her break in motel lounges and mobile-home beds under willing hot souls. She almost figured she could see it through now, all the long years ahead till death did her part.

By the time he reached the downward side of that broad crest, Wesley guessed he'd accepted the pull of fate. He knew anyhow that he barely held the wheel. The car was taking itself and him where they needed to go, which was Rosa's house—goddammit still his.

AT A LITTLE BEFORE MIDNIGHT ON THE NEAR SIDE OF ASHE-ville, Wesley pulled off finally to eat a little supper. He'd waited through a lot of hungry hours to get to this particular stop, the place where back in December a waitress had sent him to Nashville. He knew she couldn't be working tonight, but the first thing he saw when he entered the hot glare was her busy body in the far corner serving a family of six. He went toward her and asked if one of her tables was vacant.

She said "Number four" and pointed but gave no sign of recognition.

That cut him down a little, but he sat anyhow and studied the old menu.

When she got free in three minutes, she came with iced water and a sudden big smile. "How was Nashville, old son?"

Wesley grinned. "You remember?"

"Forget *you*, boy? I often forget my own name and number, but a good-looking man late at night—not me. I got a big file of faces in here" (she reached through her pink spun-sugar bouffant and tapped her skull hard). "Gives me a lot of fun. Course I don't tell Sam."

"Sam's your husband?"

"Never mind. Sam's the adult man that thinks he owns my butt. He's kidding himself but I don't aim to tell him; I enjoy his laugh. I asked you a question though—how was your trip?"

"Very fine," Wesley said. "What the doctor prescribed."

"You look healed," she said. "Well, no extra charge."

"You from Nashville yourself?"

She said "Oh no. Never even been there. That night you slouched in here looking dead, I just thought Nashville had to be your place. I've always thought it had to be Heaven. How was Opry Land?"

Wesley told her "The best," though he hadn't gone near it.

She didn't press for details. She said "How hungry are you?"

"Enough to eat a polecat."

"Ever tried it?" she asked.

"In my sweet boyhood."

"They're not what they used to be," she said, "—not nearly. Want me to bring what you need again?"

He remembered she'd ordered for him before. "Sure. But no chicken-fried steaks this time."

She stepped back and frowned. "Did I say you needed anything strong as that?"

"No, I grant you. I just feel different tonight."

"I can see that, I told you. Leave it to me."

TWENTY MINUTES LATER—FIVE SONGS ON THE JUKE BOX— she came back with barbecued chicken, boiled rice, string beans, a salad, and a basket of Parker House rolls. Wesley told her it was perfect. And it proved to be.

When he'd also finished the lemon pie and drunk more coffee, her work slacked off again. She joined him in the booth and lit a cigarette. "You headed *back* somewhere big, ain't you?"

"My wife." He nodded. "In Raleigh, still waiting. So I trust."

"Whose idea was leaving?"

Wesley said "Mine."

"She's waiting then."

He laughed and asked "You ever been wrong?"

She laughed "Oh sure but just about me. Everybody else is a plain open book."

"You made mistakes of your own then, have you?"

She said "First, you need to know my name—I've got one: Joretta Robbins. Second, Joretta tore off and left too—a man good as you and for awful reasons. We'd had a girl baby lovely as *day*. She took sick early though, pernicious leukemia. Finally one morning in the midst of her bath—me treating her gentle as a day-old kitten—I broke her leg just drying her off. In three more weeks she died, blue as ink. I watched every minute of a sight worse than World War III, let me tell you. Then I left. Morehead City, right down on the coast, views of the sky that would crank your heart on the meanest day. I left it all. And Cliff J. Robbins, a concrete mixer—sweetest damned man old God ever made. I bet he's waiting on me right now. Last person I talked to from home said he was. Said 'Cliff still acts like you're the last woman alive for him.'"

"How far back was that?"

"Three, four years."

"You gone that long?"

Joretta said "Five years this next month."

"What would make you go back?"

"A sign," she said. "Some big sign, big enough to read at least. Like the one I gave you to Nashville back when."

Wesley thought that through. Then he sat back and faced her. She was no big beauty. But if somebody ordered him here and now to stay beside her for the rest of his life, he wouldn't feel tempted to blow his brains out. So yes, he was sure. He grinned and said "Go call Cliff up right now."

Jo looked at her watch. "It's way too late. He's early-to-bed."

"I very much doubt he'll mind waking up."

She finished her cigarette and watched Wesley through his last swallows of coffee. "Got time for more coffee?"

"Better take time," Wesley said. "I'll be driving till dawn."

So Jo stood up. One sincere moan escaped her mouth as the hips accepted her weight again. Then she brought him a fresh cup and stepped out of sight with no more words.

Wesley played more songs and finished his coffee, no

more sight of Jo. But when he rose to pay his check, she appeared from the back and met him at the register. He handed her a ten-dollar bill, said "Many thanks," and told her he hoped she'd take his advice.

She nodded, made his change, then faced him grinning. "I just now did."

"You reach old Cliff?"

"Didn't take but two rings."

"And he wanted you back?"

Jo said "Hold on. We didn't go that far."

"What did he say then?"

"I guess I asked him what he'd had for supper. It was fried bluefish, homemade coleslaw, cornbread, and sliced tomatoes. He always was a good cook; most fishermen are. I asked him where he got decent tomatoes this time of year. Cliff said he never claimed they were decent." Her eyes didn't mist up or anything dramatic. She reached forward though to the penny-mint bucket and handed Wesley two mints in bright tinfoil. "On the house. Drive careful."

Wesley smiled "I can take you on as far east as Raleigh."

Jo said "Thanks. You've done enough for now. You give me your address; I'll keep you posted. I'll also put you in my famous prayers."

"What's famous about them?"

"They work," she said. "I don't burden God more than once or twice a year, so He responds by giving what I ask."

"Except your daughter's life."

Jo coiled back quickly. That had finally struck her. But she kept her voice calm. "I'm not sure this is your business, son, but I never prayed for my daughter's life. I know God's will when it's that bold to read."

Wesley unwrapped one of the mints and ate it. Then he said "I appreciate you telling me. I'm glad I've known you. I'll hope to meet again."

By then Jo had warmed back a little. She stepped round to walk him out the door. In the dark parking lot she extended her hand. "I think you're doing a good thing here."

Wesley thanked her but said "I'm trying to mend something good I broke. Or that time broke for me. That's no big deal."

"No, it is," she said. "Most breakers just run."

He suddenly saw how short she was, maybe five foot tall. He leaned way down till his mouth met her head; then he kissed her once through the sugared pink hair.

As Wesley drove off, Jo never waved. But she watched his lights till they joined the highway and melted into a fast swarm of red, all headed east. She wondered if he'd saved her life or ruined it. For that matter, what had she done to him?

ROSA WESLEY
RATO WAVE

WESLEY WAITED AT THE CORNER TILL TWENTY minutes after the light went on in Rosa's bedroom. Then he knocked at the front door. Usually she'd finished her shower and was downstairs cooking in twenty minutes. But now there was a long wait. He knocked again.

When the white door finally opened, it was Rato, fully dressed but his hair uncombed like he'd weathered a big blast seconds ago. As Wesley dawned on him, he took three steps back and looked upstairs. His face went red, he couldn't speak, he pointed with his long right fingers—up.

Wesley said "I was hoping to find you, Ace."

Rato burst out grinning. He'd always liked Wesley. Wesley had more sense than Milo or Rosa and got more fun out of life. So he came on forward again and whispered "You want to surprise her or what?"

Wesley said "What you think?"

Telling Rato to think was generally a mistake. He tended to take you seriously.

After twenty seconds Wesley said "She still upstairs?"

Rato nodded. "Go on."

"No, tell you what. You step on up there and gently say 'Wesley's downstairs to see you.'"

Rato said "It's your house. I'm just the boarder."

So Wesley stepped past him, went to the foot of the stairs, and looked up.

Rosa was there, dressed and ready on the top step. Surely she'd heard them.

He said "Morning, lady."

She took a long look. Then she turned and moved quickly toward their room.

When she didn't reappear in another minute, Wesley climbed on up and stopped at the door. He tapped on the frame.

Rosa said "It's your room."

He said "I left it."

"It sounds like you're back."

Wesley couldn't see her from there. He stepped in and she was over by the mirror at the far end in shade. Her eyes, thank God, were dry. Otherwise, she looked like the person he'd remembered. The rape anyhow hadn't marked her face. The bed was still unmade; he couldn't sit there. He wanted to do only right natural things, things he could feel were sincerely true and that Rosa could accept. So he didn't rush to hug her. He took a few steps and stopped by the chest of drawers. "I didn't plan this."

Rosa finally laughed—thank Jesus, laughed. "No, planning was never your longest suit."

"So I don't have any big speech ready."

"Me either," she said. "You come for your things?"

"I come to see you."

"I'd have sent you a photo and spared you the trip."

"Don't be mean yet."

Rosa said "I'm sorry."

"And don't start apologizing. That's my part."

Rosa suddenly frowned and her hand went up. "First thing—I'm hungry. Could we eat breakfast first?" All her life, she'd been a breakfast hound.

Wesley smiled. "Me too," though food was the last thing on his tired mind.

She said "Go take a hot shower, why don't you? Then meet us downstairs."

He said "I'll wash my face, brush my hair. Just coffee for me." When she stepped on past him, he smelled her strongly—just clean skin and soap, as old a smell as any in his mind except the one from his mother's deep breast.

IN A WHILE WHEN WESLEY JOINED THEM IN THE KITCHEN, Rato was frying boiled potatoes from the night before. He'd already browned a half-pound of bacon, made a tall stack of toast. The eggs were waiting. Rosa was almost done with the coffee. He sat at the table quietly to watch. They left him alone like he was nothing new. And for those few minutes, Wesley felt he was absolutely right—to be exactly here, this morning. No question it could last as long as he lasted. Even Rato's presence seemed hopeful. Why hadn't they brought him down here before, their own brand of Martian since Horace had turned out so disappointing? Had the man that raped Rosa touched this room? Could any place, this peaceful now, have held such a creature? A hard shudder tore up Wesley's spine.

Rosa saw it. She looked back and said "You need coffee now, am I right?"

"Nothing too desperate. But if it comes in five seconds, it might save a life."

Rato said "And how many eggs, what way?"

Rosa told Rato that Wesley just wanted coffee.

But Rato looked so baffled, Wesley changed his order. "Just scramble ten or twelve, if everybody wants them."

Rosa said "Suits me."

Rato resumed beaming and in another five minutes he had a large platter before them—firm moist eggs, crisp browned potatoes, and perfect bacon.

Rosa had taken her old seat at the far end opposite Wesley. When they all were seated, she said "Rato, you did it. Please bless it for us."

Rato's blessings had always been family treats—never ritual prayers but spontaneous entirely unpredictable responses.

As always it took him awhile. Then he said "God, You certainly kept this one up Your sleeve. But thank You all the same."

When Rosa's eyes opened, Wesley's were on hers smiling. So she laughed. The two men checked one another and joined her. Then they all ate ravenously.

WHEN ROSA LEFT AT EIGHT, WESLEY SAT ON DRINKING coffee while Rato scraped dishes. One thing about Rato, you never had to worry in his presence about small talk; Rato sometimes went months without an idle word. So

Wesley could slump back in his exhaustion and wonder just how much longer he had to pretend to be awake and human.

Finally Rato started the dishwasher and came over to sit. The first thing he said was "If you'll run me down to the bus station, I can be out of here before noon."

Wesley said "Hold it, boy. Cool your jets down fast."

Rato smiled. "I'm about as much use as a spare dick at the convent."

Wesley couldn't remember what joke that came from. He wasn't even sure it was a joke or where Rato would have learned about nuns and convents. But he smiled and said "Rato, there's still mysteries here way up to my chin —if not overhead. I may not be here more than today. Rosa and I haven't said ten words about past or future. You've been her lifeline. Don't leave her yet."

"You ain't back for good?"

Wesley said "You know not to count on me. Look what I just done three months ago."

"You're sitting here now. You look good here."

"I'd look good drinking coffee on the moon in an astronaut suit. I'm a nice-looking fellow, Rato—or so most people tell me. It's still half my trouble. People think I'm happy since I look so calm."

"What's made you unhappy? Rosa still don't know."

Wesley shook his head. "No, I told her by mail. I felt dead as this damned table-wood." He pounded once on the rock-maple top.

Rato said "This table is *life*. It's nothing but zillions of atoms all hopping like disco dancers on speed with miles of space between each one—barely seeing each other, they're moving so fast and far apart, all singing their song."

Wesley nodded. Was Rato on speed? Had a few weeks in town pressed some button in him that nobody else had ever found before? Now his old simple-minded brother-in-law knew physics. Well, no doubt the Army had taught the corporal more than the family counted on. "All right. That's me then too. Or was in December. I was dancing in space—couldn't hear the damned music, couldn't see my partner. And if I was singing, it was 'Help me home. I'm a sad lost boy.'"

"So you lit out for Nashville?"

"Not at first, not Nashville. I just left work the shortest day of the year. I thought I was headed here but wound up twelve hours later in Nashville in a motel room."

"You had a woman there."

Wesley said "Rosa tell you I was living with a woman?"

"She mentioned it, I think."

"I met a young woman well after I got there. She kept me awhile and was good to me. But she sure God wasn't what made me leave here, not by a long shot."

"You'd stopped loving Rosa?"

Wesley said "You ever loved a woman in your life?" He'd wondered before. Now he felt the right to ask.

Rato said "I screwed a good many in Germany mostly and Oklahoma, a good few Indians; they sure are warm. But *love*?—I still love Rosa a lot."

"I mean, loved her so hard and steady you just want to touch her all night every night of your life, and give her kids, and save her body from all grades of harm."

Rato grinned. "That's love?"

"When you're young anyhow. For me it was."

Rato laughed. "No sir. Thank God, I been spared."

Wesley said "I pity you. Sweetest thing yet, that feeling

I had when I first knew Rosa in high school at home."

"We all thought you were running from her hard."

"I thought so too. I joined the Navy thinking so. But Rosa had some kind of grip on my mind."

Rato said "We all thought you didn't give a damn. Thought she just shotgunned you."

Wesley smiled. "That happened, no way to deny it. It was Rosa's plan to start a baby and slow me down—you know, get my attention. Well, news of a baby with half my blood got my notice all right. But if Rosa had been patient, it wouldn't have taken a baby to stop me. She was already bigger in my mind than any ten others. With all the women I had in a big Navy town, Rosa was the real magic to me. I could get some Norfolk girl twisting in the dark, perfuming the room like a fleet whorehouse, and keep her rolling till daylight stopped us. Rosacoke though was the sight I'd see whenever I got back alone and still. I'd ride my motorcycle out to the beach on winter Sundays—anytime after those nights with girls—and take five-mile walks up the sand toward New York City. The cold salt air and seagulls yelling and all that water, powerful as God, would clean my mind and body out. What would be left was Rosa's face and strong blue eyes set on me, begging for my life. Looking back now I'd have given it to her of my own free will if she'd left me alone and trusted her strength. I still wish she had. She pushed me though and triggered the baby, and we fell in on marriage like a trapdoor. Half our trouble now— that we didn't have time to start life right."

Rato said "Don't waste all that on me. I don't understand. Save your breath for Rosa. She'll want to know. I've always thought Rosa knew more than most folks. But here since you left, she's been dumb as me. Everything I ask her, she says she don't know. I give up asking and just tried to guard her."

Wesley said "And I thank you. I owe you a lot."

Rato said "You can buy me a radio then."

It stunned Wesley but he grinned and said "Sure. What brand you want?"

"Oh, a Sony, I guess. Something big and loud. I like grand opera."

"From Nashville, you mean?"

"Hell, no. Hillbilly music grinds my *teeth* down. I mean that stuff from New York and Europe."

Wesley said "You understand it?"

"I'm not in it for the words. I can tell when they're mad and when they're peaceful. That's all you need to know. Mostly they're mad."

Wesley said "And the women sound mostly like they're about to jump off cliffs."

Rato nodded. "They are. Big as they are, they're in terrible trouble." He waited, looked down, and then asked "You know the reason I'm down here at all—in your house, I mean?"

"My wife being raped? Rosa wrote me about that but not till last week. It's what brought me back."

Rato said "I figured you didn't know sooner. Couldn't imagine you'd know and stay gone. I guess it was right hard on her. I knew it was coming, see. Dreamed about it the night it happened. Got Mama to call her up the next morning, and sure enough I'd been right all night. So Rosa come right on home that day and stayed awhile with us. Then I come back with her and been here ever since."

Wesley asked "How much has it changed her?"

"I'm no big authority on women. But I've been right

surprised. Everything you see on t.v. says they're supposed to go wild and hate themselves and all men forever, once somebody grabs them. Rosa's been different there like everywhere else. If it's tore anything up, it's her mind and down so deep I haven't seen it yet. She's still good to me like she's always been. What's deeper than that, you'll have to test yourself."

Wesley wondered if he wanted that test, but he didn't say so to Rato now. In fact, he wondered if it was fair to go on asking Rato anything—truthful answers poured from Rato at the touch; it hardly seemed right. Still he had to keep going, to cover as much ground as possible before Rosa came home at dusk and they faced one another. He said "Then the police never knew about this? She never told a soul but you?"

"Me and Mama and Milo. Now you. Why call the cops? They never catch nobody—not in real life, not once the guy's run. And all they'd have wanted was her drawers to sniff. I think she was right."

Wesley said "Maybe so. Still the fool's running loose, and he knows where she lives."

Rato said "I kept him off till now you're back."

Wesley said "For today. We'll see about the rest."

Rato asked "You want to stay? Ain't that why you're back?"

"I doubt I know yet. I'm here because she wrote me about the damned rape. I feel like I caused it."

Rato nodded. "You may."

From Rato, a mind that plain and clear, it cut like a blade. Wesley honored his right to cut that deep. "You think I caused it?"

"Understand I'm no judge but my guess is, you prom-

ised the Lord and all her friends and family to guard Rosa's
body. They trusted you at your word and looked other
places. Twenty-eight years later your eyes flicked off her.
You didn't tell us. That left her in danger, and the Devil
saw his chance."

Wesley said "You sure you believe in the Devil?"

"I'm a man, ain't I?" Rato said. "Of course I do. Ain't
you felt the damned Devil fermenting in your soul?—
when you'd be scrounging some clean girl's body just to
ease your mind or not giving all your bi-weekly pay to a
child you'd see on the street, cold and hungry? If you don't
don't believe in the Devil, I doubt you've got good eyes."

Wesley laughed. "Where you been all my life, son? I
needed you."

Rato said "Just waiting. You never asked me."

"Should I stay here now?"

"Depends on what you want," Rato said. "If it's just to
protect Rosa, I can do that good as you—maybe better. I
got infantry training. All you learned was to keep boats
floating."

Wesley said "What else should I want?"

"You're the one got married, not me. Can't help you.
Maybe you want what she gave you back when, years ago
on that beach in Norfolk. What happened to that?"

Wesley said "Oh Lord Jesus, *time*."

"Then it ain't Rosa's fault. Don't punish her for time."

"I'm not," Wesley said.

"What the hell were these last three months then? If
you'd stayed here beating her all night long every night of
three months with a bull-hide whip, you couldn't have hurt
her worse than you did. Plus that goddamned maniac
breaking in and bruising her there in the tender part of her

body and mind. I'd skin his face one cell at a time with absolute pleasure if I knew his name."

Wesley hadn't seen any man care that much about anything but Negroes in the past thirty years. He knew his own flesh ought to be cringing at the thought of what Rosa had borne in these same walls. Was it a sign of how far he'd drifted from his old first love?—that now he could think through that painful night and not force her down to the police station to pore through volumes of felon shots and find the exact face for him to hunt and skin? What he felt was sadness at an old friend's pain and considerable shame at his own desertion of family duty.

The evening to come would tell what Rosa felt, and that might settle all other questions here—staying or leaving again or whatever. Suddenly Wesley's exhaustion hit him, a fifty-year-old man with no wink of sleep in twenty-six hours. His head almost fell forward to the table.

Rato saw it and told him "You're dead."

"I told you that."

"I mean here and now. Go on up and sleep."

Wesley said "You got everything covered, Ace?"

"I'll spend my day like I always do. Don't worry about me. Got my own set of keys."

Wesley said "Good night" and was almost halfway up the stairs when the next reality struck him firmly. He walked back down, stood in the kitchen door, and said "You be using your bed today?"

"Not till midnight, no."

"Can I sleep in your room?"

"Sure, clean sheets two days ago. But you got your own bed."

Wesley said "Not yet. That's some while off."

One more thing Rato didn't understand, though he said "Be my guest."

WHEN WESLEY CAME TO, IT WAS FOUR-FIFTEEN, AND THE light outside was beginning to fade. He had an hour and a half at least before Rosa would be home, but he wanted to be entirely ready. So he got up to wash, shave, and dress. His things were still outside in the car. He slipped on his old clothes and started downstairs. Halfway he heard two voices in the kitchen—Rato's plainly and another man's. The man seemed to be in the process of leaving, so Wesley went on quick out the front door and got his grocery bag of clothes. When he turned back to the house, he could see a tall man, black-haired and straight, walking out of the back drive toward the nearest cross-street. Maybe twenty-five years old, thirty at the most—nobody Wesley recognized.

He ducked his head through the kitchen door to let Rato know he was up now and planning to dress.

Rato was sitting again at the table, watching a cheap black television comedy and already laughing hard. He said "Sleep good?"

"Like the *road*. I haven't slept that deep since 1950. Was somebody in here with you just now?"

"I go bowl a few games most afternoons up yonder at the college. A friend walked me home from the bowling alley. I give him a Coke. You don't mind, do you?"

"Not if he's a friend of yours."

Rato said "He's new but I guess he's all right. Doesn't have much to say."

Wesley asked "He know me or Rosa?—a student at the college?"

"No," Rato said, "Hasn't got another real friend in town

or so he says. Tries to buy me stuff to eat at the bowling alley—fried pork-rinds, that sick sort of mess."

Wesley said "Watch your step. Can't trust folks here like you can in the country."

Rato laughed. "Country is the last place I trust anybody, country and *home*. I notice you left it soon as you could. Now go get clean. I'll stay on guard."

So Wesley went. Neither one of them had the trace of a guess that Rato's friend was the man who had been here New Year's night.

WHEN ROSA PULLED IN AT SIX, WESLEY HAD WASHED HIS car, then himself, then dressed in clean old clothes, and was quiet in the living room reading *The Raleigh Times*. She unloaded a few groceries in the kitchen, talked a little with Rato about the day's events, stepped up to her bathroom, and combed her hair.

Then she went down to Wesley. All day at work she'd dreaded this moment—first, the chance that he'd be gone again when she got here; second, the almost harder possibility that he'd have stayed and would need talking to. She'd held herself back from thinking what to say. As she stepped over the threshold now, she silently asked the Holy Ghost to guide her speech. But her eyes stayed open, so she saw Wesley rise in place to meet her, no sign of worry on his plain broad features but no smile either.

He said "Hard day?"

"Do I look it? May be."

"No, you look all right. I just meant I'd taken *my* day easy and was feeling guilty."

"Did you sleep off your trip?"

"Pretty well, I think. Course I doubt I'll have insomnia tonight." He returned to his chair.

But Rosa couldn't sit, couldn't make herself rest till she knew one thing. She finally said "You staying for supper? You staying at all?"

"I'd be real grateful for supper," he said. "After that, I guess you'll want to discuss it."

"You're the one that left."

Wesley nodded. "I did—and told you why, the best I could in that first letter. None of it's your fault."

"Sure it was, half at least."

"But things have changed since—what you wrote me about, your New Year's and all."

Rosa sat at last but far from Wesley. "That was not your doing."

"It sure God *was*. Don't forgive me too easy. If I'd been here like I vowed to be, no man would have come anywhere near the door—much less touched you."

Rosa said "That's not the reason I told you, to make you guilty. It turned out you were just my last friend on earth. I'd kept quiet so long, I had to tell somebody. That make any sense?"

"Good sense. Thank you, ma'm." Wesley stood in place; he couldn't think why.

Rosa said "How's it changed me, in your eyes now?"

"None at all, I guess. You look fine from here."

She smiled. "That's a flattering distance though."

Wesley didn't move to shorten it. He said "Go on now and get it all out."

Rosa asked "What?"

"Your feelings about me, how mad you must be. I've been a damned scoundrel. Punish me now. I volunteer." He

even extended his hands at his side, not quite in surrender
but plainly at her mercy.

Rosa laughed at first but kept on looking, straight at his
eyes. They were what she had loved most of all in the
world, above ground or under. What she'd lived to serve.
Through all these sad weeks, she'd not doubted that. To
have them here now—deep and dark as ever, this unblink-
ing steady, this easy to meet—and not to know whether
they were offered for good or on some sort of loan was
harder than everything else so far. She said "I'm not mad,
not one iota. I just want to hear if you mean to stay. It
won't take any big panel discussion."

Wesley said "Watch my lips." He touched his dry lips,
then moved them slowly to make clear sounds. "I'm here
to ask you that same question. You want me to stay?"

Rosa said "Please sir, till I'm dead anyhow."

"No problem," he said.

In the few more seconds they could each bear to sit and
meet the other's eyes, they wondered what on earth they
meant? Had they only told two more kind lies after decades
of kindness that had brought them to this?

WHATEVER WOULD PROVE TO BE THE TRUTH DAYS OR
weeks from now, they'd left Rato home to thaw pizza and
had taken themselves to their old favorite place—the Can-
ton Restaurant on Hillsboro Street with roomy private
booths. They'd talked about their families in Warren
County, the little they'd each heard from Horace lately,
how surprisingly different Rato seemed up here in town
(what must he have been like in Germany?), some post-
poned repair work the house was needing.

Then out of the blue, Wesley poured out the full story of Wilson and his weeks with her.

At first Rosa had wanted to stop him (it was coming too fast and painful for her), but something told her she would need the information eventually, and now might be the last time Wesley would easily part with so much of the truth. She'd already used up the rape; she had nothing to give in return, nothing to balance Wilson. She did tell him about finding Rato's little shrine to her at Mary's house and about Milo's unexpected warm kindness. But before she finished with those, she was sorry. They seemed like childish efforts at making Wesley jealous, when all she was hunting was sizable fresh news.

Still Wesley listened carefully, not drifting off. When she seemed finished, he asked if she was ready for him to run her on home?

She asked "Me? Aren't you coming too?"

He said "Rosa, I'm not trying to be cute here. I just want to give you every fair opportunity to get real honest and turn against the son of a bitch that left you Christmas week to sink or swim."

She thanked him again, laughed, and finally said "Believe me, I've tried. It's not in my heart. At least I can't find it. Let's go home to sleep."

ROSA WESLEY
RATO WAVE

I T WAS ONLY NINE-THIRTY WHEN THEY DROVE INTO THE
yard, but Rato was already gone from downstairs. The
light in his bedroom was on, but his door was shut.
And when Rosa called through the door to see if he was all
right, Rato only said "Yes but wore out."

She told him that she and Wesley weren't ready for bed,
if he'd like to come back down and watch television.

But Rato said "Like I told you, I'm beat."

So she left him alone, and she and Wesley went to the
living room to watch a tired comedy on the big set. Wesley
drank a beer; Rosa had ginger ale. In a quarter-hour he had
slid into his old ease here. For moments at a time, she
could do the same. Then she'd remember herself—the
nightmare pain of the past few months—and doubt all this.

By the time the show ended, Rosa was even wondering if she could manage to sleep beside this man, much less with him. Could she ever want him again?

Somehow Wesley felt her doubts through the air. After they'd watched the first part of the eleven o'clock news (just the standard murders), bedtime was inevitable. But he knew he must wait for Rosa's instructions.

Finally she stood up and said "Remember, I work tomorrow. And you haven't slept in a bed for two nights." For an instant she extended a hand to draw him up, but then she dropped it. She hoped he hadn't noticed, but of course he had.

So Wesley was honest when he said "I can sleep right here on this sofa, no problem." There were two upstairs bedrooms, none down.

Rosacoke said "You can if you want to." She took a step away, then looked back a moment, then spoke to the rug. "In my mind, you still live upstairs."

So he rose, said "Thank you, ma'm," and followed her up.

To HAVE WATCHED THEM UNDRESS WOULD HAVE LOOKED like always, from the outside. The only exterior difference was that they moved entirely in the light of a single bulb from the bathroom and that maybe they hurried a little. They both were keyed up and scared. Neither of them knew exactly what they wanted to happen in the next half-hour.

Wesley was not sexually excited. In fact, as he stripped, his skin showed the innocent early-spring whiteness of a soft boy. Still the nearness of an attractive woman had never failed to rouse him in the past, not once. Would it now?

Rosa didn't feel the revulsion that some raped women report at the sight of the next naked man (in fact the coal black of Wesley's pubic hair against the white of his skin was a nice sight; and his penis looked familiar and entirely harmless, unchanged by its trip). So their fear was of something deeper than sex—maybe of finding that one or the other had changed in an unexpected secret way that only their coming nearness would trigger now fiercely, some bawling mouth of hunger or rage.

In a short clean gown, Rosa went toward the bathroom to wash her face and teeth. When she shut the door and sat to take a last pee, she shut her eyes to say a silent prayer. As usual, at really hard corners, nothing wise or even right would come to her mind. She finally just said a silent "Help," flushed the toilet, and stood.

Walking back through the door, through their dim old bedroom toward the man she'd lived with all her grown years, she felt suddenly and for the first time precisely like a bride. She couldn't help meeting Wesley's eyes and smiling.

He smiled back slowly and turned on the reading lamp by his hand. He was still upright on the far side of the bed in his white jockey shorts. He'd lost four or five pounds in Nashville clearly.

Rosa felt sad to see it—couldn't that woman cook? But she also couldn't help thinking how much better he looked, how much more nearly like the first lean Wesley.

When he'd stood long enough to read her smile, Wesley also grinned and began to count "One, Two, Three." On

"One" he'd taken the tip of the bedspread and begun to pull it back.

Rosa joined him on "Two." By "Four" they both climbed into cool sheets.

And by "Six," Wesley suddenly shook with a chill. He lay on his back, hands stretched down beside him; and hard shudders racked him.

Rosa lay down quickly, rolled to face him, and watched for a while. Then sooner than she'd planned, her hand had to touch him in the center of his chest. Her courage and then her foolishness began to amaze her—this man had left her without one word for a whole long winter and now, with spring, had walked back in. What she maybe ought to do was stand up now and speak all her mind. It had been nearly thirty years since she'd done as much. Didn't she at least owe that much honesty to the pain she'd borne, that one bad night? But she didn't say a word.

Wesley shuddered harder.

So Rosa pulled back and also lay flat.

But Wesley said "Oh no, don't quit" and laughed in a whisper. "I'm fine. I'm just tremendously tired and ashamed." By then he had calmed.

So she faced him again. But this time she held back for him to touch her.

He turned off the lamp and reached to her shoulder, waiting for his palm to warm to her own old usual warmth. When it did, he kissed her lightly once. But then his hand wouldn't start slowly downward. He couldn't think why. It was like she'd suddenly changed as a punishment. Lying in easy reach beside him, still she'd become a child again, lovely and warm but young and forbidden—not fouled by the rape but a possible victim all the same and fragile.

Rosa thought that of course. In another long minute she rolled back, faced the ceiling, and said "I'm as sorry as I can possibly be." She meant she was sorry for what she saw as their present dilemma—Wesley back and at hand but unable to want her, she wanting him too much to do justice to the pain that lay just behind them, still unforgiven. That revelation had come too soon, before they'd worked through all their other questions.

Wesley understood her but still couldn't say why he'd drawn back. Again he felt she was once more a virgin. And all those years ago—a real virgin—she'd lured him on her, when she thought she had lost him for good. As she seemed just now to have tried to draw him again. Was he finally taking the chance at refusal that he'd lost—what?—twenty-eight years ago? Well, now he was diving far below his own power to breathe. He said "I feel like we're back at the start, nothing worse than that."

Rosa said "Start of what?"

"Knowing each other—you and me, back when."

Rosa said "That well may be the thing that saves us."

"If we get it right this time."

Rosa asked "Where'd we go wrong, Wesley? I really don't know. I haven't known since the day you left."

"Honest to God? Was it just me then?"

"Oh I'm not claiming either one of us was perfect or any of our marriage. I do claim though that, until I got home that evening and you didn't appear, I never suspected we could end for good—not till death anyhow. What was seriously wrong? Better tell me now in case there's time left."

Wesley asked "Do you want there to be?"

"I think maybe so. If we start off innocent again, like you say. But also knowing what we both want and need, both knowing each other and paying attention. Horace is thoroughly gone from us now, Rato'll leave any minute we say, we'll be here alone together for the first time since those few months we had at the start before Horace landed. We might well get another thirty, forty years. We'd need to pay *attention*, Wesley, every minute."

"I may not can do that," Wesley said. "Every minute sounds a lot more like you than me. I honestly believe you could manage new innocence. Poor Wesley, though—he's too dirty, Rose. He's got spots and bruises that won't scrub off. I thought part of what marriage meant was just that—you could look past the grease marks and trust each other's love and promise. You could even ignore the traces of some other person's body—their stray hairs, scraps of their fingernails. And you didn't have to keep prancing around each other with cards and flowers. You knew where you stood and could lean on that."

Rosa said, "All right. But remember one thing—what you're describing is what a man wants. Women are somehow scareder than that."

"I guess so, yes. I'd have to grant that. But you know how soon Wesley starts feeling foolish with the Hallmark love poems and Whitman's candy hearts."

Rosa finally laughed and turned where she was, without moving closer, to see Wesley's face. It took awhile for her eyes to find him in the deep dark night. When the line of his forehead and nose showed at last, his mouth was moving in very slow breaths. He'd plunged into sleep backward like a child powerless to last. That far anyhow, she guessed they were safe—that trusting in one another, that free. She still hadn't asked him the final question—how had he *died* the day he left her?

Here now beside her he was clearly alive. Even fifteen inches there beyond, he broadcast powerfully every fresh odor he'd ever broadcast—all clean and his own, like no other man's she'd ever been near. She said a last prayer, to Wesley more than God—"Let this thing *go*." Then her own mind joined him in quick black sleep.

WHAT STAYED AWAKE IN THE HOUSE WAS RATO. HIS DOOR was shut and his curiosity surely did not extend to wondering what Rosa and Wesley were doing in their new privacy. He just couldn't sleep. He was racing back and forth through what this meant—Wesley's reappearance, Rosa taking him in. Knowing them both, long as they'd known each other, still it never crossed Rato's mind to doubt that Wesley was back for good. These two had grown together more than half their lives ago. They couldn't disentangle now if they wanted to—and both their sets of eyes denied any serious thought of separation. He'd known that years ago, before they did. He'd told Rosa once she knew she was pregnant and wanted to run.

But him now, Rato? Everybody would expect him to pack his little duds and head up to Mama for thirty more years of country boredom. He'd really enjoyed these weeks in a town. Not that Raleigh was Berlin or even London, but it had the main good any city can offer—*nobody knew who you were*, at least not once you stepped into the street. You could be a guy with fourteen rich fat ex-wives dissolving in sulfuric acid under your bathroom floorboards, and people would think you were just a smiling shoe-salesman or a bachelor Baptist preacher.

So if Rato could strangle his conscience well enough, he might just either rent a room from Wesley or find him a

little efficiency apartment in the neighborhood or closer in
toward N.C. State and the bowling alley, the doughnut
shop, and the movies. His Army retirement check would
probably stretch just about that far.

Or this new friend he'd met—Wave Wilbanks—had
hinted at the chance of them rooming somewhere clean and
cheap (Wave had just got a job at a textbook store).

Jobs were the main thing here that worried Rato. He
could probably hunt down some weird thing in a bar or a
pawnshop—sweeping up, washing up, being the fool that
customers called "Sarge" or "Old Timer." Rato had a special fear of *Old Timer*. The way he heard the words on
television, he understood it was the name of the new disease you heard so much about now, where people lost their
memory and lived on their family's kindness like big dirty
turnips in bedroom corners—Old Timer's disease.

Afton and his mother's house wasn't so awful. The
place would leave him alone. And his mother was all right
too, if she just wouldn't ask too many questions about Raleigh and his doings. He could tell her about all the new
things at Rosa's—the microwave and the twenty-gallon
aquarium that Wesley had bought for a hobby and then left
to Rosa. But there had been several surprising ways that
Raleigh was different from Afton, the Army, and all of
damned Europe.

The main thing was women. Once he left home at eigh-
teen, so long ago, he got his first real chance to watch
women. He had talked to Wave his bowling friend and to
Wesley about how many women he'd really been next to,
and he never flat lied. But he also never truly admitted how
lonesome that made him—the women in every other place
but Raleigh. He could pay some whore in Rhein-Main Ger-

many to touch his body any way he dreamed. Hell, he had
known one girl that—free, for no money at all—had tried
to lick off the ugly tattoo he regretted on his left wrist. But
even if she could speak clear good English, she wouldn't
ever ask what he wanted to hear.

Rato needed women to ask him for advice. He knew he
understood the whole broad world, especially men, and he
wanted women to profit from his knowledge. He could let
them know what men thought of them, what men truly
wanted from women in their private minds, how scared all
men but Rato were of the secret whirlpool buried in women
that caught men early and held them down there spinning
forever. Rato had it all thought out in terms of the strong
pull of water. Boys are *made*, from day one, in what seem
like peaceful ponds hid deep inside their mothers' bodies.
Then one day after nearly a long restful year, the mother
flushes you out like some piece of festered trash—scared
and dry and yelling. Then when you're maybe twelve or
thirteen, every other girl in the world starts hinting to you
that she's got that same warm peaceful piece of water inside her body just waiting for you—and that this time,
there won't be any trouble. Well, dive in and *peaceful*?
That's when you find out the meaning of whirlpools. By
then though you're hooked. Or all other men but a few
queers and Rato.

Rato wasn't scared because he'd escaped. Or had never
been caught. The way he escaped was, he left his mother.
From early in the crib, he understood how much he needed
freedom. So something had made him turn from his
mother—his only food!—and make her feed him a whole
nother way. He was way too young to think it out. God or
his mind had just helped him know. And now his mission

was to pass that knowledge on—to men if they'd listen (which they'd seldom do) but mainly to women. His secret of happiness for all mankind. And up till now almost nobody anywhere had ever asked—not even Rosa lately, sad as she'd been.

He couldn't decide tonight anyhow. He'd need to talk to more people than Rato ever liked to involve—Wesley and Rosa, his mother, Wave, maybe a bunch of Realtors and landladies. He couldn't think about all them at night.

He had all day tomorrow with nothing else planned. Matter of fact, nothing was planned between here and his grave. He'd save it for tomorrow then. He asked himself one last clear question—why does a young fellow like Wave (maybe twenty-five or -six) want to live with somebody old as me? Then Rato was out too.

THAT LEFT NO ONE CONSCIOUS BUT WAVERLY WILBANKS, on foot five blocks away, hoping to walk off the pain in his heart. In all the world, he was the one great mystery to himself—why he made the choices he made and when he made them. Rosa was by no means the first woman he'd forced to know him. Or to let him know them.

The idea of knowing had come to him in early childhood from Bible reading—"Now Adam knew Eve his wife, and she conceived and bore Cain." By the time Wave was fourteen, living east of Raleigh halfway to the ocean, he had determined in his mind really to *know* at least one woman.

No one that he'd met or dreamed about made him think that a woman would offer herself to him freely. Everything he could find, in books and movies and other boys' talk, convinced him that the kind of knowledge he craved—the deep dark sweetness and power—would yield only to a sudden hot thrust from his private body. Then just beyond the thrust would come an end to need and then a return flow of thanks and kindness from the woman. And the first girl that Wave ever forced responded in just the way he planned.

She was a neighbor to him and his mother in the country, a distant cousin two years behind him in school. They rode the same schoolbus every morning and evening. And one spring afternoon when he was fourteen and pressure in his groin had built to the hurting point, Wave let the girl—Christine—walk ahead of him up the track toward their houses.

The low clear sun was falling behind her; and the light struck through her light skirt, showing the strength of her legs and hips. Wave felt, for the first time plainly, that if he couldn't get there—right in the center of her true power—he'd die or fall down at least in some kind of seizure that would prove his complete failure to be a man. He speeded up and touched her between the shoulder blades.

When Christine stopped and turned to face him, she was smiling slightly. She even said "I was wondering—"

Wave never let her say what she wondered. He dropped his books by the path, took her gently by the elbow, and led her a quarter-mile off toward the tall pine woods. When they were there in the half-dark, he first had to stop her from undressing (she volunteered to strip right off). He just motioned her to lie down in the soft straw and to be entirely silent.

So she obeyed and in another twenty minutes, Wave had done everything he ever dreamed of doing—and all of it with his gentle fingers and lips. Christine had cooperated fully with his hands. It was only when he moved his mouth down on her that she shook her head no. Wave rightly guessed how ashamed she was of that part of herself as dirty and ugly (because both women and men said so).

Well, there again Wave had another chance to redeem her pride and pleasure. When he'd worked a good quarter-hour with his mouth, Christine cut loose a sigh—long and thin as stocking thread. At first Wave thought he'd hurt her. But when he looked upward, her shut eyes were happy; her damp lips were smiling.

Finally Christine met Wave's waiting eyes and said "Can I stand up now?"

Before he could say "Yes," he thought "Thank Jesus, *that's* over. I was right all the way. I won't ever worry about that again." And it did fill the big howling hole in his chest for maybe three weeks—his memories of it, the dreams he built on it, the lovely chances it gave him to serve his own clean body again and again. But by the end of school and the start of tobacco season, the goodness had worn out of the memory. And Christine herself was asking for more. She'd wait evenings for him, as he came back from the fields. And two or three times, he walked off with her. She'd lie back and watch in the cool while he fiddled with her, got her twitching and yipping like a wind-up toy.

The trouble for Wave was, he knew Christine all the way by then. He could foretell every move she'd make the instant before she made it. He could say to himself "Put your little finger there; she'll do exactly *that*." And ten times in ten, he'd be dead right. That was when he began to think of older women.

And before he got his high-school diploma, Wave had known two of them. One was his dramatics teacher. The other was a librarian (he'd discovered books by then, the best source yet of mysterious women—really frank magazines hadn't yet penetrated rural North Carolina).

Forced was hardly the right word for what he accomplished with them. He knew that, out of loneliness and hunger, they mostly cooperated. But the way they obeyed his orders for silence and stillness and just lay back and watched him proceed, the way they almost never yelled or struck him but cried gently at the end—all those signs told him to believe what he hoped: that Waverly Wilbanks had won precious knowledge through his own strong force. He might not be the only wise man on earth; he'd never heard of any local rival at least, not down in the country or once he got to Raleigh.

Wave had dropped out in his sophomore year at N.C. State before he genuinely raped anybody. And the first real rape was also his first knowledge of a total stranger. She lived in his neighborhood over behind the Raleigh Little Theater, and he knew about her in that first drop-out year because his paper route served her house—the early-morning paper.

Once that spring she had been on the steps in her blue housecoat watering houseplants when Wave passed on his bike to sling her paper. She'd said firmly but quietly "Please don't throw it" and walked on toward him with her right hand out. He stopped and waited and handed it over smiling, knowing that instant what he'd do when enough time had passed for safety. He knew because she'd met his eyes and held onto them just that split-second longer than was usual—hunting, hunting for some good answer she couldn't foretell.

She wasn't bad-looking. So he checked round enough

to know she was single, that she lived alone, and was no more than six years older than he. He learned that she worked as a legal secretary. So he figured that it meant—if he played his cards right and didn't really hurt her—she almost certainly wouldn't go to the Law for help.

Three weeks later, after planning every instant till his brain was smoking with the hopes, Wave shaved meticulously. Then he walked light-footedly to her back yard and checked her kitchen door at three-thirty in the morning. The screen was hooked but any kitten can unlock a screen. In four more minutes he found her bedroom in the one-story house, knelt on the shag rug by her knees, and began to stroke her upper thigh. It took a surprisingly long time to wake her.

But finally she came to, lay still, and said "I really do pray this isn't what I think it is."

Wave smiled in the dark and said "It isn't, no."

She said "What you want me to do then?"

"Lie flat on your back and let me take over."

She waited awhile to obey but then did. The only other words she said were "Don't cut me please."

Wave laughed gently. "Honey, never—not a scratch." Then he spent maybe half an hour slowly baring parts of her body, stroking, kissing, honoring her skin. He even reached a moment when he thought he'd put her back to sleep—her breathing steadied and slowed that much.

But when he rocked back and paused to see, she said "Can I go wash please?"

Wave wouldn't let himself think she was dirty. He had to say "No" and work himself back to where he'd been before—the aim to gentle her back to the moment when all her gates and bars went down, and he could board her quickly and *know*—really know forever—the absolute secrets of a woman compelled to take his attention, his own last secret, and then thank him for it.

For all Wave knew, that first strange woman had never complained—surely not to him and apparently not to the law. *Nor anybody else.* In fact, as he left her room before light, she said one peculiar thing to his back—"Do you know my name?" He said "Yes ma'm. It's Kathleen, right?" and she said "Thank you."

He even went on as her paperboy for another four months till he got a better job. In the two years that lay between the first rape and Rosa's, he'd forced three other women—all alone at home in the quiet dark—and not one word of a cry for help as he crouched there beside them nor in the next day's news anywhere.

Rosa was somebody he planned for delicately. He had noticed her ever since his freshman year at State, at the office and in the cafeteria. It wasn't so much that she was beautiful or even attractive. She was after all literally old enough to be his mother, though she'd worn well enough —no fat or dyed hair.

What caught Wave in her face and shape was the same first thing that had caught Wesley. Somewhere behind her wide blue eyes, she guarded closely what Wave suspected was a big grand secret. This time, it was a secret that she herself understood; it was the rest of the world she was hiding her answer from. This woman knew the last little thing that Wave had missed. Week by week as he watched her—crossed her paths on campus, saw her smile eight times—he convinced himself that the two of them had a world to give each other. He knew every volt he had for her. And her rare smile said "Waverly Wilbanks, I can give you rest."

Just by occasional questions at school and in her neighborhood, Wave gradually put together the sense of a friendly woman with a cheerful-enough husband that didn't seem to fit her looks and her nature. It was that which gave him the most hope. Wave had discovered early that he somehow gave girls and then women more than most other men even began to offer—he *attended* to them.

He listened in stillness, heard their private needs, and filled them. Or so he believed. And didn't his safety, his freedom from jail or the fear of capture, prove him right?

So more and more in the days before that New Year's, he came to the urgent conclusion that not only could he get at Rosa but, without maybe knowing it, she wanted him to. How he was going to meet her with her husband in residence—that was his only big problem. Would it have to be his first attempt in daylight? (he'd noticed that Wesley worked till nine on two or three nights, usually late in the week).

But the first night Wesley disappeared, Wave picked up his absence—his car was gone from the drive and stayed gone right through Christmas. So his guess was right. Rosa wanted his attention. So did the sky, maybe God Himself —*the way was cleared*. It had seemed that plain, that wanted and right.

Even now—months later with her friendly watchdog, her guard-dog brother that couldn't hurt a gnat and her husband back home—Wave couldn't much doubt he had been flagged on, *led* on to face her. What had ruined him ever since New Year's was, he hadn't really finished. Out of all the women he'd really been near, Rosa was the only one who cried out and stopped him. She'd somehow lied in all those smiles and misled him badly. His mind couldn't leave her.

So now Wave stood in the midst of the night on the street outside her house, her room, her simple brother, and now this husband who couldn't deserve her. He suspected, even now, that he might be crazy. He'd read enough books, seen enough television, to know his kind were pitied and feared and dreaded by all. He himself might better off be locked in a cell, or hanged or gassed, than left out here on the streets free to roam. Yet he knew one thing more urgent than all—he was not a member of any common *kind*. He was a man in possession of a talent.

Surely what he had—a kind sweet gift that women seldom got, for all this pain—more than earned him room and air, the right to roam in darkness and strike where his hands knew best to strike. Surely nothing, in heaven or earth, meant for Wave to be this unknown and lonesome— this dreaded. Now that Wesley was back, surely Rato and Wave were the only two live adult souls in this town who wanted companions but took their rest with no warm shape to touch in the night.

He sat there opposite Rosa and Wesley's on the now chilly curb and tried to make his eyes pierce brick, thick drapes, and plaster to see their sleep. He knew they had to be unconscious by now, not talking or touching.

Just when his mind had made out the trail of Rosa's hair sideways on her pillow (her back to Wesley), a car roared around the nearest corner. And Wave had to jump back and find the dark—his own narrow bed, hopeless and dry. He who had this gift to give, this permanent pleasure, the actual worship that all women dream of—the one man alive who knew that secret in pure perfection and longed to give it night after night to willing women, every woman on earth, and no trace of harm.

ROSA JEAN RATO
WAVE WESLEY
BRONNY

THE THIRD FRIDAY IN APRIL WAS AS FINE A DAY AS any live soul in Raleigh remembered. In the past week the trees had advanced from that day when new leaves break as a pale green mist, almost a hallucination, on the highest limbs. Now there were actual yellowish leaves. The dry warm air fell gently down through them, bearing a light sweet odor that seemed an actual promise from the sky—that one more winter had truly ended, that life was given one more round (earned or not).

Americans, Asians, smoky combinations of all the large and small, pink and brown races—the tens of thousands of students at N.C. State University had begun their annual grateful response to the single visible wheel of nature that responds, on time, to human hopes. The vernal thanksgiving consists of many acts in many stanzas, but the first is a sudden and forthright strip-to-essentials. The limbs of a race of well-fed children burst from the grim winter padding into a nearly blinding glare of grace and rank eros—a forest of gorgeous parts. And the upward rush of desire in their bodies is all but visible in the lilac snaking of arteries as they circle one another in the slow dances of noontime splendor. And though final examinations are hardly more than a week ahead, physics and calculus, hydraulics and architecture have slid from their minds as thoroughly as the grays and mists of February torpor.

ROSA AND HER OFFICE MATE JEAN GILLAM (WHO'D GIVEN the New Year's party) had brought their lunches outdoors near the English Department. They'd eaten and now they were savoring the last minutes of freedom on a brick bench in the direct light that—for all the eons of human abuse—was as unscreened, kind, and caring as ever. Jean was no more than six years younger than Rosa; but her eyes frankly consumed the passing male bodies in the welcome new fashion of short-shorts and converted the bountiful information into a line of comment that (for all her good humor) Rosa could never have issued, though she laughed right along.

But finally Jean burst out with "First prize, no question! You could tear the last few threads off that child yonder, spray him white, and stand him up in Athens, Greece right this minute with no objection from anybody, least of all me."

And Rosa had to say "Nobody but the vice squad, you dirty old woman. That child could be yours."

Jean nodded. "Thank Jesus he's not. It was hard enough not stroking my own baby boy before he left home—those little running shorts of his, those curly gold hairs on his big calves!"

Rosa could still smile but she had to say "Jean, you may need a good long day in church on your knees. I never had one trace of trouble with Horace."

"No offense intended, Rosa—Horace is a sweet boy—but he can't compete with the Pillsbury *Doughboy* for beauty."

Rosa said "He didn't inherit Wesley's looks, I'll grant you."

Jean chose to let that one lie dead behind them. "Remember you promised to show me your old photos of Wesley? You never did."

"I'm afraid I burned them early last winter."

"General Sherman, you didn't! Lord, Rose, it's a sin to burn up history."

Rosa waited a good while. "Not *burn* really. I did fish them all out, shut them up with hot sealing-wax in a brown envelope, and bury them in a box in the basement."

"Well, rescue them now from the silverfish and bring them to the office for me to enjoy."

Rosa said "I'm not sure it's absolutely safe, not yet awhile. They may need to be something Horace finds when he's shoveled me under forty years from now."

"Or tomorrow noon. You and Wesley seem fine." Jean and her husband Hal had grilled burgers on their patio for Rosa and Wesley the previous weekend.

Rosa said "Did we really?"

Jean nodded emphatically. "Hal and I discussed it later. He said 'You'd never guess Wesley had missed a beat at home, would you?' I don't offer Hal as one of the world's most sensitive observation-posts (he's been known to miss a few H-bomb blasts in our own backyard). But he has got a pretty good sense of other men, when they're happy or sad. And Hal said 'Wesley Beavers is a lucky damned sucker; he knows it now if not a day sooner.'"

Rosa laughed. "You're lying."

"Swear to God on high." Jean raised her right hand with a last crust of bread.

Rosa said "Anybody swearing on Wonder Bread can't ask to be believed."

Jean flung the bread toward a pair of horny pigeons and swore again.

"He hasn't told me."

"He's showing you, Rose."

"How please? Tell me."

Jean said "He's here beside you smiling, not in Nashville or east Madagascar or Akron. Not with some bleached-blond X-ray technician in a mobile home cheap as sardine cans, eating cheese puffs and marshmallow whip on crackers. Wesley's promised you his life."

Rosa said "You've heard words I haven't heard, not from Wesley *this* year. The last plain thing he told me was, he was dead."

"I'll bet he's not dead when the lights are out."

Rosa faced Jean squarely, thought through the truth, then decided to tell it. "We've no more touched than brothers and sisters these past three weeks."

Jean said "Some brothers and sisters touch a lot. Read the paper every day. Fathers and daughters—"

"I can joke fast as you when it's joking time, Jean. It's not that yet, not at our house yet."

"But it's your house together, Rose. Wesley came back home. He knew what was his."

Before she remembered fully, Rosa said "Because he found out about—." Jean had never heard a word about the rape. So Rosa stayed calm and continued. "Wesley found out in his own heart how big a wrong he'd done."

Jean said "Shoot, that wouldn't have fazed Wesley. Wesley's as modern as any stud dragging Main with a Playboy Bunny insignia on his mirror and a pair of fur dice. Wesley's wild, Rose. One look at those eyes the other night, and I knew deep down that Wesley was as different from my Hal Gillam as Hal is from Nancy Reagan. Wesley won't say one word he doesn't mean."

Rosa nodded. "—Which is why he left."

"*And* came back."

Rosa said "He never changed his mind that fast before. I still don't know what happened with Wilson."

"Who?"

"That mess in the mobile home."

Jean said "I was scared you meant a man there for a minute."

"No. In this case, Wilson is a girl. We're talking about Wesley, Jean."

"I told you he was wild. Wesley gets *me* riled—pardon the personal confession."

Rosa smiled. "Careful or I might begin to wonder who *doesn't* rile you."

"Don't be mean now." Jean laughed the low gutter chuckle that won her forgiveness in so many quarters. "No, believe me, Miss Rose. If Wesley wanted or needed to be with that blondeened bitch, he'd be with her now."

Rosa said "The bitch may have had a word to say about

it. She may have thrown him out. He's twice her age."

Jean said "He could be four times my age, with those dark eyes. God, Rosa, those eyes can see on through me and every wall between me and Peking, China."

Rosa said "Me too but that's because those eyes aren't looking for you or me."

Jean said "Not me, for damned sure. But who?"

Rosa said "I've wondered since the day I first saw him. And so does he. He no more knows than you or me what he's hungry for."

"Then why did it take him thirty years to see you weren't it?"

"It didn't. He knew it well before our wedding. I forced his hand."

Jean said "The two of you got pregnant. Wesley wasn't exactly standing on the other side of the room when Horace cranked up in your tender womb. And Wesley knows that. Stop beating yourself."

Rosa smiled. "You ought to been present a lot earlier in my life."

"You might not have been such a woebegone sheep dog."

Rosa said "We're due back at work."

"Cool your jets," Jean said. "That office ain't going a step without us. We've earned a tardy, today anyhow."

"So you're telling me to take him back—Wesley, here and now? You're saying he won't bolt on me again? Won't ever surprise me? I couldn't stand that."

"I'm saying that much. But I'm not Wesley. Sit him down, sweet Rose, and ask him outright."

Rosa took ten seconds to study Jean's face in the frank sun, still as lovely as before. With all the fine young

bodies around them, there was nothing in sight more generous or plainly trustworthy than the hands and face Jean
Gillam had constructed in her years. So Rosa grinned
broadly.

Jean knew it was a compliment. She responded gravely.
"I love you too. But are you really telling me you haven't
sat Wesley down and asked him the facts?"

"I haven't told you that, no. But you're guessing it
right."

Jean waited an instant, then pointed sharply back toward
their office. "Get your dumb ass in to that word processor.
You no more deserve another minute of God's sun than
these pink worms gnawing our feet."

Rosa smiled, studied the soles of her own shoes and
then rose. "My shoes are safe."

Jean laughed and joined her. "Nothing else is though.
You count on that."

"You just said the opposite. You said I was fine."

"I was lying," Jean said. She trotted three steps before
looking back, younger in spirit than any student near them.
"I don't do nothing but lie, old Rose. I'm sick as a dog, but
oh please love me. I need human care."

Rosa said "I'll try. It'll be damned hard."

Jean stopped and said "You've done nothing else all
your natural life. You're a pluperfect martyr. You *know* you
know it, and you love every minute." She stepped back
slowly till she bumped into Rosa. Then she took her kind
but innocent friend's pale bare arm and steered her, like a
lost untrained blind child, back to work in the world.

Rosa felt like a new-washed window in the light.

* * *

Two hours later just across the road, Rato sat in the bowling alley drinking a Pepsi and talking to Waverly, his only non-family friend in Raleigh. Rato had always lived on the policy of asking as few questions as possible of anybody—first, because he had the world's minimum of curiosity about other people and, second, because he didn't want to concede anyone else the right to question him. But after nearly a month of quiet job-hunting in the N.C. State neighborhood, Rato had about shot his bolt.

Home, the deep country, and more long years with his mother were staring him hard in the face. And while it wasn't all that bad an outlook, he did want to make one last few days' push to stay in town and keep the gains that a big city gives—excitement to watch, good noise to hear, more stuff than squirrels and foxes to study. It had pretty well come down to asking for Wave's help, so Rato said "Is there any work down at your place?" (Wave had said, a few days ago, that now he was working an early shift at a computer typesetting outfit.)

Wave waited and then said "Don't get me wrong but can you read good?"

"Ain't had a complaint since the third damned grade. What you want me to read? Anything but books—I can't stand a book."

"Oh nothing right now. What I mean is, a typesetter spends his time copying sentences from one piece of paper to a word processor. Could you do that?"

Rato said "You telling me they still have to do it that old way? Where the hell's the progress in that?"

Wave laughed. "Son, it would take a month to tell you." He'd called Rato *son* since the first week he knew him. It just seemed right, though Rato was old enough to be his natural father. Wave hadn't known his own father long enough. He'd been killed in some fast shoot-out with a deputy sheriff when Wave was five, a kind wiry man with a head of tight curls and a sweet gift of harmless practical jokes.

Rato was in no way like Wave's father except in one respect, his stillness. They both had the capacity to sit and watch some part of the world (a little thing nobody else would pause to snapshoot) till it opened up its inmost secret, if it had one. And neither one of them felt the need to report their findings. So Wave had grown a fondness for short doses of Rato's company, nothing intense or worrisome though. Now he said "It's a real small place, full of dumb-ass PhDs that think they're Einstein frosted with Jesus. But they might have some janitorial work, something like that."

Rato stared him down. "I pushed enough broom in my country's service to last me on to the grave and beyond."

"No offense. You asked."

Rato nodded. "I did." Then he sat still to down the remainder of his drink. "See, all it is—I'm aiming to stay here in Raleigh. Get me a job and a little place, maybe room with some quiet guy. Not have to go back to the miserable country and watch leaves develop."

Wave said "I wish I could *see* a leaf, just one more clean leaf."

Rato pointed to the big plate glass behind them. "Step out to the damned campus yonder and look."

Wave sneered. "They're so damned filthy they ain't even green, just a sick yellow-gray."

Rato said "I love them. City leaves deserve extra credit.

They got to work harder. Up home they're lazy, get everything free."

Wave said "I was wondering what effect it would have —your sister's husband coming back."

"It don't have to have any effect on me. I'm welcome to be anywhere Wesley is; he said so plainly. I just plan to give them air to breathe."

"They still having trouble?"

"Ask them," Rato said.

Wave said "Cool down. I was just well-wishing."

"They'd be glad to know it. Go tell them so."

Wave laughed. "Thank you, no. I'll give it to her though, your sister is a lovely lady."

"Glad you noticed. I didn't know you'd seen that much of my sister."

Wave said "I haven't. Just two or three minutes—it don't take long. She shines out fast."

"She's naturally kind. Like natural curly hair. All her life and mine, Rosacoke has been kind from the roots of her hair."

"Rosa*coke*?" Wave asked.

"That's her full official name."

"Where the hell did that come from?"

Rato said "From God to our mother—you know, inspiration. But she dropped the *coke* when she moved here to town. Too country, I guess."

Wave smiled and nodded. "People might have thought she was dealing drugs. Just yesterday out here on Hillsboro Street, I saw a black dude in a big limousine with guess-what license plate?—S-M-A-C-K."

Rato said "Like I said though, my sister is *kind*."

"And she's been well paid, far as I can see."

Rato flushed. "What the hell does that mean? She don't work for pay. She's had real pain—a baby born dead after one live boy."

Wave said "I'm sorry. And I didn't mean money. I mean she has won her a happy life. I thought she had; now you say otherwise. I bow to your wisdom."

Again Rato took one of his pauses, time enough for atoms to race back and forth from pole to pole a few dozen times, making unseen auroras in the gloom of Greenland. Then he leaned forward. "Listen, how does this sound? If I head home in a week or so, would you come by the house the last night for supper? A little kind of party, my way to thank Rosa for letting me stay?—I'll buy all the food. Course I'll probably stay on."

Wave thought it through, then smiled sincerely. He knew Rato would have to leave soon. "If your folks don't mind, I'd be real honored."

Rato said "Anything I want is fine by them."

Wave said "I thought your sister has been kind of sick."

"Nervous, not sick—just from Wesley being gone."

Wave said "I thought you moved up to join her once she got sick."

It didn't raise any suspicion in Rato. "I never said that. You must have dreamed it."

Wave waited, then laughed much longer than he planned. "I dream so much I sometimes wonder if I'm ever awake."

Rato met his eyes head-on, then leaned closer quick and pressed a long fingernail hard in Wave's wrist. "Feel that?" he said.

Wave drew back. *"Yes."*

"You're awake now at least."

Wave said "I hope."

THE SAME AFTERNOON AWHILE PAST FIVE, THE SPRING
light was holding at the rim of the sky; and the younger
boys at Wesley's garage were dropping their equipment and
heading home. His old boss Bronny walked up to Wesley,
who was tuning a Volvo, and asked if he'd join him for a
beer across the road?

Wesley said "Sure. Just give me ten minutes."

Bronny said "No longer. That woman can wait."

"I promised her I'd have it ready today. She's leaving
for a wedding tomorrow at nine."

Bronny said "Yeah, her own—her own third, ain't it?
You'd be doing both her and the guy a favor if you quit
here and now, with the damned thing broke."

Wesley laughed but Bronny left him. And in another
half-hour he'd finished the job, washed up, and was sitting
with Bronny in the cool dim back of the Top Hat Lounge.
Bronny had ordered Michelob, his idea of the finest in
European beers; Wesley was nursing a double Jack Daniels
on the rocks. After two long draws, Bronny said "It looks
like you're deep back in the groove and happy—am I
wrong?"

Wesley said "I'm grateful to you for the raise. There's
some few things I'm glad to have back. But Bron, I left
here feeling cold dead. I won't lie to you and say that's
changed."

Bronny pressed a dark enormous finger against the back
of Wesley's hand. Blood flushed out of place. The flesh

shone livid. Then the accustomed red streamed back. Bronny said "That's a test for life. You pass, flying colors."

Wesley smiled and pressed both palms to his temples. "The dead's up here between my ears."

Bronny asked "Since when were you any big genius? You live in your hands like me, not your brain. You're younger than me but you're still, what?—fifty?—and the store's shutting down. Got to slow down your dreams."

Wesley nodded. "I've got dreams old as my eyes, older than any cell alive in my body I need one thing fulfilled at least. Then I'll shut up and die like everybody else."

Bronny said "Will you tell me?—that last thing you need."

Wesley said "Then give me your flat Bible oath, deep secret or death."

Bronny nodded in silence.

Wesley said "I need a strong woman maybe twenty-three. She'd work at home, keeping everything straight— no kids, just stuff: nice clean useful stuff. Good wholesome plain American food, no same dish more than once a month except sweet potato pie. Fine sex every night with a low light burning in the bathroom maybe—a good hour's worth, both of us repaid. Then the lights go out, I say my prayers, she tells me—I think her name may be Sandy—every last lie I need to hear. She makes it sound sincere as scripture, I trust every word, I sleep like a three-year-old and rise strong and rested to live more days like my best boyhood. That strong, that certain Wesley knows his way, that proud he's satisfied God and his family and will still not fail."

"That who you left in Nashville?"

Wesley's face clouded over.

"—Sandy, the girl? Is that who you lived with all those weeks?"

Wesley had to wonder. But he answered truly. "Some parts of her, yes. Her real name was Wilson. Wilson had some things I never saw matched—the sex part at first was like sweet magic: night, dawn, noon (if we got a day off). Wilson knew ways to lie there, facing my eyes, or even better ways to get up and *work*—ways I pray I never forget but can't never hope to meet again, not in this world. But then she stopped on a damned cold dime. The first day of spring I reached over to her and, Bron, she had *quit*. She said she quit lying, the real girl Wilson."

Bronny said "How'd you know?"

"She told me so. Said she'd been giving in to help me 'recover,' said now I'd need to manage myself. 'Work out your own cure—you're too old a guy to be rooting in just my skin for salvation.' Lying there that instant, my hand in her hair, I knew she was right. And it hurt worse than stabbing. I tucked tail and came on back here fast."

"I wondered what brought you."

Wesley nodded. "That was it." He hadn't yet mentioned the rape to anybody.

"And you're meaning to stay?"

"I don't think of anywhere else right now."

Bronny frowned. "I was hoping home had got some better."

Wesley said "Don't lose a good minute on me. I can still tighten bolts good as I ever did. I just can't face up to being grown. See, nobody but me ever knew how high I aimed—for happiness, I mean. Not money or power, nothing like that. Just a steady perfectly happy ride for my body, right on through this life to Paradise."

Bronny laughed. "Anybody ever get it? Anybody you've watched?"

"Course not," Wesley said. "I told you I was crazy."

"Then why not give up, admit you're normal, set back here with that fine wife you've got, and count your blessings once a year at Thanksgiving?"

Wesley nodded but then faced Bronny gravely. "Because I hurt too goddamned much."

Bronny said "I'm not exactly gliding on morphine. But hell, my mother warned me in the cradle. She said 'Ernest James, your dad and his brothers have ruined every woman's life that ever brushed past them. When you get grown enough to notice girls, remember your mother and let women *be*. They are just human beings, not angels in pearls. They can't make up to you for your bad luck. You'll be damned fortunate if you find one, in all your years, that can softboil an egg right four times in five— much less mend your broke heart every night.' I remembered her too, every word all my life. It saved me a lot."

Wesley smiled. "Ernest *James*? Who in God's name is that?"

"The first two-thirds of my whole name. I let it slip out. Tell a soul and I'll kill you."

Wesley said "What you pay me?"

Bronny grinned at first and reached for his wallet, then put it back, and leaned to Wesley's eyes. "I've already give you a priceless gift—my good mother's words. You step on home now and live her advice. You might yet have a nice day or two in the thirty more years you're liable to get above ground."

Wesley said "Is it that long? Please say no."

Bronny said "May be longer, if you don't shape up. Something else Mama said, 'Whom the Lord loves, He kills.'"

Wesley shook his head. "Hot-damn, old Ernest! Your mama shot *straight*."

Bronny stood up to pay. "And is still aiming right this evening at fools. She'll be ninety-six this fourth of July."

"Then God must love her sweet butt to death."

Bronny said "He does. She's been stone-blind for the past ten years. But you knew that."

Wesley shook his head. "I didn't, no sir. I doubt I could have stood it."

Bronny strode on forward to the bleached cashier. "Sure you could. You'll stand far worse and be glad."

THEY ALL GOT HOME WELL BEFORE DARK THAT EVENING. Rosa came first and when she had parked in the drive, she took the small bag of groceries and headed for the house before she thought to look. In all the months that Wesley was gone, she'd forced herself not to study homesights (the details of where they'd spent their life—for instance, the dimestore white azalea that Wesley had brought her the week they moved here; now it was almost a neck-high tree).

But Rosa's right foot caught on a rock. When she paused to gain her balance, she saw the sun in the upstairs back-hall window ablaze. For an instant she thought the house was burning out of control, and for one more instant she felt relief. A leveling fire would bless them all—flush Rato to Afton, force Wesley's hand (to turn loose once for all and leave or to seize hold finally and rebuild a life).

Rosa's eyes brimmed water and the big can of yams in her grocery bag tore through the paper and struck her foot. She hollered "Oh!" and realized then that the fire was mere sunset, a commonplace. Next she thought "Thank God, it's all here—a lifetime's surroundings ready and waiting to work. Now we'll each take hold." By *each* she meant herself and Wesley.

FIVE MINUTES LATER WESLEY PULLED IN BEHIND HER, paused at the wheel to spray his mouth with a sweet disguise to hide the bourbon (knowing Rosa still hated even one strong drink, whatever she said; it had killed her father). He tested his breath on the back of a hand, winced at the whorehouse stench, then aimed for the kitchen door. By then the sun had sunk enough to cool the back windows. What showed upstairs were the lamps Rosa had lit just now as she climbed up to change into kitchen clothes.

Wesley suddenly thought of the years he would race home here from work, hoping young Horace would still be playing and that Wesley could stretch out with Rosa ten minutes and fly back in time to their good first days before they stood back up to be parents. Could he do that now? Would his mind give the order and his body obey? Granting all that, would Rosa consent and not just laugh?

He kept on walking in the clean gray gravel. And in three more steps, he was saying again and again to himself Bronny's mother's old words—"You let women be. They are just human people, not angels in pearls." Was a word of it true? And if so, did Wesley want such a world—with no better dream?

Wesley prayed he'd know a workable livable answer by the time he reached for the door. But no he didn't. Still he went on in, with his own old key, and called upstairs to let her hear his voice. "It's nobody else but your old bud."

From somewhere farther away than the moon, what seemed Rosa's young voice said "Dear bud."

Wesley's dry heart leaned toward the flame. But no cell took fire, no answer came—not there or then.

RATO SAID GOODBYE TO WAVE AT THE CORNER TWO blocks away and scuffed on to Rosa and Wesley's in something very much like a trance. He'd counted as a last resort on Wave having job ideas or, at the least, an offer to bunk in with him. But Wave had met him with blank refusal. He'd seemed a real friend, almost like a son. Now Rato had scared him and flushed him off.

That had been the story every time in his life when Rato tried to open up to somebody. Something someway scared them. His strength was too big, or so he suspected. What he hadn't allowed for was another plain fact—that his own big eyes were wide as holes in the ocean floor off the Philippines sucking in all life, all rocks, boats and whales. People, men especially, scrambled for high ground when Rato got anywhere near serious.

He'd tried fifty-odd years to change the problem— laughing more often, when nothing seemed funny, and letting folks know the last thing Rato needed was human help. But they still ran from him. All right, he'd take that as God's own will.

His mother once asked him not to get married. He didn't ask why at the time and had never asked since. She was bound to have had her own good reason (she never asked anything big without reason, generally good). When he got back home this time however, he'd ask her at last—

just tell me why. And unless she barked back or sang a long stanza of partridge calls, Rato knew he'd obey. He was not a real human, not yet in this world.

But a voice said his name. "Horatio Junior Mustian."

Rato stopped—Wesley combed, clean, and dressed on his front-door stoop with *The Raleigh Times*.

Wesley also said "You look kind of lost."

Rato said "I'm not. I know my place."

Wesley said "Tell me mine."

"That's your next problem," Rato said, "nobody else's."

Wesley walked on to meet him and hugged his thin chest with one long arm.

Over his shoulder, from Wesley's mouth, Rato thought he could hear Wesley's deep voice whisper something like "Guess though. Guess where I belong. Please guess hard now. Help any way you can. It's got that bad."

Rato was confident he understood the words—Wesley was howling an S.O.S., something they'd never done in Rato's hearing in all the past years. Rato couldn't guess why though or what would help. His own hands stayed flat down at his sides. And in his natural voice at normal volume, he said "Just tell me what you want and when."

Wesley said "Take over, Ace. You lead from here."

Rato said "Then Jesus, we're blind in the night."

Wesley stepped back, turned loose of Rato's arm, and stared. Then he burst onto one long high laughing note.

By then Rosa had opened the front door behind them on the porch. She asked "Anybody but me bad hungry?"

Both men turned to face her, and Rato said "I may have to fall down here till you feed me with some kind of tube."

Wesley said "We both need you to save us."

Rosa smiled in their faces and said "All right." Her lean

chin nodded again and again, the same agreement they'd seen her give throughout their lives when people (sometimes the two of them) needed her skills as badly as now.

Rato stepped forward, drawing Wesley behind. By the time they reached the screen door and entered, the last weak light had soaked back into the sky, and night swept up around all their tired legs.

IN HIS OWN ROOM TWO HOURS LATER THAN THAT, WAVE lay in the dark and stared at a large hole of black night beyond him—his one clear window. He somehow knew that Rosa and Wesley, and Rato beside them, were still at their dining table still talking. He went on to think they would soon join hands and sing one song, not a hymn but some sweet statement of their care. They'd never have done it—Rato couldn't sing "Jesus Loves Me," much less harder songs—but the thought alone was sufficient to ease Wave off into sleep.

Fully dressed on top of his light army blanket, he slept five hours without turning once. Two or three times he spoke strange sentences plainly to the ceiling and woke himself briefly, long enough to realize he'd either said nonsense or told his dark secret to the walls and the window—that no man but Wave in all this state could serve lone women as fine as he, with his nice brand of tender care.

Then at one in the morning, Wave woke fully rested but chilly. He sat straight up. Rosa's face swam up at once in his head. He wanted above all things on earth to see her now and make up to her for all she'd suffered, all the world had kept from her.

He couldn't imagine how to break through the circles of

guards that kept her—Rato in his room, yards down the hall, and Wesley right by her (he couldn't cut or kill; Wave had never cut yet).

But his wish was so strong, it took him to the street and in sight again of Rosa and Wesley and Rato's house—medium size and in need of paint—before he pulled up and saw his error. *This woman is happy. She's chosen her life and is glad to have it. Or it's chose her and she's bowed to take it.*

Wave had not shed actual tears since childhood; he shed none yet though his eyes felt full. Was his whole life wrong, founded on some sad or ridiculous mistake? What if the whole world out there, including all women, was happier than Wave? What if Wave was just one lonesome ludicrous clown out by himself in the cooling dark night acting on a simple boyhood mistake that everyone but he had long since corrected?

He still hadn't wept, not actual tears. But he couldn't have bet you his head wouldn't burst—in a screaming utterly silent explosion—in the next few seconds leaving Waverly Wilbanks no longer alive and present as a friend and no one noticing the hole he'd left or caring at least.

ROSA WESLEY

FIVE NIGHTS LATER AT HALF-PAST ELEVEN, ROSA climbed to their room, scrubbed her face, and was in her gown and robe before Wesley joined her. She'd spent a good part of the past few days thinking through her campus talk with Jean. Jean had even tried to keep up the sales pitch for Wesley. But Rosa had asked her to pull back please—she needed quiet air to test her own feelings and choose her own path. Jean had gladly agreed, saying only one more thing—"Don't even dream of finding another man that sweet to be around, that tried and true. They threw away the mold in 1945."

And by now it had come down pretty much to just that. If Rosa hung onto Wesley, and he to her, time might well be expected to sweeten their bodies again for one another. But *tried and true*? They'd sure God tried each other all their lives and might well have thought there were no surprises. But there were. Oh Jesus, there were awful shocks. And in all the problems the world could throw you, a surprise—anything from telephone reminders that you've missed a PTA meeting to announcements of death—was what Rosa dreaded most. She was living proof that a woman can walk into the house one evening to find it dark and cold and vacant, your long-trusted mate speeding west for Nashville and (whether he knows it or not) a young radiologist with fresh gifts to give him.

How could that be counted as something *true*? How could any such human be trusted again, much less lain down beside every night—even if he was the veteran of all you'd felt and done since early childhood? Maybe trust wasn't something anybody ever had a right to feel. Maybe all you could hope for was strength and courage and a steady share of luck.

One thing seemed sure—the rape hadn't made Rosa dread him or anyone except the sick rapist. She hadn't felt powerful bodily need for any known man in maybe ten years. That need had just slid from her for no visible cause. If Wesley badly needed to rekindle that, Rosa truly guessed he was welcome to try; she'd cooperate to the limits of her mind and present body. If a better life—deeper truth and trust—flowed forward from that, then praise all the angels, praise God (day or dark)!

By the time Rosa worked her way that far, she was sitting in the little straight chair she'd brought to Raleigh from her childhood bedroom, her grandfather's dark oak corner-chair (all rounds and slats, no foolish springs or stuffing and padding). She picked up *Quiet Time* from a low table, the devotional magazine that Mama gave her every year for her birthday—a scripture passage and a

half-page meditation for each day. Rosa seldom kept up. In
fact she hadn't so much as opened this month's copy yet.

Today's Bible verse was "Jesus wept," the shortest verse
in either testament. When she was a girl, kids used it in
Sunday school for all grades of fun—comic rhymes for
instance. Milo could spin them out for the best part of a
Sunday.

> *Jesus wept,*
> *Peter crept,*
> *Moses came a-crawling.*
> *Adam slept,*
> *Eve leapt,*
> *Cain came caterwauling.*

That night's meditation acknowledged that the verse had
been cause for fun through centuries past but that now it
was time for every believer to pause a long while and think
of the meaning.

"Jesus weeps at the grave of his friend Lazarus. He
weeps though He knows that, in a moment, He will raise
His friend from the stench of death into radiant life. It is
the only time in the gospels when Jesus is shown to sorrow.
Elsewhere He shows anger or consternation that evil has
gained access to human flesh; but only here does he pay
the tribute of tears, the fruit of love.

"Later, in the cool dark of Gethsemane when He fore-
sees tomorrow's hot dust with the crowd jeering and cold
spikes pounded through His tender flesh, He does not
weep. In full awareness that tomorrow He must suffer, as
hard as any man or woman ever, what rolls down is not
tears but sweat, sweat like drops of blood streaks His flesh.

The mystery in that! Tears for a friend who suffered death but will rise again, sweat for Himself who will die and rise. The fruit of sorrow, the fruit of labor—our deepest glimpses of what He paid to save all souls."

Wesley stepped on past her to the bathroom and brushed his teeth, gargled, combed his hair. By the time he was ready, Rosa had set her book down. Wesley stepped again past her to finish undressing. And again he took no notice of her, neither looking nor speaking—neat as she was.

In fifteen seconds he was bare before her, and he held there a minute—not preening or even aware of her eyes but wholly absorbed in a spot on his forearm. He finally licked at it lightly with short strokes of what seemed the tip of a puppy's pink tongue. Then he reached into his drawer, got a clean white T-shirt that once had been Horace's, and pulled it on. On the back it had Rosa's favorite message of all—

If you love good music,
Follow me home—

and he stepped toward the left-hand side of the bed. Rosa had already stood to follow before he turned to speak. But when his eyes met her, Wesley said anyhow "You planning on getting tired any night soon?"

Rosa said "No sir, I was coming for the music."

He didn't catch her meaning at first.

She pointed. "I mean your T-shirt. I'm following you home."

By then Wesley had thrown all the cover back. You could plainly see he was thinking of *home*. Was this really home she'd followed him to, his home anyhow? But suddenly he faced her from the edge of the mattress, pulled the hem of his shirt down in front, and blinked at her shyly. "I'd have dressed up better for a real lady-guest if you'd warned me you were here."

"I hoped I wasn't that much of a lady."

He was honestly baffled. "Why would you say that?"

"I sometimes think I hurt us with that, all my sense of what's fitting and right. I never was sure I could do it sincerely, be that easy at night with you."

Wesley waited awhile. "Oh no ma'm, you were—sincere all right. Eleanor Roosevelt was white trash next to you."

What could Rosa do but grin or run?

Before she could bolt though, Wesley laughed and climbed in the sheets and covered his body right to the chin.

Wesley stayed shy in the face, looking down. Steadily he moved from joking to gravity. Rosa's upright pride and dignity were things he'd also admired and sought in her. What was she meaning here now—cut and run? Was she saying they ought to bail out this Friday and drive to that sex motel near High Point and rent a big room with closed-circuit television, video porn, and maybe some hot deals with other starved couples to right and left?

Even though they never planned to try for more children or go to church regularly, Wesley knew he would hate it now if Rosa tried to rip out the broad base of decency they'd stood on. He couldn't even dream of a Rosa in make-up and crotchless panties from Frederick's of Hollywood (with all-night Saigon ticklers for Wesley to use by hand while he lay here lonesome and sad and watched her writhe). He said "Rosa, hush up and step on to bed." But he didn't turn the cover back and wave with his palm.

Rosa studied him in place for what seemed upward of half a minute. The front of his T-shirt was blank but clean (no other known housewife ironed T-shirts). Still she knew the back—*Good music . . . follow me*. Wasn't that what he'd said always since the Sunday she saw him up the tree staring off?—and not with his own voice but in some silent message from the empty air around him. Wesley was a promise and had evermore been. A promise of what? Well, she still didn't know. She had never really figured in nearly forty years. And had never really asked. Rosa couldn't stand here now and ask, outright.

That left two choices. She could dress again warmly and leave for good. There were probably as many jobs for good secretaries in Nashville, or Charleston, as for good mechanics—well-combed women of the sad damned school that would water the office plants and cook for the Christmas parties on top of every well-spelled word she typed. Or else she could strip off further still and join that mainly strange man beyond her, begging her presence for his own secret need.

So eventually she did take the first step toward him. She switched off all lights, laid her robe on the chair, and made a slow chilly way forward into cold cotton sheets till the zone of Wesley's established warmth broadcast through space and found her skin—just the warmth, no touch.

Rosa had time alone to say her night prayers. They were mostly calm requests for her mother as the one lone person in her family tonight. In the silence that followed, she could hear Wesley's body beside her awake. She figured it was she that would now have to talk. He was trapped as usual in his own natural quiet. But their hall door was still wide open, and next she heard Rato's big footsteps outside. His television was finished.

He paused by their door and listened for life or the rhythms of sleep.

Wesley was finally the one who spoke. "Hey, bud."

Rato said "Y'all asleep?"

Wesley said "For hours."

Rato said "Sleep on" and moved toward his room.

But Rosa said "Come back, hon. We're wide awake." She wondered if she'd ever called him *hon* before. Would he take offense or notice?

He noticed. He waited awhile and then began buzzing loudly like a bee. "Bzzzz."

Finally Wesley asked "What the hell is that?"

Rato said "I'm just cooking Rosa more honey."

Wesley said "Good business. Then you won't need me." He began to snore.

Rosa said "You two please hush; it's *night*. Rato, you got something to tell me or what?"

Rato said "Both of you. I'm leaving here soon."

Wesley said "No you ain't" and snored again.

Rosa said "Rato, why?"

"I got to head home."

"Something calling you there?" Rosa's voice by then was genuinely urgent.

"Nearest thing to home *I've* got, I guess." Rato was the last man alive who could say such words with no trace of self-pity.

Wesley said "You can live here long as I'm here." He meant it entirely.

Rosa said "Me too." And to her surprise, she was serious also. The peculiar brother who had been her good watchdog was suddenly now her friend and companion, a sure thing to lean on.

Rato said "Look, I've thought about it long as you two. I'm a retired U.S. soldier-boy and Afton's my address. Afton, N.C. is where the Army sends my check. If they come looking, they plan to find me there."

Wesley said "They won't come, Ace. They've used you up—you and me both, believe it. They're looking for men a lot younger than us."

Rosa smiled in the dark at both of them using the service for excuses. She said "Mama's making out all right alone."

Rato said "I ain't even studying Mama. God help the rapist that stumbles on Mama."

All three of them were struck dumb by that.

But Wesley broke the silence. He burst out laughing and the other two joined him.

Rato said "Wonder where he is right now?"

Wesley said "Out yonder in the bushes, hearing us."

Rosa said "Poor boy."

Rato said "I always thought he was grown."

Rosa said "Maybe so. He's a man anyhow; he was sure no lady." She could even laugh again.

Rato said "I can't find a job down here."

Wesley said "You ain't looked."

"I have, a long time. Nothing's turned up but pin boy at the bowling alley. And pin boys don't really work anymore; machines set the pins. They're just guys policing the floor backstage, picking up all the shit people throw with the balls—excuse me, Rosacoke" (excuse the word *shit*).

"Excused," she said.

Wesley said "I might could help you downtown."

Rato waited again. "Thank you, hear? But look, I worked a good hard thirty years for my country. Look how good a shape the damned country's in. The last thing my pride needs now is the minimum wage for a job some teen-ager dying of acne needs a lot worse than me."

It was the nearest anybody had ever come to hearing Rato admit publicly how his strangeness affected the world's opinion of him. Rosa was too puzzled to respond. But Wesley said "You are a fine ranger."

Rato said "Beg your pardon?"

"—Forest Ranger, old Smoky the Bear."

Rato said "That I am. Can't say that I love it."

Rosa asked "How much you think we love our work—typing letters, tuning cars?"

Rato said "You don't?"

Wesley said "You'll notice I ain't gone wild with excite-ment. If I never had to touch one more sick Porsche, I wouldn't miss a beat."

Rato asked "Where would you rather be?"

Wesley didn't speak so Rosa said "I could be happy in my mother's house, once she's gone to Heaven, raising most of our food and watching the sky slide through a year's changes."

Wesley still didn't speak so Rato said "Wesley, you ain't said."

Wesley laughed. "I take what the Lord sends down."

Rato said "You ran."

Again they all were struck dumb. This time they knew they'd heard real judgment from the only one present who was fit to judge, a true bystander who (far as they knew) had never hurt one human soul for one instant. At last

Wesley said "—Ran like a shot dog, then turned and came back."

"Ran from what?" Rato said. He was asking out of pure curiosity now with no trace of malice. They all understood.

So Wesley said "Rato, I was scared to death. Maybe scared *of* death. I'm three-fourths there anyhow; we all are—fifty's three-fourths of seventy on anybody's scale."

Rato said "Just about." When they'd all paused again, he said "I'll get the bus late tomorrow morning."

"No you won't," Wesley said. "The least I can do is drive you home Sunday. Please let me do that."

"Me too," Rosa said. "The bus is too sad."

Rato said "I've met a lot of girls on buses."

Wesley said "Well, now we don't want to butt in if you've got a hot plan."

Rato said "I'm joking. A ride would be nice."

Rosa said "I'll pack us a picnic lunch so Mama won't go into a big cooking tizzy."

Rato said "You do and you'll ruin her week. You know that's all she's living for now."

Rosa said "That's one place I learned we were wrong. Notice how very much Mama's liked these months of not having you to feed."

Rato said "O.K." but he didn't sound pensive. He said "Good night, hear? And thank you both."

Wesley said "For what? It's us that thank you."

Rato said "I'm thanking you for all this much time in town. I've learned some things."

Wesley said "Name two."

Rosa said "No don't. We'll all be a lot better off with sleep."

Rato said "Maybe so. Good night again, hear?"

Wesley said "We hear you. Go get yourself dark."

Rosa heard that it was the most times Wesley had ever said *we* in his life. And calm as they were, it came as a shock. By the time she'd recovered, Rato was gone; and nothing else seemed important to say.

In a minute Wesley rolled to his left side, facing her. But still he didn't reach out or touch her skin at any point. He listened for a hint of sound from her, then he asked "That suit you?—what we just said?"

"I think so, yes."

"You want him to leave?"

Rosa said "I wouldn't need to put it that way. But I see what he means about his chances for work. And he couldn't stand to have us support him now. Long as he was guarding me, he let me keep him."

"I could leave again."

Rosa was also facing him. Even dark, she could see the dim lines of his features. "I won't ask that, just to keep a brother."

Wesley said "I'm absolutely serious. Understand me."

Nothing in his flat tone gave her the handholds to grasp a complete meaning. Was he claiming he needed to leave again? Was it that easy for him—to take *Go* or *Stay*, whichever she demanded? Eventually she said "No I don't understand. Can you go that easy?"

He said "Rosacoke, I think this is home. When I came back last month, I couldn't say that. Tonight though I almost think I can. It don't make me all that happy to admit it. It's not the real best I've dreamed to have; and whether you believe it or not, I've *dreamed*. I know that can't make you glad to hear. The trouble's not you, not the main part at least. The trouble's just life, the way it's made and *me* made in it—the turns I took and can't correct. With my mind now though, the way you've trained me, I don't think I can strike out and find better. That may mean I love you and that this must be home."

She thought "That's the longest speech he's ever made near me." And at first it promised to be a good thing, a new brand of freedom. But then she realized she'd heard two things. One was fine, the verge of a firm commitment for the rest of their lives. The other was as bad as she'd dreaded since Christmas week, the honest confession that what they'd had was not just imperfect but less than sufficient. To face Wesley now and accept all he'd said was somehow to lay down everything she'd fought for in knowing him and struggling to keep him. She faced the blank ceiling and waited for words. Not a clear true word rose up through her mind.

Wesley waited, slid into wheezing sleep (which Rosa could hear), then woke again to hear that she was silent. His brain's own clock couldn't tell if he'd lain there a minute or thirty. So he said "You still haven't said *Go* or *Stay*."

She told herself "If you cry now I'll kill you dead." But she said to Wesley "Better stay on tonight. I need to pause here. Tomorrow, or some sane day soon now, we both may have to pack up and go into separate rooms. I simply never heard your feelings before, not as clear as you laid them out just now. I've got to be sure I understood you right. Then I've got to be sure I can live with the meaning."

Wesley asked "You sure my meaning is all that different from yours?"

"I think so, yes. I think it's got to be. It *has* been all these years anyhow."

Wesley said "Mine too. That's the main thing I said. I

think—and hope—I can trim my sails and live like a
human, not an angel on fire gazing off toward God."

Rosa said "Is that it? Maybe so. Oh Lord. I know I've
felt on fire a lot."

"And burned, third degree."

Rosa nodded. "You too?"

"No you. I've watched you close, don't forget."

Rosa said "You're bound to have hurt."

Wesley said "Oh sure. But slower."

"Maybe deeper."

"I won't swap scars," he said. "It won't make sense."

Rosa touched him then—not thinking and never again
knowing why. She'd been on her back; and when she
turned, her left hand was uppermost. It went to his right
shoulder and stroked him gently there.

At first he was startled, but then he lay still and waited
for her gesture to clarify. In a minute he'd calmed to the
point where he dreamed he had a fine tattoo under her
palm, a sizable tiger stretched on the ground of Wesley's
still-taut white hide. For so many years it had felt alone
and not realized the danger in that. Now it roused and met
Rosa and welcomed her notice.

Then for the first time in all his years with women,
Wesley lay on quiet and let Rosa work her own slow will
—partly because he started so tired but also because he
was gambling there might be something to learn.

Rosa didn't share the hope. She'd learned all this, every
move and sound, in her bedtime thoughts and dreams long
ago. These were the ways she'd always loved Wesley, in
her mind at least. The main thing she made was slow circles, small circles with her hand and (though she could
only see a little) the syllables of tranquil comment and as-

surance that are most men's favorite of the sounds on earth.

She didn't assume he would somehow ignite and take over from her. She just kept going and he kept lying there. They'd got to a place that amazed them both, of mutual trust and precise alignment—lovely harmony, perfect rhythm.

And somehow they both moved on into sleep. In both their cases, it was sleep so profound their minds heard nothing from the house or street. Neither one knew a single thought or dream.

AND WHEN, BLOCKS AWAY, WAVE WILBANKS WOKE SUD-denly, he sat bolt upright in hot stale sheets and said their full names in one short prayer. It was a prayer for their life together hereafter, and it served to deepen the rest they'd earned tonight and enjoyed.

ROSA WESLEY RATO
HORACE PRIS WILSON

◈

THE NEXT WEEKEND—THE LAST IN APRIL—HORACE called from Charlotte on Saturday morning while Rosa, Wesley, and Rato were finishing breakfast. Because Rosa was cooking a last round of pancakes, Wesley was forced to answer the ring (he'd rather have drunk rat bane than answer a telephone). He said "Hey, son" and several other pleasantries, then "Sure" several times, and finally "Plan to stay for supper. Drive careful, hear?" He sat down again without comment, and stubborn Rosa decided not to ask.

Rato broke down finally. "Who else is coming to supper? And is it today?"

Wesley ate a whole mouthful before he said "Horace and, I think he said, Pris. They're leaving now and said they'd be here in maybe three hours. That'd be one o'clock."

Since they hadn't let him buy the groceries, Rato knew he lacked the right to object. But he did think how this would complicate the evening, his last one in Raleigh. Rosa had planned him a farewell supper, and he'd invited Wave (Wave's first meal here). Well, Rosa could handle it all someway.

Rosa had not returned to the table. She was still at the stove, cleaning up there. But finally she couldn't restrain her anger. "I sure do wish you'd asked my opinion. I've already got to shop and cook for Rato's farewell supper tonight, and now two extra mouths to feed—one of them, that Pris! I'd rather cook for the baboon-squad at the N.C. Zoo than that mean-mouthed bitch."

Wesley shot a look to Rato. They both raised their eyebrows—having grown up in homes where, whatever you thought of your kin, you never spoke quite that frankly about them. Wesley though was the first one to laugh.

Rosa said "She is. You prove I'm wrong."

Wesley said "I'm not her lawyer, no ma'm. I'll grant you Pris is no tender shrinking vine. But our only son married her. What choice have we got?"

Rosa said "—The choice I've made all year, when Horace kindly volunteered to come and help me. I told him I'd handle my trouble in place. I didn't have to say 'Without your spouse.' Horace knows I tried to like his pick. But who, in their right mind, could warm up to Pris? Hell, a polar bear doesn't crave warmth that much."

Even Rato broke down then and laughed. "Don't worry. Pris knows you're more than her match. If they do stay for supper, you'll hold her down. Wave'll think she's just a clean dog in a muzzle."

And Rosa had got to the point of a smile. "Pris has always been respectful to me. If they stay, I trust she'll act all right."

Wesley said "Remind me to lay in some booze."

Rato said "Since Wave is my guest, I'll contribute. He likes foreign beer." That meant a real outlay, maybe Heinekens. Never mind. Wave had thoroughly earned it.

Rosa said "I'll put my foot down now. That way, nobody gets mad later on. You can bring in maybe a case of beer, nothing too expensive. But stronger than that, we better not go. I'm not slaving my lovely bubbies all day over this hot stove for a table of drunks. Anybody not sober enough to taste my cooking, can get up and walk. I serve notice now."

Wesley said "Understood" and winked at Rato.

SIX HOURS LATER THEY WERE ALL BACK THERE TOGETHER in the kitchen. Horace had kept Pris downtown shopping from two till four. Rosa was laying out supper supplies. The men were drinking beer at the table, Pris was serving the nachos she'd just learned to make from *Family Circle*, a big success.

Rato said "I learned to love spice in Spain. I can't see why it don't work in America."

Pris said "It does now, at my house anyhow."

Horace said "She's got me *massaged* in garlic. I can't see how I grew up without it."

Rosa said "Well, you did. Somehow against all odds you survived. And look at you now, strong and healthy to watch."

For an instant, pure misery swept through Horace's eyes. Not only had his whole childhood been darkened by the fact that a sister younger than he had been born dead; but once he'd quit college, gone to work, and found a classy wife, then his wife and mother hated each other. And *hated* was not too strong a word. Whenever they were apart (which he arranged to be more than a hundred percent of the time), they each survived by pretending that the other one didn't exist. But when he couldn't help bringing them to the same room, then he had to face truths about humanity that nearly stove him in.

Horace had his father's gentle heart. He couldn't imagine jealousy this harsh. What was in such short supply in his heart that two smart women had to fight like Siamese fish in a bowl to get their threatened portion? He knew he'd never find out. And anyhow he and Pris would be leaving shortly. So Horace took his old way out. He grinned and said "The women in my life have kept me hopping. I'm grateful to them both." He bowed to Pris and then to Rosa.

They each eyed the other—noticing the order of his recognition—then bowed back to Horace. And Pris said "Glad I made up the pallet."

Wesley said "Beg your pardon?"

"A pallet in the car, for Sabu to sleep on the back seat homeward." Sabu was Pris and Horace's dog, a King Charles spaniel that Roger hoped to eat. She'd left it in the car to help keep peace but found a way every hour or so to remind everybody of her sacrifice. She bent herself double to see out the window; it was almost dusk. She said "Who is this eating dinner with y'all?"

Rosa said "A very rich friend of my brother's."

Rato looked to his sister, unbelieving.

But Rosa shot him a smiling signal, "*Hush!*" She knew how Pris worshiped money in life. Then Rosa thought "O Lord, now she might stay." So she added "Course he won't come into his trust fund till when, Rato?—ten years?"

Rato said "Twenty-odd. He's flat-broke still. That explains the bugs."

Pris went lilac-colored at the ears but Horace said "Bugs?"

Wesley said "Rato doesn't mean real bugs. His hair does look like it's got legs though."

Rato said "I'm not sure what I mean." But he left it at that.

Pris began to rise. She brushed herself off carefully in place, then headed briskly for an upstairs bathroom where she suspected no visitors went.

And Rato, for his own unexplained reasons, all but ran out the back.

By then Wesley, Rosa, and Horace were seated at the kitchen table. Horace said "We'll need to get on the road, got just tomorrow to rest up in, then work again Monday."

Wesley smiled "Like everybody else on earth. You all that tired?"

Horace said "No sir, I didn't mean that. I just meant I didn't want to drive past midnight."

Rosa said "We well understand that, son. You've got no need to feel guilty with us. You've been a good boy. You don't owe us one single thing more."

As if his mother had tripped a switch he'd dreaded all day, a gallon of blood flushed through Horace's face. A vigorous red, then a strangulated purple—it passed through the visible stages of health. Then he finally said

"You both look safe. Am I right or wrong?"

Baffled thoroughly, Wesley looked to Rosa. "You feeling in danger?"

Rosa smiled "Not a lot." Horace was one more person who didn't know about the rape.

Wesley said "Me neither. What you talking about, son?"

Horace's blush had calmed a little but renewed itself now. "I meant are you two feeling good together? You've been back under the same roof now for—what?—four weeks. Is it going to take? Have I got my parents back together again, or are you two staking out separate tents?"

Rosa wanted to answer quickly "Parents, two of them, back together." But something kept her silent, waiting.

So in his own time, Wesley said "I think this tent'll be big enough. Don't you, Mom?"

Horace grinned. "Outstanding."

But Rosa was staring serious at Wesley. "Please never call me *Mom* again. I've asked you before. I'm Horace's mother, nobody else's yet."

Wesley nodded. "*I'm* ready. We still got the crib." He wasn't being cruel. The dead little girl was so far behind them, and they'd talked so long about other solutions. "Call the orphanage Monday."

Even Rosa could smile. "Maybe this tent does need a big annex—a few concubines, years younger than me."

Pris was back in the door, hair sprayed again—a hard-sugar helmet—and a clean new white blouse stiff at her neckline (she always brought an overnight bag of change-ables, in case of filth or perspiration or a big change of mood). "There haven't been concubines since the Old Testament."

"There may be again though," Wesley said. "Any day,

here and now. Brace yourself and come on forward toward me. My first wife just now give her permission which is all it takes, in the Bible at least."

Pris looked to Horace with a taut sick grin.

But Horace was already rising to leave. He'd grown up here; and he liked his parents, especially his father (a kind burdened man). But the wife Horace chose and all but worshiped was made for a better world than this—different at least, according to her. All her dreams were of order, of cut-glass chandeliers, mint-green velvet rugs, and everybody dressed for the hour of the day. It was time to rescue Pris and drive her and Sabu home to Charlotte. He and she both were prepared to work hard years—ten, twenty, thirty till arthritis crushed them—to buy their tickets toward her brand of taste.

WHEN THEY'D SAID GOODBYE TO HORACE AND PRIS AND were still in the yard, Wesley turned to Rosa. "I'm going to run in and buy me some magazines. Anything you need to get for the supper?"

She said "Bring me something decent to read."

"Whoa, what would that be? Most reading's indecent these days—whole point about reading."

Rosa said "How about *Southern Living*?"

Wesley said "That's decent but tame as hell, recipes and how to restore your old johnny-house."

"Bring it anyhow. I'll stay out of trouble."

He asked Rato when the friend was due.

"Six o'clock. He'll be here early though."

Wesley checked his watch. "Then I'll beat him back. Wouldn't want him to feel like he didn't have a host."

Wesley wished they hadn't but Rosa and Rato stood

there to watch him out of sight as if he might be going for good. The whole point of the errand was, he wasn't. He was making the last arrangement to stay. And only that certainty made him push on through this little last afternoon deceit.

HE STOPPED QUICKLY AT A NEWSSTAND NEAR N.C. STATE, picked up fifteen dollars worth of magazines, and rushed on into the middle of town (near Capitol Square) to a pay phone he'd checked out the previous Friday. You couldn't see it easily from the street, and Wesley had laid in a big lot of change. As the number rang the first time, he did what he'd hardly planned to do—for whatever reasons, he prayed she'd be there.

It seemed she wasn't or the number had been changed. A strange woman answered and repeated the number.

He said "Look, I'm trying to get up with Wilson."

She said "Who are you?"

"An old friend, Wesley in North Carolina."

She said "Hey there" and yes, it was Wilson.

"Boy, you sure don't sound like the Wilson I knew."

She laughed a dry cough; had she started back smoking? "Maybe that's because I'm not. Leave me alone and I go all strange. You're not the first guy to run across that."

"Nor the last," Wesley said.

That was her turn to say "Look, what's the problem? I don't want to sit here and ruin a nice memory. You got something kind to say, say it or let's quit."

"You got you some company?"

"I'm curling hair," she said. "But just for tonight. Me and Eunice Dean are supervising permanents on each other's heads."

"I bet you look grand."

"And you win!" Wilson said. "By dark I'll look like a million in cash."

Wesley said "It's pretty here, a long bright Saturday."

"That's nice to know."

Then he couldn't think further. He forgot the reason he'd gone to these lengths.

Wilson still remembered him well enough to know that, if she was ever going to get back to curling hair, she'd have to spring his trap. She said "You miss me?"

That did it. In his mind Wesley felt a strong click as his meaning cleared up. "Wilson, I missed you before I ever left. I'll miss you every day long as I live."

"It's fun to hear," she said. "And I'm grateful. But don't overdo it. Your brain's got to have other memories by now."

Wesley said "It does. What I mean is, there'll be whole sets of minutes every day when I think of you as one real blessing in my sad life."

"That's so sweet, Wesley—you could've called collect!"

He laughed edgily. "It's every word true. But beyond it I also got to be honest. I'll be staying on here at home in my old stable."

Wilson said "I understood that. It's no kind of shock."

"I just didn't want it to be. I felt like the decent thing was to tell you myself."

In her privacy in Nashville, Wilson smiled to herself (even Eunice Dean near her couldn't have seen it). But she said "You were decent right along. I won't forget that. And you gave me eight or ten pictures yourself that'll stay with me always."

"I hope I did. It's about all any old boy can hope."

In an unguarded attempt to quit, Wilson said "So if you're back up here anytime, give me a ring for auld lang syne."

Wesley said "I won't be. Not unless I wake up one dreadful day turned overnight to a country-music star."

Wilson laughed. "I'll sit here waiting for that!"

"You do," he said. And his errand was ended. As he headed on to Rosa, he felt lighter weight by twenty pounds. He even whistled every country song he knew, smiling one or more times in each block.

Yet when he had entered the kitchen, given Rosa her *Southern Living* and Rato his *Playboy* and *Hustler* and *Cheri* (provisions for country life), Rosa said "If I didn't think it would mean I'm crazy, I'd say you've been out crying like a dog."

Wesley glanced at the small mirror by the refrigerator. By God he had but he said "No ma'm, just the breeze in my eyes."

Rato said "It's as still outside as Hell on Monday."

"That's still," Wesley said.

But they all quit there and turned back to supper tasks.

ROSA WESLEY
RATO WAVE

AT FIVE MINUTES TO SIX (EARLY AS RATO FORE-
told), Wave knocked at the kitchen door. Rosa
was upstairs dressing, Wesley was watching television in the living room, Rato was nervous waiting beside
him. And at the sound of the knock, Rato shot up like
somebody struck with lethal voltage—"Goddammit, I told
him the *front* door."

Wesley said "Be nice to him now. It's no big deal.
Maybe he just ain't a front-door man."

Rato said "But it's my damned party, the only one ever.
If I don't make the rules for this one, I won't get another
chance."

Wesley laughed. "And if you don't go on and let your
company in, you ain't going to have *this* chance."

So Rato went and there Wave was in black corduroy pants a little too short (with red socks showing), a dark blue shirt, and a grass-green tie. It was more than any of the family men were wearing.

Rato said "You can take off half of that stuff."

Wave said "Is it that ugly?" Never having been a supper guest, he was genuinely unsure.

Rato stepped aside and waved him in. "Hell no, walk in. You look so expensive I barely recognized you."

Wave smiled and entered. "I was hoping for that."

With no other word, Rato walked off toward the living room; and Wave fell in behind him shaking.

Wesley stood up to meet him and thrust out a hand. "Rato's told me you've been a good friend."

Wave said "Nothing hard in that" and looked around quickly. This was one room he'd never had time to see on his other trips here, in light and dark.

Already zombied by the television eye, Rato dropped on the sofa to watch the ball game.

So Wesley had to say "Take a load off your feet. Can I get you a beer?"

Wave said "Oh no sir, help yourself. I don't touch beer."

Wesley laughed. "You wouldn't have to touch it. I could bring you a straw."

But Wave shook his head and sat next to Rato neatly. In another second he was watching hard as Rato, though he knew less about any ball sport than a well-bred lady. Something in his mind said "Grab this hard, this moving picture. It'll get you through till she appears."

All the way over, he had wracked his brain to see if Rato had said where his sister would be. Maybe this was some sort of bachelor event? If so a whole door in his life would shut. He might never get to do the big thing he needed to do, the thing that might yet keep him alive and in hope.

But Wesley stood up and repeated his offer. "Last chance at a beverage." He loved the word *beverage*. It came into wide use after he was grown, and it fit his mouth nicely—*bev-er-age*.

Wave said "All right, sir," quickly dug two quarters out of his pocket, and held them toward Wesley.

Wesley grinned. "Lord, son. Be my guest. I'm a well-paid professional. I can handle the outlay, one night at least."

Wave blushed so fiercely it seemed to warn a hemorrhage. But then he smiled and Wesley went out.

THE GAME HAD NEAR ENDED, AND THE BEERS WERE FINished when Rosa walked in. She came so silently nobody heard her but Wave, and he stood like a galvanized child —bolt upright, shivering. He thought she looked younger than ever before. He had never seen her smile up close, and it almost shook him past his power to resist. The thought that he'd touched her closely in darkness not four months ago—and run when she yelled—seemed more unlikely than world peace or Jesus walking through the front door next with several blind children all reading the news.

Rosa didn't think she had seen Wave before. But of course since he was the one stranger present, she risked his name and offered her hand.

He seemed to inspect it before responding. But then, with his face still grave, he held it longer than either of them intended.

Rosa didn't pull back but when he'd released her, she took a long instant to search his eyes. There was something strong here, way stronger than she'd looked for in Rato's friend. But no, no clue of the source came to her. She said "I'm glad you were free to join us. We wanted to let Rato know how we'd miss him. He said you were his best Raleigh friend. So you seemed the right one to share our sadness but celebrate the chance he'll be back soon."

Rato said "Don't hold y'alls' breath too long."

That let Wave laugh. But he told Rosa how glad he was to share. Then he said the first truth he planned to reveal. "I've never been asked out to supper before."

Wesley said "Son, how old are you?"

Wave said "Twenty-six."

Wesley reached for his beer (a good heavy bottle—he hated to drink anything from a can). He toasted the air and said to Wave "Consider yourself asked, again and again. We're here most nights, clicking against each other like dice on a board—Rosa and me, old married folks. Drop in when you're lonesome."

Rosa smiled, understanding how loosely it was meant.

But Wave stayed earnest. He said "Whooee, if I came that often, I'd move on in."

Wesley said "We got a spare room from tomorrow noon onward."

Wave said "Oh well, my rent's paid up. I better stay there and leave you be."

Something told Rosa to change the tune, so she said "Anybody need a refill here? Otherwise I'll head on back to serve supper." She faced Wave again.

And again he was swept by her actual power. It no longer drew him onward to her skin but warmed him lightly all over—spring light, though by now outdoors full dark had fallen.

Wave said "No ma'm. I'm saving myself. Home cooking's a general mystery to me."

"Don't hope too hard," Rosa said. "I'm a typist. My mother's the last great cook in our line."

Rato said "You're better than all of t.v." (television chefs were among his favorite actors).

Wave said "I've counted on that now for days." He risked confronting her eyes again.

She was laughing and shaking her head, "Don't believe him." But every watt of her energy reached him and said "Your chance is still here waiting." Then she left for the stove.

DESSERT WAS THE LAST OF RATO'S CHOICES, AN EAGLE Brand condensed-milk lemon pie of sufficient richness to sink most battleships, not to mention submarines. When everyone had surfaced and Rosa had stood to start clearing plates, Wave spoke for the first time without being questioned. His face went urgent. "You going somewhere?"

Rosa laughed for the hundredth time. "No farther than the dishwasher. Why? What you need?"

Wave said "I just need to get on home and—"

"Home?" Wesley said. "The night's still young."

"Thank you, no sir. I got some homework to do—I'm taking a course in the night school at State in Creative Writing. Got a story to write."

Wesley said "No sweat. I'll just tell you mine. That'll hold you through three or four more semesters."

Rosa sat back down and said "Please spare him."

Wesley said "You got you a story already?"

Wave nodded. "These nine things land on Earth next year from the Fourth Dimension. They look so much like humans that nobody thinks they're strange. But one or two smart people notice their eyes, which don't reflect light. The eyelashes are about an inch long and straight, and the pupils are so flat black you can all but fall in and drown. Anyhow the things spread to all the real continents."

Rato asked "Are they men or women?"

"Neither one. They can be whichever they want—plus others—as the need arises."

Wesley said "Hot damn, it's going to get dirty."

Wave said "No sir. My class is mixed; most of them are working women with kids. Anyhow my spacelings each know one skill that the whole Earth lacks. They can heal fatal cancer or negotiate peace or prevent divorce by help-ing grown people in their bedrooms at night. The only thing all nine can do together is stop child abuse, just stop it dead. So the whole story shows how they each try to train their whole assigned continent the main thing they know. Their idea is, if all nine succeed then the continents can turn around and train others once the spacelings have left. Well, as you can guess, some of them succeed, some fail, some are killed—they can all be killed as easy as us; you just have to aim at their hearts or heads. They don't really have much muscle or bone. They're mainly just gris-tle. So their mission is not that big a success. As they leave all of them but two are in tears."

Wesley said "Don't get me wrong now please. But what kind of story would end like that?"

Wave said "Beg your pardon?"

Rato said "I like it a lot. It'd make a good show."

Rosa said "Me too. Do they teach some progressive people how to cure cancer?"

Wave said "No ma'm. That's another place they fail."

Wesley said "See there. That's all I mean. If you're making up a story, why the hell say that? Why not let the whole thing come out right? If you're making the story, you're the God of it—right?"

Wave smiled. "I guess so."

"Then *be* God, son. Do your best by the Earth. If I'm going to shell out hard-earned dollars to buy your book, I sure God don't want the Earth to end up with cancer and men's poor peckers still falling off from syphillis and such."

Rosa said "We're at the table, Wesley."

He said "Oh damn, I thought it was the pool room" but went on genuinely facing Wave, for an honest answer.

Wave said "I hadn't thought of it that way. My teacher neither—or at least he hasn't said so. I guess it's because we're telling the truth or trying to. The Earth's got cancer and even worse problems—"

Rosa was stunned to hear her mouth say "Women get raped too night after night."

Everybody was stunned. Rato and Wesley knew they understood. They figured Wave at least would be mystified. Finally Rato asked "You saying that's bad as cancer?"

Rosa said "Can be, in some situations."

Then Wesley got scared she had broke some leash and would, any instant now, throw her last room open to this strange guest. He said "Sugar, we're just talking school talk. It's no big deal."

But Wave faced Rosa too and dared a short smile. He said "Mrs. Beavers, two-thirds of raped women don't even call the cops when their bodies get forced."

Rosa waited a long time, still mystified by her mind's direction. Nothing had told her who this boy was, no clue in his voice or the line of his face "No, Wave, they don't. I understand why. They don't want to share that awful a secret."

Wave said "You sure it's always awful?"

"I'd have to say yes. But I haven't finished polling the rest of my sex." By then she'd found the breath and will to manage a laugh. She knew something she hadn't known before supper, not even ten minutes ago at this table. She couldn't yet say what it was or why. She just suspected a broad black weight, like a dense canvas tarp, was lifting back off her—her face and neck, her legs and feet. With grace and luck, by bedtime tonight she'd be drawing freer air than for months, for long years maybe. Was she crazy or not?

The whole room wondered, all the three men around her. Her skin and eyes were brighter and younger. She had the low still radiance of girls with the first baby in them, nested deep down and growing steady. It looked to them all that, if they could just wait here—minutes, not months— she'd give birth before them to something worth watching and helping to live.

Wave suddenly broke his eyes off her face and turned to Rato. He said "Old buddy, you let me know. I'll hop on a bus any weekend you say. I ain't seen the country for several years now. But I'll come on up and you reacquaint me."

Rosa said "Wave, don't let me ruin it. Stay on yet awhile. Rato's got a good movie picked out on t.v."

Wave said "I'm serious, Mrs. Beavers, truly. That story of mine's due tomorrow night at eight."

Wesley said "O.K. Just let them cure lockjaw or whip Ronald Reagan's dyed hair at the polls or something as good. Make my dollar worth spending."

Rato said "You're showing your ignorance, Wesley. No book's cost a dollar since you were a boy." Then he stood and offered his hand to Wave. "I'll write you that postcard real soon, hear? I've got sights up yonder, country or not, that you'll never guess till I've got you in hand and can give you the tour."

Everybody stood and watched Wave turn toward the back door slowly.

Rosa said "You go out the front way, Wave."

Wave smiled. "The back door won't shame me, Mrs. Beavers." He headed on as planned.

So Rato, Rosa, and Wesley followed—standing in a crescent to shake his hand once more and wish him well as if a spring night outside were threatful, a trial to be faced.

As his face got to Rosa's, Wave's own face paled. He thought "In this last second, she could hurt me." He prayed she wouldn't say more than "Goodbye," and it seemed for the moment his prayer had won.

Wesley said "Don't speak to no girls in the street."

Rato said "You taught me some things," the highest thanks he knew how to give. What he meant was the air of kindness from Wave, the way Wave showed his good intentions in every move of his hand or eye.

And at last Rosa said "Whatever you felt in other times here, Wave, you're welcome next time. We'll be here to greet you."

Wesley and Rato barely heard her strangeness. If they had, they well might not have understood.

Rosa wasn't sure she understood herself. Something that was still a deep secret in her own mind had formed her meaning and sent it on out in words.

But to Wave they sounded clear as great boulders heaved off a tall cliff into water way down in the night and deep. One by one he felt their weight and power and plea. He had hurt this woman, not helped or pleased her. How on the Earth had he failed to know that? Was he meant to go home now and cut his own throat? Whatever strange planet had sent him here, it had also clouded his mission for now. He'd done more harm than he ever intended.

No number of years of life on Earth would let Wave make up for all he'd ruined. The kindest act would be to leave now. Nobody left but his mother would mind. Or maybe this woman here three feet beyond him, his friend Rato's sister—the main one he'd harmed. He couldn't turn from her, the big blue eyes. He said "I'm sorry."

Rosa said "Thank you, sir."

Wave took a whole minute to squat down to Roger and tell him goodbye. Since the first day he came here as Rato's friend, Wave had noticed how Roger pulled back from him. No snarls or barks but a cold-eyed stare. Wave couldn't remember if Roger had seen him New Year's night (there were surely no barks). Still there'd always been this stand-off between them. So now he extended a bare right hand to Roger's big mouth—lick it or rip off two or three fingers.

With much more dignity than came natural to him, Roger kept his seat and sniffed at the hand from a courteous distance. Then he touched the back of the palm with his nose, no slobbering kiss.

Wave said "Thank you, sir." Then he rose up quick, facing no one else, and trotted off.

Roger stood to escort him at least to the curb.

But by then full darkness had folded Wave in. He was almost down to the corner before they could hear his final "Thank you all. Rato, hold it in the road." Then from farther still, they plainly heard a last "I may love you." Who was that meant for?—the few stars already straining to shine?

Rosa wanted to run, touch Wave's shoulder lightly, stop him, and say "Think it over. Love who?" But of course she waited, and then he was gone. She faced the room and moved on in toward the cluttered table.

Wesley was making strong coffee at the sink, and Rato was already testing the new Sony FM tape box that Wesley had bought him—their farewell gift for a child that had maybe saved her life.

Neither man in her family looked up to watch her. And certainly neither one asked what they'd meant—Rosa and Wave in those last few words. They were just that tired. But when, in a minute, the loneliness struck her and she asked for help, they both turned to help. The three together had all dishes cleared in under ten minutes.

ROSA WESLEY
RATO EMMA MILO
SISSIE MARY

◊

THE NEXT DAY WAS SUNDAY. AFTER ANOTHER SUB-
stantial early meal, they hit the road at eleven. For
the first twenty minutes, they rode without talking
since Rosa was tuned to a Presbyterian service on the
radio. But finally Wesley's imitation of the minister's des-
perately maintained Scottish brogue (by an American citi-
zen who hadn't seen heather for forty years) forced even
her to laugh and give up the effort. They spent the next
twenty minutes watching the countryside before Louisburg,
as all the after-shocks of Raleigh calmed down and the
woods deepened out on both sides of them. There were
some few oaks and shag-bark hickories, looking old as al-
ligators stuck upright in the sandy ground. But mostly there

were what seemed endless pines, each lovely as individual trees in Chinese paintings meant to teach us stillness and constant strength in adversity.

Nobody in the car thought quite that way, but all three had spent their lives close to pines a lot like these. So the lesson and the lonesome moan of the limbs in any slight wind was as much a part of what they knew as their mothers' names or the plans of the rooms they were each born in.

When they'd crossed the high bridge and cleared the long Main Street of Louisburg (the only town), then Wesley could say "Everybody remember now—no dirty words, no speed or crack, no crotch-shot magazines flashed in public. And Rato, no mention of your friend Brenda Walters."

Rato laughed, grinned at the woods on his side, but kept his own counsel.

Rosa finally turned back and said "Did I meet her?"

Rato shook his head no.

Wesley said "Sorry, Ace. I'd have never brought her up. I just thought Rosa might have walked in on her the way I did."

Rosa said "Walked *in*? What's been going on?"

Rato didn't meet her eyes. "Nothing you need to rile your mind with now."

Rosa said "It's my house and will be tonight when we get back home. I need to know who to call Monday morning—the flea exterminator or the health department." She gave a nervous laugh but was plainly interested.

Wesley said "She looked right clean to me." He craned up to catch Rato's eyes in the mirror.

Rato just nodded.

Rosa turned back to face him. "Rato, I'm a grown woman. I know you spent your young years in service. So don't look to hear any sermons from me. I'm just surprised to hear of a lady visitor while you were there with me. I'd have been pleased to meet her and welcome her in."

Wesley said "Two of your words there need a little tuning—*lady* and *welcome*. Scratch those two at least. I thought she looked like she had an education till she said she loved our 'old antiques' and that she still hoped to have 'two twins' and quit."

Rato said "She's no big scholar, no. How about when she said 'I've worked extra hard to keep my virgin's license, but I just keep failing the hand-signal test.'" He meant it to be the purest nonsense and laughed like a moron.

Wesley joined in the laughter.

But Rosa said "Boys, hand jokes are out now we've passed Louisburg. That's big-city talk. I've told you before. Don't forget hereafter."

Wesley said "She did have petal-soft hands."

"You'd better say how you know," Rosa said.

"Strictly eye-inspection—ain't I right? Back me, Rato."

"Absolutely," Rato said. "I had em both busy the whole time you saw her."

Rosa said "Stop here and let me out. It's still not too far for me to walk."

Wesley knew she wasn't serious, but he pulled to the shoulder and faced her gravely. It was then that he saw they'd pushed her too far with a manufactured joke. Nearly forty years of identical jive hadn't immunized Rosa to the rank male strut of their favorite fun.

She somehow still held on to the hope of men's sweetness, a hope for single-eyed devotion to her and her own fierce brand of love for them that would sweep the air clean of rival girls and their filthy threats. Wesley put out his long-boned index finger, pressed her left thigh, and kissed her cheek. "We made this whole thing up to cheer you. Won't you ever learn that?"

Rosa searched Wesley's eyes till she knew he was earnest. Then she turned back to Rato. "You backing him up?"

Rato nodded. "If you force me to, yes ma'm. I wish to God I'd met Brenda Any-Damned-Body in Raleigh or Rome. I wouldn't have brought her to your house though. So don't burn any of your towels or sheets."

"Or strip up the rugs?" Rosa asked and laughed.

"You might want to buy new rugs," Rato said. "I walked through them barefooted day after day. All sorts of my germans are teeming in there."

It was the first time in forty years she'd thought of Rato's *germans*, the word he used for *germs* through the war. She reached back and stroked his long dry cheek. "New rugs then," she said, "and cheap at the price—all the free care you gave me."

Rato said "No I didn't."

She said "You're not the soul to know the truth of that. I'd almost surely be dead of the blues or choked in my sheets if you hadn't been there those weeks of dark winter."

Rato said "You mean it?"

"You know I do. Don't forget it was *you* called me New Year's Day. You knew I was bad-off and volunteered help."

"That so?" Wesley said, slowly joining the road.

Rato nodded to Wesley's eyes in the rearview mirror.

Wesley drove a whole mile, then at last swallowed down a wad that blocked his words. "I owe you a lot more thanks than is easy."

Rato said "Why's it hard?"

Wesley said "Goddamn. I'm the cause of it all—me running, her pain."

Rato said "You're crazy."

"No he's not," Rosa said.

That silenced them all, right to Emma's front porch.

BY THE TIME THEY'D CLIMBED THE GULCHES OF THE LONG drive, Emma had seen them and was out on the front porch waiting by the steps. When Rosa caught sight, she took a sharp breath. She hadn't seen her mother in exactly four Sundays, and in that time it seemed Emma had shrunk several sizes inward. And near the five steps, there seemed a good chance that the slightest breeze would tip her balance and fling her down broken.

Again Rosa suddenly felt she should come here and spend the rest of her mother's few years giving constant care and learning everything her mother had kept in. There was no real way to manage it though and stay close to Wesley; she forced back tears.

Wesley hadn't seen Mrs. Mustian since Thanksgiving, so the change came even more clearly to him. "You two didn't tell me she'd been so sick."

"She hasn't," Rosa said, "—just fast old age."

Rato said "She knows how to outlast us."

Wesley said "Then I just beg her not to tell me."

"That's the reason I dread coming back," Rato said.

Rosa said "You told us you'd be happy here."

Rato said "The main thing you learn in the Army is

lying. I could tell you the sky was raining port wine, and
you'd say 'Pour me a big slug quick.'" But by then he was
already out of the car and waving at his mother.

Rosa and Wesley got out, stood, and watched Rato give
Emma his standard greeting. He brushed her cheek as dry
as sandpaper, said "I got to stash all this mess," and pushed
on past her with his suitcase and grocery bag of new
things.

Then Emma looked to them. "Wesley, I been afraid I'd
go to my Maker without seeing you. You look good as
ever—course I'm going blind." But she held out two long
thin arms to take him.

Wesley had always liked her (she laughed at his jokes,
none of them too risky). So he loped up the steps and
hugged her hard till Rosa suspected she'd hear joints crack.

When she got to her, Emma said "Ain't we all lucky?"

Wesley was standing there but Rosa said "Why?"

"To have him alive."

It still scraped Rosa's throat to say it but she nodded.
"Big as he is, a coffin would break me."

Wesley gave an old-fashioned boy's bow from the
waist. "Miss Emma, many thanks. Miss Rosa, kiss my
heiny."

Emma reached out and straightened Wesley's brows
(like most men his age, he'd begun sprouting grasshopper
eyebrows like tentacles tuned to the farthest planets). She
said "I've cooked everything on the place, all but boiled
the wood bowls."

Wesley said "Let's start" and they all moved in.

BY ONE O'CLOCK WHEN DINNER WAS READY, MILO AND
Sissie had rolled in from Henderson. So there were six

around the table, all of Emma's live family and in-laws
(the youngest child, Baby Sister, had died twenty years ago
of Hodgkin's disease—divorced with no children). In
Emma's generation when family gathered, a woman absolutely never said dinner-grace. But today when they'd all
unfolded napkins big and white as old baby-diapers, they
faced Emma silently.

At first she went cold—did she even know a grace? But
then she accepted her duty and right. She even composed
her speech as she went. "Good Lord, I'm proud to be here
today. I thank You for the mind and hands to still work.
Thank you for these strong children that have grown up
doing good mostly. Let them outlast me and never be sorry
they were mine and knew me." She looked straight up and
said "Everybody eat till they fall out asleep."

Rato said "Amen."

Emma said "Beg your pardon?"

He said "You never ended the blessing. God's still on
the phone."

Emma laughed. "Oh He's not. He invented the phone.
He knows when to hang up, even when I don't."

Wesley reached for the biscuits.

But Rato wouldn't quit. He said "Alexander Graham
Bell made the phone."

Milo said "But he credited God for the dialer."

Rato said "Say what?"

"Bell always said it was him made the mouthpiece, but
God made the dialer—the really hard part."

Sissie said "It *is*. I still have trouble dialing numbers
with zeroes; my finger gets stuck."

Milo reached out and squeezed Sissie's dialing finger.

"Poor child, shut up now and eat till you drop like Mama said."

Sissie had heard such nonsense all her grown life, but she knew not to fight. So she quieted down and ate big helpings.

Everybody else did. In families like this only a few years past, hard and poorly rewarded labor in the fields was consoled by plentiful hot food. And in those who contributed their share of the outdoor work, a great deal of personal oddness or nonsense had always been allowed to pass in amused silence, if not laughter. Only genuinely frightening symptoms like filthy clothes and stinking skin or a failing appetite would be mentioned at once and warned of.

Emma continued watching. Silently but with eyes that still needed no glasses, she patrolled the various recipients of her food. Who was falling behind on this or that? And if so, was the trouble her own (too much salt, too little vinegar)? Or were Milo or Rosa dieting (a development of her own lifetime that Emma thought as foolish as it was unneeded)?

The only person present that she'd hesitate to warn was Rato at her left, and that was only because words spent on Rato might as well have been puffed up the chimney for all their effect. Still she was glad to see him and to know he was back. Not that she'd worried about him or been scared for herself in his absence. But now that his long tan horseface was back, Emma could check every few minutes on its peace and be reminded (as nowhere else) that she'd done a fair enough mothering job. To raise such a strange child, lose him for years to the faceless Army, and now have him back here—at this much ease, blaming no one

for nothing—was some reward for all her own pain, even
if she hadn't had Milo and Rosa (she barely ever let herself
recall Baby Sister; that was too far to go, for too much
heartache).

Milo carefully reloaded his plate, then turned on Rato.
"And now, Big Ace, forget these ladies here, and tell all
you can about big-city life."

"I knew it," Wesley said. "Now you've breeched the
damned dam. We'll all be swamped."

For the first time in anybody's memory, Rato looked up
grinning and began to speak at once as though in fraternal
affection and obedience. "The first morning there I asked
Rosacoke, and she checked the phone book—those yellow
pages; I could read those all night—and by noon that same
day, my lifetime heart's desire was filled. I was enrolled in
the Ajax Bible College learning God's whole will for my
sinful life. So every day since then, that's where I been—
just sitting there with my poor face scrubbed soaking up all
the wisdom and goodness I've missed for so long. To be
sure, I wish there'd been a few girls in at least one class,
But no, I guess they know what they're—"

Emma said "Rato, sundown's not but four hours off.
Don't spend all our daylight on one big lie." She was
plainly not mad.

Milo said "You always wanted a preacher."

Emma gave a high sharp laugh. "Not here, not under
my roof. Once a week, at Delight Church, is fine by
me—no more, thank you please, here lately anyhow."

"Hell," Milo said, "we'd have had a lot more fun if
you'd lost your religion back when we were kids, in time
for us to enjoy the world."

Emma said "If you'd enjoyed it any more, your heart

would've stopped. You well know what I mean. I hold onto all I ever believed. I just don't see the need to harp on it so."

Milo began to harp with both hands and to sing a tenor chorus of his personal favorite hymn from childhood, "Shall we gather at the river?"

It had all rubbed hard on Sissie's nerves, and her determination to stay shut-mouthed had worn thin. So to change the subject, she smiled at Wesley. "Is the new Opry Land good as everybody says?"

The fact that he had never set foot there didn't slow Wesley. He said "Yes m'am, every word's more than true. If Milo won't take you, then save your own allowance and hop a fast bus. Whatever you do, don't miss the Jacuzzi part."

Milo was already grinning in hope.

But Sissie was earnest with expectation. "You better explain."

Wesley said "You give them your name as you enter before the main show. Just say 'Ms. Milo Mustian, a widow.'"

Sissie said "But I'm not."

Milo touched her wrist. "Just do what he says. Wes knows how it's done in those big hillbilly towns out west."

Rosa caught Wesley's eye. "Have a heart now, hear?"

But Rato said "Sissie, you'll love this fine."

So Wesley lit out. "Once they have your name, they take you to your seat in the plush-lined box. You listen and eat on your complimentary cheese and crackers, and you drink your Cold Duck if so inclined. Once the last song's over at midnight—Kenny Rogers, Loretta Lynn, Mother Maybelle Carter—"

Sissie said "Mother Carter's been dead long years."

"Well, whoever else—it's all big stars. Once the music's done, your private attendant comes to lead you back. You change in your own spacious private lounge, then walk out into your own dimmed cubicle—deep blue mirrors on all sides and ceiling. Your private masseur, a young Christian gentleman in modest tights (they have to have bare chests, the work is so strenuous), he steps on in and commences his craft. Child, they are *well*-trained. The girl I got on my first visit had studied at Bob Jones University in South Carolina, and I still feel relaxed—the stiff neck of mine just laid down and died for good and *all*."

Milo said "I'll bet a dollar it did. But now just for curiosity's sake, could Sissie get a lady masseur herself?"

Sissie said "They have their rules set, hon, by the state boards and all. Anyhow I'm no kind of missionary."

"There have been times," Milo said, "when I wondered. But steam ahead, Wes."

"You got it," Wesley said, "—the steam comes next."

Emma said "No it don't. Sounds like a trip I might need to take, with my bad knees. But you and Sissie finish this plan in the yard, the details especially. What comes next at my dinner table is cake."

AFTER DINNER RATO TOOK HIS NEW RADIO AND WENT TO the woods. Sissie napped (one of her punishing headaches). Rosa and Emma headed for the kitchen, and Milo asked Wesley to take a good look at his new Pontiac in the yard. The day had opened out on a seamless bright sky and shirtsleeve temperatures. Both men, for all their middle age and stopped hopes, felt fine with each other. They'd known and liked each other since the days when Rosa first

fell for Wesley, and they'd played baseball together at John
Graham High School. So now they could crouch down
over an engine, study it like abstract iron sculpture, and
barely need to speak.

Milo said "Tell me I didn't get a bargain."

Wesley said "Wait now. I'm a pro at this. You don't
really want to hear a real pro's truth."

"What you think I'm standing out here with ugly you
for, when I could be canoodling upstairs with my lovely
wife?"

"If you touched her," Wesley said, "she'd *run* to
damned Nashville, with your credit cards."

Milo said "Let's don't get mean and personal both. If I
opened up on you, you'd be so full of buckshot you'd die
of lead poison."

Wesley laughed. "You win. No, Milo, look—you love
your new car. It's exactly what you wanted, and it matches
Sissie's hair. Just roll back, cross both hands on your belly
(it's swelling nicely, by the way), and try to forget that day
by day Wesley works on Mercedes, BMWs, Bentleys, and
moviestar-customized Alfa-Romeos. Every now and then I
lower my standards, double my prices, and tune up a Jag.
But it's been six years since my soft hands even touched a
piece of Detroit tinfoil dogshit. I done you a favor by looking at this." When he faced Milo, Wesley saw that wide
jaw clamping down hard. He'd been too cruel, one more
time. So gently he rocked all the sparkplugs for tightness
and checked the dipsticks. Then he could say "It's a clean
neat baby and, sure, it's a bargain. I'll accept it right now,
as an Easter present—you forgot me last Easter—and
drive it straight home."

Milo smiled and nodded. "See, I'm real sorry about

your Easter. But I didn't get any word from you, so I just assumed your ass would be as invisible then as it was at Christmas."

Wesley grinned. "No it wasn't. Me and Easter Bunny sat home all day waiting on your basket of eggs to show."

Milo said "Hold your breath. Anyhow if I'd sent so much as a biddy, Miss Sissie would've shot me in cold blood in bed."

"Might have been a welcome change," Wesley said, "—little noise and violence in you all's bed."

Not a note of that was meanly intended, and both of them knew it. It was their original mode of conversation. It meant how long they'd liked each other, how long they'd known each other's secrets and destruction buttons. The fact that in nearly forty years of such scuffling they'd never cut a serious wound in each other meant simply that they hoped to grow old together—old and even more knowing, more nearly each other's mirror-self like the best male friends who stop short of touch. (Wesley understood that one of the mysteries about himself was, though he'd had good times close to several queer men, it never crossed his mind to touch Milo or any other friend on his own initiative.)

Finished, Wesley stepped back and wiped his hands on a clean white handkerchief. Then he stepped aside to let Milo take the owner's prerogative, closing the hood. It gave the satisfying crunch of a new metal catch, and Milo said "You glad to be back?"

Wesley looked to the house, the dining-room window— no sign of Rosa or Sissie or Miss Emma. He said "You know what your own answer would be?"

Milo said "Sure I do."

"Then mine's the same."

"I'm sorry," Milo said. "I figured as much. She *is* a fine girl. It still shows in her. I noticed just now—how she sat there letting us play the tired fool. She laughed and winced but never tried to stop us. Looks damned good too for— what?—the change of life."

Wesley nodded. "The last lady left."

"Her and our mothers," Milo said.

Wesley took a step toward the house.

Milo said "What's wrong?"

Wesley kept his head turned and still watched the front door. But then he thought again and came back to Milo, within breathing distance. When he felt his breath echo off his friend, he said "What's wrong? You're bound to know. We're the same kind of man. We're near the same age."

Milo shook his head hard. "You're way past me. Wesley, your whole luck went way past me. Don't ever forget you had the big sense to leave here long enough to serve your country. You saw a whole lot, touched a lot of young women, and got back here with your hide in one piece. And your mind still hot with all that good memory, all that clean good hair you tasted."

Wesley smiled. "And some that went a long way past clean."

Milo waved a careless palm in the air. "All the diseases back then, they could cure. Just a juice glass of warm penicillin, and you were right back on the streets set to nail one more señorita by sundown."

Wesley said "So you had your share. Don't go get bitter."

"The hell you say."

"What?"

Milo's face was as pale as a veal cutlet, drained and tan. "I never told this to nobody but you. So if it ever gets back to me, I'll know where it come from. And I'll shoot you straight down the minute I find you." He clamped both eyes shut. "In all my whole life—boy and man—I touched one woman."

Wesley said "You mean Sissie?"

"I don't mean Rosa."

It shocked and hurt Wesley more than he'd have guessed, even that much of a hint about Rosa (who had always been Milo's choice kin). He said "I'm sorry. I thought you'd enjoyed yourself much as me."

"No boy of all that we grew up with was as lucky as you, Wesley. Look at Lonnie Williams—he went to Campbell College for two years. Got him right much of that sweet Baptist pussy, or so he claims right up to this day. And I for one believe him. Lonnie's too dumb to make it all up. Right today he can tell you what every gal said when he touched her left nipple for the first time. He said most of them—even then, that young—had hair on their nipples. Like to made me lose my dinner on the spot. You believe that?"

"I don't just believe it. I know it's true."

Milo shook his head, kicked in the dirt, and then laughed. By the time he met Wesley's eyes again, he could say "Makes me almost proud to be a virgin."

Wesley laughed in relief.

"Almost but not quite."

IN THE KITCHEN EMMA AND ROSA HAD FINISHED WASHING dishes, and Rosa was storing everything away for the twelve millionth time. It was just in other people's houses

—helping other people, especially her kin—that Rosa felt the real deep awfulness of housework. How it consisted almost entirely of wrecking something you'd built, clean and neat, just hours before. A drawer of knives and forks or shelves of dry plates, each one waiting to be fouled again. How had Mama stood it a whole life long?

She suddenly felt full of a question she'd never dared to ask her mother till now, "Are you ever sorry this is how you've lived?" But Emma's back was broadside to her, narrow as a dusty sparrow in the ditch; and her whole frame was half a head shorter than when Rosa was a girl. Pounded mercilessly down toward the earth by decades of walking from that sink to this green table here, on these pine floor-boards that had someway not been worn to air by the traffic. Rosa opened her lips and what she said was "Go lie down a minute. I'm tired myself."

Emma said "You know I can't rest in daylight. You go yourself."

Rosa smiled. "That old room of mine is too full of sad ghosts."

"I always thought this house was good to you. It tried to be."

"Oh it was," Rosa said. "I didn't mean that."

Emma said "Then it's got to mean you're sad now."

Not really being sure, Rosa waited on that. Then she said "No ma'm, but I've been pushed back."

"Where to?"

"Years ago, the Sunday I first saw Wesley."

"Up a tree."

Rosa said "You remember?"

Emma grinned and gently slapped her own thigh. "You

told me times enough. Lord knows, I can near about recite every move."

"I'll bet that's more than Wesley can do."

Emma said "He'd surprise you. Wesley's got a sweet heart."

"So sweet it could start home a few days before Christmas, take a little detour that lasted four months and saw me raped, saw a new woman on him, and the whole world ended."

"The *world* kept going up here," Emma said. "Least I thought it did. Check round and see."

Rosa actually looked around slowly. "It did, same as ever. Thank you again."

"Not me," Emma said. "I had no more to do with it lasting than this ant did." She'd seen a black ant pause on the counter. She crushed it slowly with the palm of her hand and then wiped the hand on her damp apron.

Rosa tried to conceal a wince.

But Emma laughed. "Get on back to town. You've lost your country nerves."

"Wish I had," Rosa said.

Emma asked "How so?"

Rosa smiled all through the answer. "Because if I had, me and Wesley wouldn't be here together today. I'd have told him to get his tail back to some place as common as Nashville, Tennessee—and that girl he found with the steaming butt and the big mobile home."

Emma said "Rosacoke, I didn't raise children to talk mule manure."

"Mama, I'm talking the plain truth now."

"Very little that's plain true is worth bringing up."

Rosa said "That was my whole problem from the start.

You taught me to be so Christian polite, I never told Wesley what the ground rules were."

"Rosa, that's a black lie. You been giving rules, to Wesley and me and the dogs on the porch, since you could stand on your own legs and say 'Shut up.'"

"If Wesley had truly known what I could and would stand for, he would never have put him and me through this pain." Big tears ran for the first time in months, surprising Rosa far more than her mother.

Emma said "Sit down at the table a minute"—the first real order she'd given in years. She herself sat first and Rosa slowly joined her. Then Emma said "I trust you've got some memory left, way beyond you and Wesley. If so you'll recall that suffering didn't start when you two met. You loved your daddy. Remember him? He had parents as kind as any child ever had. Him and me were good in our iron bedstead as any three whores on the modern t.v."

Emma blushed ferociously but still had to say it. It was a part of her truth, confirmed every hour now in every newspaper. "But Horatio Senior was ruined from the cradle somehow, just ruined. A terrible seed was born down in him. He needed liquor like the ground needs rain. And fine as he was to look at and touch, the seed bloomed gradually when he was fifteen. I already knew him and I saw when it started. The church picnic that year was nearby. Nobody had cars then to truck up the road to nice lakes or cabins. We went to the deep woods back of Mr. Isaac's house and pitched down there, spread our quilts in the shade, and ate a feast fit for the kings of the world and ample for the full five thousand plus orphans."

"You were how old?" Rosa asked.

"Thirteen, just turned—and already watching him like

quail watch foxes. He didn't seem to know I was live on the ground, though no other girl seemed to have his eye either. What happened in the shank of the afternoon was, an older fellow—Dim Waters, a lawyer that practiced in Warrenton—came up and tapped your daddy on the shoulder. The two of them and one other boy, that died in the war, loped off farther in the woods. With my two parents, I'd barely heard liquor mentioned (much less seen it drunk). But right that instant in my heart I could say the two things I suddenly knew. I said 'Dim Waters will fry in Hell, and Horatio's going to be a drunkard for life.' I was as sure as I've ever been about any fact. But it seemed like my love was a train that, whoever was driving, it wasn't me. It just plunged hot right on down the line till I married him six years later, to the month, and had all of you and watched him kill himself way too slow."

Rosa waited, watching Emma closely so the words would register in a way that lasted—stamped onto one long moving-picture of faces, her mother and father's (with Milo, Rato, herself, and poor Baby Sister pale behind them, sucking strength). Then she thanked her mother simply.

Emma stood up and said "Wesley's right lucky. But so are you, Rosa. You forget that and you know you do."

"You want to tell me where the lucky part is? Just the fact that Wesley's not a falling-down drunk or hasn't ever beat me?"

Emma said "Thank you, no. I tell you what I see, from way out here in my seventies. You ought to be glad. And so ought he. Course I may be blind or crazy or soft-brained. You got to recognize your own damned luck."

Rosa had only heard her mother say *damn* maybe five

times through the years, times that mattered. In Emma
Mustian's mouth it had the force of the wildest outbursts in
others less restrained. So then and there she decided to
honor it at least, to search her own life hard for luck. She
said "Please teach me."

Emma said "What you think I been teaching all your
life?" But then she laughed and stepped toward the door,
time for others now.

BUT BY THE TIME EMMA COMBED HER HAIR IN HER BED-
room, her poor ears heard the others beyond her. Rosa had
joined Milo and Wesley on the porch. No word from Sissie—she would still be asleep. And Rato would still be
gone in the woods. Emma Mustian was all alone again, the
way she'd been these past four months—the way she'd
stay in the grave forever. She'd promised herself not to tell
another soul. But while she was here alone in this house,
she'd finally come to the hard conclusion that had tempted
her since Horatio died.

There is no Hell or Heaven. There is no afterlife. We are
here, one by one, with the pigs and chickens, the beetles
and snakes. We work like miserable coal-black slaves, with
the hope of some final gold-watch reward. Well, Jesus
looks nice in the Sunday-school pictures (and can put you
to sleep fast in the one-page devotions like the ones she
sent Rosa every birthday that came). No doubt Jesus, the
man on earth, was kind and polite. But the secret that
Emma thought she'd learned these past lonely months was,
Jesus himself wouldn't be her reward. Now she knew it
was bound to be better than that. It was pure black sleep,
perpetual *rest*.

How had Emma known, after all the wrong years? She

couldn't quite have told you. Maybe by a kind of reverse revelation. Some saints in the night get gleaming pictures of God's throne with angels in endless harmony. Ten days or so after Rato left her, she settled back into new deeper silence. Life in the country—with no children home—had been quiet enough. But now, with even her last son gone, day and night passed in a quiet so deep that even a bird call got to be offensive, a raucous scrape down a perfect sky.

Then well before dawn at the end of two weeks, Emma woke in the dark surrounded by silence. Something had called her, she well knew that—no voice, some *absence* with a plain truth to tell. She lay in her warm sheets and waited, not scared. Maybe three blank minutes, then a long high scream. Beginning loud, then shrinking in size— some squirrel or rabbit seized by an owl and borne through the night farther off to be torn and swallowed. So she knew.

That was it. The final shock that was really such relief. It was all she'd waited for. All bets were off. The last easy truth was plain before her. There was nothing else to come. The world, the sky, the core of the ground was nothing but two things—eaters and food.

In the nights alone also she'd sat up late, doing additions with the little hand-calculator Rosa gave her last year. She figured up how many times in her life she'd done so and so—changed baby diapers, made love to Horatio, cooked hot meals (and for seven mouths generally), washed all their dishes, emptied slop jars till they got indoor plumbing. Could any old mule in the county say more, assuming you could still find one live mule?

The meals for instance. Emma started at age fifteen for her daddy, when her own mother died. And not one time had any black woman ever lent her a hand. So till now, she punched the plain facts on her keyboard—well there, it came to more than thirty-five thousand cooked hot meals. Every one of them laid out with at least good conscience. Could anybody, even her most loving child, recall one single dish and taste it in memory? She'd said it to the empty house when she finished, *Don't everybody fall down laughing at once.*

So *rest*. Lord Jesus, you lie back now and calm yourself—and thanks for your time—but bring on my *rest*.

The sound of Milo's laugh from the porch caught Emma where she spun far out on the string of her new lonely knowledge. She checked her face again in the mirror. All things considered, for its age, the mirror was in worse shape than she. Again she touched the wings of her hair, still bunned in the back and tight on her ears. Since she had never smoked so much as one cigarette, it was snow white and soft—a glory at last after long years of looking like packing straw.

She would step out now and join those children as if she was who they'd known all their lives. They'd be almost right. Very little changed except that now she had this surety—rest like the finest hospital anesthesia, black silent sleep. No eternal glare on her tired eyes, no big reunion of all her old kin, grinning and singing and ready to eat.

By the time the children reached her age—if they ever did—they might well share her joy in the news of rest, pure rest. They would have to learn it without her help though. She'd given them the slim faith in God that sustained them this far. She wouldn't feel right now to walk out toward them on a nice spring Sunday and strip that off their ignorant faces. Let time teach them in the night like their mother. It would come with age, if they earned it at all. And by then, thank the stars, Emma Mustian would long since be underground. Or nowhere. *Nowhere*.

She went toward them smiling.

WHOEVER DIED, HOWEVER MANY LEFT, IT STILL TOOK AN hour to withdraw from Emma's. First there were all the gifts to pack—the home-canned goods, the caramel cake she'd made for Wesley and kept hid till the last minute, the pan of her rolls laid out and ready to bake for Sunday supper as soon as they were home (the possibility of rolling in and defrosting a pizza would have horror-struck Emma), Rosa's tenth-grade autograph book she'd found preserved in a trunk.

Then the farewells—tying Rato down long enough to say goodbye and to hear Rosa's serious repeated thanks, extricating from Sissie without further insults, assuring Milo he'd be welcome to visit anytime he could come (he always asked, ever since the one good time, but still never came), facing up to what might be the last sight of Emma.

Then the lingering small talk through both car windows, then at last the slow drive downhill through gulches back out into whatever dream of freedom they could manage once they'd struck hard pavement and begun to thread the last country roads before they could aim unblocked for Raleigh.

IN A WHILE THEY PASSED MR. ISAAC ALSTON'S, THE BIG-gest old house in Afton. When Mr. Isaac died it had run down badly till the long front porch had fallen in. But now they'd heard of a rich Warrenton lady who fixed it up and moved in lately. Wesley figured they had daylight enough to see it, so he took a sharp right and rode on past.

And yes, she'd fixed it—brand-new gingerbread brackets in corners, fern baskets all along the porch ceiling, and every board painted a jaundiced yellow with barn-red trim. In the yard—instead of bird dogs, chickens, and sand—was thick lawn-grass in an unreal chemical blue dotted with painted concrete figures of colored boys wearing red sombreros and adorable matching yellow burros hauling carts of watermelons. The porch was hung with a new rope hammock. None of it looked like a human hand had participated. Rosa said "Sometimes I hope the dead *die*."

Wesley said "Why so?"

"At least Mr. Isaac wouldn't have to see this."

"He's in Heaven. To him it's all one more joke."

Rosa said "In my very humble opinion, it would take more than Heaven to make this a joke."

By then the insulted house and dirt were gone behind them in the dusk, but Wesley missed the first two chances to turn. At the third, Rosa started to ask were they lost. But "No," she thought, "I'll sit this out. Wherever we go, and I bet it's not Nashville, I guess I could find my way back home if Wesley fades on me."

The days now were longer; and every rock in the road was clear, every cone on the trees. The road had been paved twenty years ago, and the car picked up speed to pass Delight Church. Fine as it looked in its new white paint, its tall storm windows, Rosa didn't let herself think back to the night when there, in a Virgin Mary costume, she had watched her mind find its slow pained way to accept Wesley's offer and take his name for the bastard child they'd started growing in her secret womb. She made the only sane guess she could manage, "We stopping by to see your mother?"

"I called Mother three or four nights ago, remember?"

"You know she'll be home."

Wesley said "She'll be home, Rosa, when you and I have *flown*."

"I'd be glad to see her. Don't think I wouldn't."

"Rosa, don't go tell a king-size lie. We've had a nice day."

"Your mother has never been less than kind to me."

Not glancing toward her, Wesley's right hand reached out with perfect aim, found her mouth, and shut it gently. "I'm looking for something you long since forgot."

Rosa said "I remember how Mama's ribs looked from inside with the sunlight slatting in through her skin when she pulled off her nightgown each dawn at the window. I can still recall my daddy's voice through Mama's belly when it reached me treading in her warm dark lake every night when he'd find his drunk way home and bunch up beside her and beg her hot pardon, worn out as it was. So don't tell Rosa she's forgot a damned thing, not anything old enough to matter tonight up here in the woods."

Wesley nodded. "Yes ma'm."

"What?"

"We're looking for woods."

Rosa still hadn't followed his line of thought. "You've found them, Columbus—hearty applause." Pines and cedars stretched on both sides, so deep beyond them that they might almost reach Canada unseen if they set out to walk.

Wesley pulled to the edge of the ditch and slowly stopped. He was looking past Rosa into the trees. Then he faced her at last. "You game to walk a ways?"

She had on new panty-hose. But this was so strange, she wouldn't have said no if her new hose were spun-gold thread. And even with all the past year's history, it never dawned on her that Wesley meant to harm her—the Afton Strangler. She set her purse in the glove compartment and said "Better lock this please—credit cards, a little cash."

So he turned the lock, came around, and politely helped Rosa out. Then he took a slight lead and walked on to where the trees began to thicken and strain out light. The sun that reached them was a pale blue, but it gave their features a clarity that seemed to stream from within.

Wesley noticed it first. He turned to Rosa, studied her face, and said "You don't know where you are." Even he could hear that his voice was strange, more than the usual space between words. But his smile was normal.

Rosa had already checked the surroundings, a small circle in the tallest trees they'd seen all day. She said "You win this time. I'm lost."

Wesley's smile deepened. "But you brought me here, lord, thirty years ago. Remember?—the night we saw those deer out on the road and walked back in here, hoping to find them, and then laid down on the ground and did it. First time of all."

Rosa looked around once more, then checked his face for laughter. "It can't be so. The trees are too tall."

"You don't think they've stood still anymore than us?"

Rosa said "I've never been back here since."

"I have," Wesley said, "every five years or so."

"What for?" To Rosa it was all but incredible.

"I had a good time that night," Wesley said. "I hoped you did."

Rosa looked to her feet. The ground was clean, just dry leaves and sticks. "Can we sit down a minute?"

"You want to risk chiggers?"

"Too early for chiggers." She sat down slowly and pressed both hands in the compost beneath her, down to where the ground was still cold and damp.

Wesley sat clear of Rosa but in reaching distance.

"You're sure?" she asked.

"I'm sure you're you." He reached toward her face, then stopped his hand short in the darkening air. "Yes ma'm, I'm sure as I am that you're Rosa. This is where we were."

So they'd seen the buck out there on the road, in deep fall dark. It had been at a time when Rosa thought she was truly losing Wesley and must move fast and furious to stop and hold him. She'd asked him if they couldn't follow the deer and his two does on back in these woods, meaning— God, whatever million things had she meant? *Let's live forever, let's die right here, don't ever let's tear apart again, there'll never be any place better than this (any better night) to join together and make one thing.*

It had been her idea, she understood that, but Wesley had agreed in mind and body. And if he was right now— surely he was—this was where they'd done it (as he said), *made a thing.* She dug with her short nails deeper in the earth. Well, let it be true. Let this be the place. They'd made a real thing. And only part of it was Horace, a baby. This big part was them. Why cancel them here or anywhere else in this world or life? She met Wesley's eyes. "It's bound to be." She meant the place. He'd apparently found it, something she could not have done.

Wesley waited a long time to nod his thanks for what he

thought was her final agreement. By then the sun had dropped another three notches toward night. If Rosa had just now seen him clearly, he could barely find her when he stepped on forward and leaned to give her his right hand again.

She found it though and rose to its strength. Far stronger and more certainly than all those years ago, she followed him out to the car and toward what might yet be home— no longer the old Mustian place (her mother's, with room for Milo and Sissie, Rato and Sister) but Raleigh, the house she and Wesley had bought with their earnings to shelter their own heads and the one child they'd started with young lovely bodies on the hard ground they'd just now touched in the woods.

THEY TURNED FULL-CIRCLE AND DROVE TOWARD THE HIGH-way. Then in a half-mile the lights struck a tall shape coming against them with what seemed to Rosa no visible head. Then she saw it had to be a black woman.

Wesley recognized her first and began to pull over.

Rosa said "Who?" Then she saw it was old Mary Sutton alone in a heavy green sweater. When Wesley had stopped, Rosa cranked down her window. "Can we drive you home, Mary?"

Mary didn't know the car or the voice, but she said "Not unless this car's a damned *tank*." Mary's house was far too deep in the woods for a car, and the *damn* had to mean that she'd had a big drink.

Wesley laughed and leaned over. "It's Wesley and Rosa-coke, heading to Raleigh. How you doing, Mary?"

So Mary relaxed her guard, walked over, set strong arms on the window ledge, and craned in to see them.

"Right," she said. "I'd a knowed both of you if I had good sense." The odor of cheap fruit-brandy was clear but not rank.

Wesley asked "You got me a drink of pain-killer?"

Mary took two steps backward, then laughed loud. "What's hurting you, boy?"

"My whole life till now. I'm an *old* man."

"You a baby next to me. And I'm still grinning." Then she came near again. "Miss Rosa, don't tell me you hurting too."

Rosa said "I'm younger than either one of you. No, I'm proud to say Rosa's in fairly good health."

Mary said "Glad to hear it. You the only one left. Everybody else up in the sticks here's miserable." She looked past Rosa to Wesley. "You back I see."

"You knew I was gone?"

Mary said "Me and every sick sparrow in the trees. You was big bad news—in the paper, on the radio."

"I told her," Rosa said.

But Mary ignored her and went on to Wesley. "Where'd you go?"

"Nashville, Tennessee."

"Learn anything new?"

"Not new."

"But good?"

Wesley's eyes knicked the side of Rosa's taut face. "Neither one," he said. "Mary, I'm a plain boy. Can't handle rich food, these fast rich towns."

Mary said "Lord Jesus, then give me a chance. Give me a bus ticket out of here and I'll fly. Won't see me back." She'd never been farther than Baltimore, for more than a week during World War II.

Wesley said "I doubt you know what you're saying."

Mary held out her palm, again past Rosa. "You try me and watch."

Rosa knew Mary Sutton had always been hard. She'd gone to Mary several times years ago, when everybody else lied, for clear rough truth. But now was worse. Time had walled Mary off. Now was mean and useless. Rosa wanted to say a fast good night and leave.

Mary felt it someway. She laid a hand on Rosa's lean shoulder. "You proud of him, ain't you?"

"I'm used to him, Mary."

Mary drew back her hand and faced Wesley again. "That good enough for you?"

Wesley smiled. "May be the best offer I get."

Mary said "Think it over then. You a fine man. Still young enough to pick."

So Rosa firmed up. "You get home, Mary. It's not safe out here alone in the road."

Mary said "You used to ask *me* for advice."

Rosa smiled. "Yes well, I'm a grown woman now."

Mary stepped back again, took a good long look, and laughed. "Ain't it so, yes madam!"

Rosa said "You're bound to sleep good tonight."

"Ain't it so. Ain't it so!" Mary slapped her own firm thigh over and over.

Wesley said "Mary, come round here to my window."

She put a long hushing finger to her lip and tiptoed with obvious caution toward his side. Then she leaned in his window and gave him a pecking kiss on his ear.

He laughed but said "I'm spoke for now. Don't go tempting me." He dug in his wallet and handed her a bill.

Mary walked due left till the edge of the headlights

shined on her hand. "This'll ease more grief than most folks I know." Then her voice broke up into chunks like concrete dumped from a loader. "Wesley, you too good. I'm praying for you."

Wesley said "I'm a saint in glory—believe it! But don't stop praying for us both anyhow. God loves you. You're so big a sinner, he's bound to."

Mary waited awhile to understand that. Then she said "I'm going to laugh at that once I get back home, and the sting in it don't hurt nearly this much."

Wesley said "You do that." He blew her a second kiss, released the brake, and rolled ahead.

MILES UP THE ROAD WHEN THEY SIGHTED THE HIGHWAY'S chain of lights, Rosa said "Who is *both*?"

"Ma'm?"

"*Both*—you asked her to pray 'for us both.'"

"You and me," Wesley said. "You object to that?"

"Not really. She was drunk."

His voice wasn't angry but patient as a father's. "I knew that, Rosa. I also know Mary Sutton's prayers work. They've worked for me since I was a boy. I need them again and I thought you did."

"Thank you then," Rosa said.

IN THE DARK THEY REPEATED THE MORNING'S TRIP—silence between them till they threaded Louisburg (all but deserted, a few young black men propping up buildings with their tall fine bodies). Then in full dark beyond it, with Raleigh ahead, Wesley said "Please tell me what you believe."

Rosa asked "About what?"

"Everything—God, Heaven and Hell, the fleas on dogs. You recall that radio show of Edward R. Murrow's, 'This I Believe'? He'd ask—you know—Einstein, Mrs. Roosevelt, General George C. Marshall. They'd answer too and fast."

Rosa said "I believe the Apostles' Creed and Jesus' Lord's Prayer."

"Don't be a damned missionary all your grown life." Wesley knocked her knee.

"It's true though, Wesley. What do you doubt?"

He said "Most of it. Oh, I guess there's a God. But it sure as hell looks like He's so far gone, He can't see us and barely hears even our loudest begging—when we beg help for children that are twisting in pain."

Rosa said "We had good luck with Horace, nothing worse than that one long bout of strep throat the winter he was two."

"—And being a pitiful jackass now."

"Wesley, that boy's the one thing we made together. Give him some little credit."

"For what?—marrying a beehive hairdo with legs?" Wesley hoped he could hear Rosa strangle a laugh. He paused to see if she'd show her true colors, but she was watching the right side intently. So he went on and said "I'm ashamed now to think Horace was what forced me to marry you, a piss-poor shotgun."

She finally laughed and slid a few inches toward him but not quite touching. "He's got a sweet heart. We're not old yet. He'll be there ready when you're feeble and gray."

Wesley said "For you. You'll outlast me."

Rosa shook her head. "I don't take wear. I'm wrinkled, creased, threadbare in the seat."

"You're the thing I watched all those years ago. You're still broadcasting the signal that caught me."

Rosa smiled. "Thank you." But then she remembered. "You died though, Wesley—signal or no. You said you died toward the end of last year, and Rosa didn't save you."

"I did die truly. But I never blamed Rosa."

"She was there right beside you, the same girl as now. Nothing in me has changed."

Wesley said "*Me* then. I'm a different piece of work." He stared on at the road.

So Rosa looked carefully. And yes, he had changed again. All their time together, it was what had held her closest—the slow unpredictable speed at which each day he was turning like a tall plant into something, more or less different anyhow. Times without number, she prayed he would stop, stand still, and *be*.

She'd tell herself she needed a fixed human star to plot by, a tall lone tree on a hill to watch as she cut her own path toward him or away. But he'd never been that. He'd always brought home peculiar faces (some scary, some grand) that she had to watch or at least learn to bear— faces that would vanish next day with no warning.

Could she—hell, *should* she—spend the next thirty years shifting the grounds of her care every few days to match Wesley's shifts. Well, first, he couldn't help it; he was built to change. And finally surely, it was what she loved deep down in her dark heart. It was what she had learned maybe from her father and two older brothers. She herself really needed that restless ground—a light that *burned* but wavered and sank and nearly dimmed out but always somehow, in her own eyes, demanded care. She'd watched Wesley's profile all through her thought.

Now he glanced over toward her, from as far off as that first day she'd seen him—grave as a watchman on the highest lighthouse. Then he faced the road.

Rosa said "All right"—meaning *All right,* change. *I can try to watch.*

IN ANOTHER QUARTER-HOUR OF SILENT DRIVING, THEY could see the gleam of Raleigh on the sky. It was still twenty minutes ahead at this rate. But either one of them, or both, could stop here. Turn back, choose another destination together or part company finally and go different ways. Wesley said "We could streak off right now for elsewhere. Just send Horace the keys and a letter saying where the deed's kept."

"And then go where?"

Wesley said "You choose."

"Together or apart?"

He smiled but ahead at the road and the dark. "You choose."

Rosa let a whole extra mile roll behind them. The gentle pad of the tires was left. Then she said "Well, Raleigh. The same warm house. Us same two old dogs, the same old basket."

Wesley thought a whole minute, then gave a nod, pressed his foot down slightly, and the car took speed.

WAVE ROSA WESLEY

THE WHOLE DAY SUNDAY, WAVE HAD STAYED IN HIS room. He'd slept a lot—long naps with dreams that changed faces so fast he never got to know who his actors were, much less what they needed from him or had volunteered to give in return for the use of his brain and time. Then he would wake up and read awhile in the short stack of books he always kept by his bed. His favorites were mysteries and science fiction. The mysteries were not detective stories but real human bafflements—the Bermuda Triangle or the Holy Shroud.

Wave had first run into the Shroud in *Time* magazine years ago, and ever since he'd pursued its truth. Since he left his mother, he'd never darkened a single church door and had no plans to. But that didn't mean he was an atheist or that he came anywhere near spitting on what others believed. If the Shroud was the actual cloth around Jesus in the thirty-odd black hours in the tomb, then all those yelling Baptists had one thing right anyhow—man had conquered death and would do so again.

Wave Wilbanks's body (this ramshackled five-foot-eleven-inch house thrown together of meat, bone, and hair) would stand up one day out of the grave into God's own actual truth-seeing eyesight and hear those final words, "Well done, My good and faithful servant. You have honored My loved ones. Accept My thanks."

Then Wave would climb out of worms and cold clay, his big skull bored by tunnels of rot, and stride into hot clean light that streamed no longer from the sun but from God's own eyes. As his legs gained strength with each forward step, Wave would see on all sides the other human eyes— eyes that, in his life, had hated and jeered: other children, his uncles, some women he'd tried to touch and help.

But now every eye would be weeping with thanks, begging somehow to stay near the risen Wave (stronger than ever) and finally share what he'd offered again and again in the past—his harmless gifts that could bring such joy, all permanent now in the land without death. Even his father, that had died so long ago (God knew how), would step up now with identification and show true pride in this great son—pleading for just a seat at his side, to share the new glory. And Wave would let him.

He got through the whole day till sundown like that, a good restful time in sweet-smelling sheets. And unlike most healthy young men at ease, he felt no need to seize on himself and masturbate. After a few times in early adolescence, he'd come to see how sad that was—that lonely showing-off. He preferred to wait for a warm other body.

Then in late afternoon—just before he would need any

light—he climbed out, showered, shaved, dressed in his only suit and prettiest tie, and started his plan. The plan had not formed till the night before, as he walked home alone from supper with the Beaverses and Rato Mustian. They would all be out of the house Sunday from morning till bedtime.

Wave would wait till dark, go over unseen, let himself in, and finish the business that Rosa had balked on New Year's night. There would be some risk. Neither Wesley nor Rosa had said when they expected to be home. Wave was guessing on the basis of what he'd watched in other people's family visits—eat a little supper with them, take your leave slowly, mosey on back in time for bed. But risk had been the main excitement of his grown life, and it didn't slow him now.

So it was past seven when he jimmied the door-handle lock in the Beavers' kitchen. They'd left on at least one light in every room, and one quiet radio to fool the burglars. He had good company then and a nice steady glow for the thorough inspection he needed to make—every corner, every drawer. Wave had learned years ago how to do it invisibly.

Housebreakers in general leave a hateful mess behind, not Waverly Wilbanks. He could open every envelope, read every letter in a filing cabinet, and leave behind nothing but clean fingerprints (he'd never feared those and had never been caught, not even suspected). Methodically then he fingered, read, and memorized the souvenirs and hoarded junk of two lives no longer young as they'd been.

But Wave loved the chance. The thought that he, more than any old friend (even Rato himself), knew the hidden trail of two married lives and all they'd thought worth saving back—it drew him on through the downstairs and up like a bright warm light.

And then in the bedroom he found Wesley's secrets (a dozen new rubbers, three oldtime books with pictures of sailors with cocks like underground prize-winning State Fair tubers in their white blocked hats and short black socks screwing star-spangled whores, and a red rubber-dildo painted with a motto—"Forget your hairdo! Hang onto your heart!"). That was good, almost good enough.

But before Wave could carry out all his plan, he had to find something just right that was Rosa's. Some unmistakable clue, after Sunday night's kindness, that she wanted Wave to finish up here.

Her own drawer was nothing but a clothes drawer though, just neatly-folded underwear and blouses, stockings and scarves. Wave sifted those quickly with no sick interest in their feel or smell. Her bedside cabinet held nothing like the modern-day working girl's shelves (a diaphragm, modernistic battery-powered massager, or copies of *Playgirl*) but straight-trimmed recipes from family magazines and one moldly scrapbook with clippings about Horatio Beavers as a high-school student (the Audio-Visual Club, that sort of thing).

Wave's heart sank a notch. He might have to leave and not accomplish his one main hope. That would sadden him far more even than leaving here fast on New Year's night without the chance of showing Rosa his inmost meaning, his hope to ease her.

As he turned from the cabinet, he saw an old Bible. A thin *New Testament and Psalms*, dusty with the yellowed

edges of clippings and photos kept there for safety. He sat
on the edge of the mattress and opened the book, hoping to
find any verses she'd marked for special memory or for
help in trouble. Find that, in anybody's house, and you've
got a key to their deepest back room. Nothing here though,
not even real signs of wear and tear. None of the darkness
of long needy use. Could she be the sort of person for
whom a Bible was just a filing cabinet, a place to keep
birth certificates or insurance receipts? It didn't seem likely
but here were the facts.

Then Wave turned to his own favorite passage of scripture, St. Paul's Epistle to the Romans, chapter 8: verse 18
(*I consider that the sufferings of this present time are not
worth comparing with the glory that is about to be revealed
to us*). And laid in beside it was an old tan photograph, no
writing on the back. So Wave had no idea of the subject.

It was Rosa's father, with two other boys, as a very
young boy at Ocean View—long before liquor found his
mouth and burned out the core of his body and soul, long
before Rosa herself ever saw him, before he dreamed that
this body of his would ever bloom in its own grinning
babies. Yet it was still her favorite picture of him, of his
innocence in the days when he had live dreams of a useful
life—when his own four children were patiently waiting in
the dry-seed fork of his strong bare legs.

Somehow the force of it tore through to Wave. Somehow he felt like that same boy, in his own life now. He also
stood up smiling like that, in a strong counter-wind, with
his mouth wide open trying to say something helpful and
kind to a world that could see him but would not take his
meaning. He even had the boy's dark eyes and hair. There

seemed to be a bruise on the boy's right knee. Now, this day, on Wave's own knee was a brown mark big as a baby's palm—some permanent sign of who he was and had always been.

Could it someway be him, here in Rosa's Bible? Had he lived back there a whole life ago? Maybe without her knowing it at all? Was it why he'd felt so drawn to her life? Maybe that was why he'd known he could help her.

And had Rosa treasured him all this time? Whoever she thought the old picture was—a kin person?—she knew by now that it looked like him. Surely she'd plan to follow that up? Had he ruined his chance at knowing her again by forcing himself too soon or too late? He needed to know. Maybe someday he could ask her.

Or maybe he had to swear off here. Leave it to patience, time, and fate. And hope that at last Rosa would know that—whoever he was now, had always been—he'd stood at the edge of her whole recent life and wished her well. Surely she knew she could call for him and get all the help he'd saved for her?

How could he vow to leave her now though and make himself obey? What would convince his mind in the nights, when it brought up Rosa's face again and begged him onward, that she'd already known him?—that she had a version of him pictured by her pillow and would surely think of him whenever she opened the book in reach?

He could hide a penciled note here now on the back of the picture—*This old friend came back in once more but has left for good thinking you are happy. If that ever changes and you want him again, just say so quick. He will be nearby.*

Then a better way dawned. Wave stood up, borrowed a comb from the cabinet, and smoothed his hair in the glass of a picture near the bed. Neatly he checked his fly and all buttons, then straightened his necktie.

He sat back down on Rosa's edge of the mattress. He shut his eyes and said "Dear Lord and God, I was here once before in the hopes of doing Your will by one of your saints. I made some mistake and hurt her badly. You've let her give me a real second chance. And also I've found out she's known me before and values my face. Let me bless her now, once for all in her life, by resting in the place where I tried to touch her and begging Your strength to leave her for good unless she needs me."

A voice clear as anything on FM broadcasts said in a deep tone "Thank you, son. Now do the right thing." Next it gave him the right thing to do.

He lay back on Rosa's side of the mattress, slid himself to the center on top of the spread, touched both their pillows, shut his eyes again, and said "I'll never be back here again, not of my own will. I'll wait for her." He waved both long arms beside him like wings, the angel wings he saw so often in the night in dreams or awake above him in the dark overhead.

The clear voice said "Get up now and go. You've got three minutes. You were right. Amen."

Wave stayed another instant, sweet as any in his whole past life. Then he sprang to the floor, leaned back, and neatly composed the spread and pillows to where even Wesley and Rosa herself could never guess he and God the Judge had been present there and done great deeds. He went to the door, looked back once quickly. Then helpless to resist, he turned and bent and pressed a long dry kiss deep in the spread. In under a minute he was downstairs, out the back door, and gone—no trace behind.

AND IN ONE MORE MINUTE, WHEN WESLEY DROVE IN AND Rosa faced the house, she could say what she said at the end of most trips but with real truth now "Home. Safe again. Thank heavens."

Wesley said "So right" and was also true.

Whatever the sky was—at least the cause of birth and death (all hardness and ease)—it had secretly honored the unlikely choice of two normal creatures to work again at a careful life. They could not know they were safe till their endings, which would be hard and slow a long way off. This modest house would be home till then. It had room enough for the small calm pleasures that would not be rare. They would live here till death. Death would find them with ease.

ABOUT THE AUTHOR

Born in Macon, North Carolina, in 1933, Reynolds Price attended North Carolina schools and received his Bachelor of Arts degree from Duke University. As a Rhodes Scholar he studied for three years at Merton College, Oxford, receiving the Bachelor of Letters with a thesis on Milton. In 1958 he returned to Duke, where he is now James B. Duke Professor of English. His first novel *A Long and Happy Life* appeared in 1962. It was followed by *The Names and Faces of Heroes* (a volume of stories), *A Generous Man* (a novel), *Love and Work* (a novel), *Permanent Errors* (stories), *Things Themselves* (essays and scenes), *The Surface of Earth* (a novel), *Early Dark* (a play), *A Palpable God* (translations from the Bible with an essay on the origins and life of narrative), *The Source of Light* (a novel), *Vital Provisions* (poems), *Private Contentment* (a play), *Kate Vaiden* (a novel), *The Laws of Ice* (poems), *A Common Room* (essays), and *Good Hearts* (a novel).

THE CELEBRATED AUTHOR

REYNOLDS PRICE